OTHERWISE OCCUPIED

Second Edition

All characters and events in this publication, other than those clearly in the public domain, are fictitious and any resemblance to real persons, living or dead, is purely coincidental.

Published by Shay Savage

Cover Design: Mayhem Cover Creations

Interior Formatting: Mayhem Cover Creations

Editing : Chaya & Tamara

DEDICATION

To all the Evan Arden lovers out there.

Special thanks to my team – Chaya, Holly, Tamara, and Chanse Lowell for their tireless efforts in getting this book to production!

TABLE OF CONTENTS

CHAPTER ONE
Hired Relief

It's fucking raining.

Again.

It wasn't that I minded the wet or the cold – I really didn't, but it screwed with my aim and I was still trying to get back into the boss man's good graces. I couldn't really afford to miss. Against my better judgment when it came to an easy escape, I had put myself a little closer than I liked to be for this sort of job. I had to be sure to be successful, and if it cost me my life…well, that was better than failure at this point.

With my left eye closed, I looked through the scope of my Barrett M82 rifle. The crosshairs focused on a set of double doors made of glass and metal. The doors led inside of an office building, and there was a large "space available" sign over the entryway with a phone number to call if you wanted a thousand square feet, which was just right for your office needs. If you were to call the number, someone would answer, but you'd find there wasn't *really* any available space.

Not unless you had the right connections – preferably Russian, quite probably illegal Caspian Sea caviar, and definitely heroin. Those connections might get you a little corner office, but they would not, however, endear you to Rinaldo Moretti – my boss and sole owner of all the Moretti businesses. Some of those businesses were even legal.

Well, one of them was.

Sort of.

I shifted my hip and stretched my back a bit. I had been in the same position for a good seven hours, and I was hungry. I brought a couple of protein bars with me, but they were long gone. This job wasn't supposed to take this long, and I was getting frustrated and annoyed. I forced my breathing into a slow, regulated pace.

Frustration and annoyance were not my friends, not when I was on the job. I needed to keep my shit together long enough for my target to walk out the door and die.

Maybe the weather was causing a delay.

I reached up with my hand and tightened the cloth around my forehead. It was doing a decent job of keeping the rain from my eyes, but it wasn't helping with the whole comfort level. I didn't stop watching the door as I adjusted the bandana – never that. I had to be quick, efficient, and deadly.

No fuckups.

The last fuckup nearly cost me my life and had ended with me exiled to the desert for months, and that was just for killing the wrong guy. Missing the right one would be a lot worse. Of course, I couldn't hit or miss him if he didn't show up where he was supposed to be when he was supposed to be there.

"Calm, Arden." I blinked as I realized I was actually talking out loud to myself. Not good. I didn't like that shit, so I clenched my teeth a bit to remind myself not to do it again.

Everything had been perfect up until this point. After a week of scouring the Chicago city skyline, I had found the perfect building with the perfect view of the front doors. No visibility from the street directly below and nicely shielded from view of both the Willis Tower and the John Hancock Observatory. I only needed to be patient until…

…there he was.

I had no doubt the man in the grey trench coat was my target, though I had never met him before. I had studied his picture for hours yesterday to be sure I wouldn't make a mistake. I'd probably been through his family photos more often than his wife had.

I blinked once, placed the crosshairs in position, and smoothly pulled back on the trigger.

Only a muted thump could be heard as I sent the bullet down the barrel and into his left eye. Before he hit the ground, I was already back away from the ledge of the building and disassembling my rifle to shove it into a gym bag. I moved the clothes around inside to cushion the metal and make it undetectable from the outside of the bag and then headed swiftly to the rooftop entrance.

Three minutes later I was on the other side of the building, out the door, and then taking the stairs into the parking garage across the street. At the top of the garage was a gym where I held a membership, and I made my way to the locker room inside. With my bag padlocked into a locker, I hit the Nautilus equipment.

It felt good to work out a bit. I had been slacking.

All thoughts of Thomas Farmer, chief board member of Electro Industrial (now deceased), vanished from my head by the time I had done my third set of weights. If it sent the right message to others about which crime lord you should align with, I might get a bit of a break, and Moretti might put me back on my normal pay scale.

Probably not.

Sweat replaced the rainwater in my hair, and after I'd done a rotation on the Nautilus, I went for the treadmill. From the front counter, there was a chick there who kept giving me the eye. She even brought me a towel when I finally got off the machine. She'd done the same thing the last time I was here, but I didn't see her do it for anyone else.

"How was your workout, Evan?"

"Fine," I replied. "Thanks."

Great – she even bothered to look up my name.

She was twenty-four or twenty-five, five-foot-seven, blonde, and she had recently gotten a haircut – the ends were crisp and blunt – but she didn't like how it had turned out. She was trying to pull off a little ponytail for a hairstyle that was far too short, using a rubber band from around a newspaper. She didn't normally wear it that way, or she'd have one of those scrunchie things.

The first thought in my mind regarding her hair was to agree – it was too short. It also wasn't dark enough. She didn't have that classic Italian beauty look I preferred.

Preferred?

I wasn't actually aware I had a preference, and I considered this as I gave her a smile, a quick thanks, and then headed to the shower. While the water poured over me, images of long, smooth dark hair – almost black, but not quite – and matching dark eyes flooded my mental vision. I could almost feel her smooth skin against my palms.

I shook water from my head and quickly changed my thoughts.

I was probably going to have to change gyms even though I had only recently joined this one. I didn't need anyone paying attention to me, remembering me, and hitting on me. It was too bad, really, since the place was big enough to have a short wait time for the machines. Oh well. I could always work out at the gym adjoining my apartment, but the wait time for a treadmill meant spending half the day there for a sixty-minute workout.

Home again.

My apartment was a high-rise building right near the Chicago River. My boss owned the place, and it came with the job, so I didn't have to pay any rent or anything. It was a nice perk, though I would have preferred living in the country somewhere. I had never lived in the country, but I always thought I would like it – open spaces for target shooting and enough room for Odin to run around and chase squirrels and shit.

I nodded at Pete, the security guard, as I walked by. I had no idea what his last name was, but he was on Rinaldo's payroll. He smiled back at me, but the smile didn't reach his eyes like it usually did.

I glanced over him and quickly took in other changes. He was usually dressed pretty nicely, but on this day his normally ironed shirt was wrinkled, and the tie didn't match. His eyes were a little bloodshot from either lack of sleep or possibly actual crying – I couldn't really tell the difference.

It made me wonder if the wife had left him or if he left the wife, and then I decided it was probably the former. He had a kid, too – a young one not yet in school. I wondered if she found out about who he worked for and walked out. I wondered if I'd have to kill him.

Or her.

Maybe the kid.

Nah, probably not. Rinaldo was a businessman, and killing a kid rarely achieved anything that couldn't be achieved just as well by killing the parent.

The elevator dinged, and I pressed the button for the seventeenth floor. My apartment was the perfect location as far as I was concerned – right on the corner of the building, up high enough for my rifle to be very effective from a distance, and just two stories above the adjoining building. If I needed to get out via the balcony, I could. I usually took the elevator up and the stairs down but not for any particular reason. I was used to doing little things like that to keep myself in shape, and it was just a habit.

My eyes traveled over the door to my apartment, automatically looking for any signs of forced entry. There were none, but you couldn't be too careful. I slipped the key in the lock and opened the door.

"Hey, bud."

Odin jogged his way across the living room to greet me, and I rubbed his shaggy head. It was good to see his hair growing back in again – he looked better with it longer. Well, he at least looked more like a giant mop, a.k.a. a Great Pyrenees. When we had been out in the Arizona desert all that time, I had to keep it closely clipped to keep him cooled down. His buzz cut had been nearly as short as mine.

Maybe dogs did end up looking like their owners. Or was it the other way around?

Whatever it was, if dogs were man's best friend, Odin did his best to live up to the job. He had been with me for years and was about the only living thing around me I felt like I could actually count on. He would always be there when I got home from whatever

I was doing. He never judged, never asked me a bunch of questions about why I was the way I was, and he never looked at me with fear.

He was my buddy, and it was one of the few things that scared me. I kept quiet about him because making it known I had something to care about – even a dog – was enough to bring those who had something against me out of the woodwork and into my private life. I didn't need that shit, and I couldn't always be around to protect Odin. As big and ferocious as he could look to some people, he was an easy target to others.

I started up my netbook computer before heading to the kitchen for some orange juice. It was the good stuff – fresh squeezed. I had been splurging on little things like that since returning to Chicago from the cabin in Arizona. The little things were so much more important than people realized when they had to go without.

Not that I had taken any of the small creature comforts for granted beforehand, either. It had been like that in the Iraqi desert, too, even at our base. Ration everything was the rule. It sucked, but it beat being left for dead in a hole.

Odin rubbed up against my leg, and I realized I had been lost in thought for a moment. I patted him in thanks and wondered for the hundredth time how he knew to do that. Like those service dogs that would get epileptics to lie down on the floor before a seizure starts to keep them from hurting themselves, Odin always seemed to know when I was thinking too much about the past.

He worked better than the drugs the doctors had prescribed.

I finished the OJ, took Odin out for a quick walk, and checked my email.

More lotto winnings.

Amazon would like me to review my purchase of a new set of headphones. I hadn't actually tried them out yet, but I'd be hanging out with Jonathan tomorrow and would probably need them. The dude smoked a lot of weed and usually started babbling when he was stoned.

A dating site called *Lost Connections* wanted to hook me up with an available woman in my area. I licked my lips and thought I was going to need a little company for the weekend but not from a fucking dating site.

Lost Connections.

Before I could stop it, expressive and soft brown eyes in the center of a heart-shaped face invaded my thoughts. Long, dark hair and a fucking luscious ass came next, but I pushed the rest of the memory away before it could really take hold and turned back to my email.

Pizza Hut had free cinnamon sticks with any large pizza.

"That's what I'm talking about," I muttered to myself. I clicked on the pizza link and quickly ordered a large stuffed crust with mushrooms and pineapple to be delivered.

Hey – it's what I like.

Fucking sue me.

When the pizza showed up, I sat on the floor of the living room with my back against the couch and dug in, tossing bits of crust to Odin as I ate. It was a good thing I had gone to the gym today because I had eaten a shitload of pizza since returning to the city.

More thoughts about the simple things spun around in my head. Pizza, beer, coffee – even a gym where I could work out properly. For some reason, my pleasure at the thought of the mundane alarmed me. My tongue moistened my lips, and I grabbed the remote to find something to watch on the television.

I was definitely thinking too much. I had to stop.

Television wasn't a necessity; it was a luxury and a way to pass the time. I never really liked television much as a kid but found it was good for helping me relax now.

This History Channel was always good for a few z's, and it was playing something about dinosaurs. I tossed the half empty pizza box up onto the coffee table and lay down on the couch. The throw pillows picked out by Luisa were soft and comfortable, and I wondered how Rinaldo's youngest daughter was doing. I hadn't seen her in a while.

Not that I would go too close to her – I wasn't stupid. You didn't date the boss's daughter unless the boss told you to. He hadn't done that, though she was my age and I was considered one of Rinaldo's favorites.

Had been, anyway.

If he ever gave his blessing, I'd do her. She was hot and had a smart mouth that made me laugh. It didn't seem too likely now, not with me on the shitlist indefinitely. It was enough to make anyone paranoid, and I was already a little bit on the unstable side.

An animated T-Rex took a bite out of a Stegosaurus as my vision blurred.

Head throbbing…and the taste of dirt in my mouth. On my stomach, coughing, trying to get the dust from my lungs…but only inhaling more of it. Hands bound behind me, and I can't turn enough to the side to get my face off the ground…

I woke, startled, and glanced up at the television to see a bunch of World War II footage on the screen. I quickly shut the damn thing off. I sat up and put my head in my hands, trying to clear the memory-dream from inside.

A large wet tongue against my forearm centered me, and I reached over to scratch the base of Odin's ears.

"I need a better distraction," I muttered to myself.

Odin huffed at me as I grabbed my jacket and keys and shoved a Beretta down the back of my pants. He was probably looking at the clock and assuming I was going to work, but I'd gotten my job done earlier. Now I needed to spend some of my cash.

My parking spaces in the garage held two vehicles – a used black Mazda hatchback I had purchased on my way back from Arizona about an hour after my old Chevy truck died and a silver Audi R8 convertible that I rarely ever took out unless it was one of the high-end social occasions I sometimes felt obligated to attend.

The public transportation in Chicago was awesome, and I was a big fan of it ninety percent of the time. Every once in a while there was a need to get from one place to another door-to-door, though, and that was what I needed on this night. I slipped behind the wheel of the Mazda and headed south to the area where the gentlemen's clubs tended to spill out onto the street corners.

There were a hundred reasons I loved Chicago. Someone could live here for twenty years and still have new stuff to do. Jobs were everywhere, despite what the dudes sitting in the doorways of rundown buildings holding out cups and signs claimed. They might not have been good jobs, but there was shit to do and ways to make money. I loved the buildings the most – the whole concrete jungle idea. I loved figuring out how to get to the top of them and look down over the whole city. The Skydeck on top of the Willis Tower was an awesome place to relax.

Okay, maybe not to everyone, but I loved it.

I slowed the car as I approached the corner, and a half dozen girls and one guy took a few steps closer to the passenger side door. One of the girls actually came around to my side and laid her boobs over my windshield, smiling and grinding away at me. She was way too skinny though and had that junkie look about her. I checked the rest of them out quickly, and it didn't take me long to decide on the one with the biggest ass. My finger depressed the window button, and the guy placed his hand on the roof of the car to lean it.

"You lookin' for somethin' special tonight?"

"All-nighter," I told him. "Gimme the dark-haired girl with the round ass."

The dude leaned in a bit more, and I tilted my head a bit so he could get a good look at me.

"Yeah, I know you," he said. "One of Rinaldo's guys. Arden, right?"

"You got it."

"You sure you want that one? She's new and givin' me a bit of trouble." He snickered. "Nothing you couldn't handle. Fuck, might use you to make an example out of her, ya know? You do side jobs?"

"Yeah, sure," I said with a shrug. "She won't give me no trouble, though."

"Well, you give her a little discipline if ya need to, 'kay?"

"'Kay," I repeated. Like I was really going to fuck up a girl I was fucking. Pimps were assholes, no doubt about it.

"Employee discount!" he announced with a laugh and a wink. "Come over here, Bridgett."

The black-haired girl walked over to the side of the car, and the pimp opened the door for her. She looked up at him with a bit of concern.

"You're gonna be taking care of Mister Arden tonight," he said as he gave her a little push inside. "He's a good customer, so you be good to him."

She only hesitated a moment before getting inside. Her tiny skirt rose up and gave me a view of her little black panties. She had on stupidly high heels – like they all did – which were going to look pretty good over my shoulders. She shivered, but I didn't know at first if the motion was from the temperature change or from nervousness.

I gave the pimp half the cash before I drove off with her. I'd owe him the rest when I brought her back, assuming she took care of me the way she was supposed to. I knew she would. However she ended up in this business, they all knew better than to piss off a client. Those who didn't know the rules ended up in the river or the lake.

"What's your name?" I asked. I knew what it was – the pimp had called her by her name – but I wanted her to say it.

"Bridgett," she replied quietly. She looked down at her hands on her lap and then tried to pull her skirt down a bit. I saw her hand tremble slightly before I looked back up at the road.

"I'm Evan," I told her. "Evan Arden. You haven't been doing this long."

"A while," she responded.

"You've never had anyone take you home before."

She glanced sideways at me and then shook her head.

"I'm not going to hurt you," I told her. "That ain't my thing. I'm an ass-man, though. You take it in the ass?"

She blinked rapidly a few times, and her fingers tensed around themselves.

"I have," she said quietly.

Her throat bobbed up and down, and her eyes tightened along with her jaw. She'd been hurt – I didn't have any doubt about that. Hookers often were, and I didn't think there was such a thing as one who wasn't broken in some way or another. This one was new, though – recently damaged.

I pulled the car over to the curb and turned sideways. Her whole body tensed up, and she pushed herself a little towards the door. I reached over and took her chin in my hands.

"Hey," I said. "I told you I wasn't going to hurt you, right?"

"Yeah." She nodded rapidly as her eyes widened.

"I meant that. I got lube, we'll go slow, and if you decide you don't want it, we'll stop. I can always just fuck you from behind – I'm good with that. Okay?"

She nodded again and relaxed slightly. I leaned over the console and placed my lips against hers firmly. She responded like she was on autopilot, which she probably was. After a couple of kisses, I backed away and looked her over once more as I tried to decide if she was going to be all right with this or not. She looked good, though – the right hair color, at least. Her eyes were light brown, though. I wasn't sure what her nationality might have been, but she wasn't Italian. Regardless, I really wanted to keep her. It was too much trouble to go all the way back and pick out another one.

"You okay?" I asked.

She nodded her head a few times, so I pulled back into traffic.

Bridgett was obviously new. She was young – maybe twenty or so – and definitely didn't have the demeanor of a street-hardened hooker. If I was a different kind of guy, I would have just taken her to some motel and given her the night off or whatever, but I was more pragmatic than that. If I wasn't doing her tonight, some other guy would be. Maybe he'd be a nice guy and maybe he wouldn't, but at least she wasn't going to get hurt with me.

At a red light, I looked over at her again, and my mind immediately began to catalog information. Long, soft-looking black hair – maybe Latino, but no accent, so she wasn't an illegal from Mexico or Cuba or anything like that. She was dressed in the typical whore attire – red mini skirt, thigh-high stockings, black lacy top that showed her lack of bra quite clearly. Nice, big, round nipples.

"Bridgett?" I asked quietly. It took her a moment to look from the window over to me. Bridgett wasn't her actual name, and she hadn't been going by it for very long. People responded very quickly to hearing sounds even remotely like their own names, and her delay was far too long. "You hungry or anything?"

"No, thank you," she replied. "I'm fine."

"There's a restaurant in my apartment building," I said. "We could eat first, if you want. It's a nice place – good food, maybe get you a drink or two? I know I could use one."

Come on, baby – go with me here.

"If you want to," she finally said.

Very complacent.

It was almost ten-thirty, and the full menu wasn't available after ten, but I ordered a couple of sandwiches with chips and a beer for me. I got her one of those vodka martinis that were a lot stronger than people realized. I tried to get her to relax a bit, but she kept glancing around the restaurant.

I contemplated for a moment.

"No one here cares what you're wearing," I told her.

Her eyes found mine.

"I look like a hooker," she said quietly.

No shit.

"You *are* a hooker," I said. I waved my hand towards the two servers near the bar. "They all know that. They'd know that if I put you in a cocktail dress, flats, and one of those little old lady red hats, too."

"How would they know?"

I laughed.

"Because you're with me."

I managed to get her to settle down a little after that, and she did eat part of her sandwich and polish off two martinis while we talked about the weather and the Chicago Fire soccer team. Mostly I talked – she didn't seem to know shit about soccer. I finished my beer, tossed cash onto the table, and led her by the hand to the elevators. As soon as we stepped inside and the doors closed, I could feel her tension mount again, so I leaned over close to her ear.

"Not going to hurt you," I reminded her, and my lips pressed lightly against her neck, just below her ear.

Bridgett nodded slowly but still jumped a bit when the elevator went ding, signifying my floor.

I led her out into the hallway and to my apartment door. Her eyes widened a bit as Odin came up to sniff at her. He could be a little intimidating, and he didn't usually let people touch him. However, since he didn't bark much, he didn't often end up frightening anyone badly, and Bridgett was no exception. I didn't give them much of a chance to get to know each other as I grabbed two bottles of water from the kitchen counter and brought Bridgett to my bedroom.

My foot connected with the edge of the door, blocking Odin from the show as it slammed shut. I could hear him snuffle at the crack before he gave up and moved away. Placing the water bottles on the nightstand, I sat down on the edge of the king-sized bed and started to untie my boots.

"Those look like army boots," Bridgett observed. "A friend of mine went into the army. Are you in the army?"

"No," I said. Her babble amused me a little. "Ex Marine. Don't you know what *ARMY* stands for?"

"Um…no."

"Ain't Ready for the Marines Yet."

She snickered at the lame joke, which I figured was a good sign. Laughing brought people's guards down, and if she didn't relax, it was going to pretty much ruin my evening. I smiled up at her, and she returned the look before walking up to me and standing between my knees.

She placed her hands on my shoulders, and I tilted my head up to meet her lips as she bent over me. She tasted like vodka and pomegranate juice in my mouth, and she felt soft and warm in my hands. My fingers moved up to her shoulders and then back down again as our tongues moved around each other.

She pulled at the hem of my T-shirt, and we broke apart long enough for her to lift it over my head. Her hands came back to my shoulders, and she stroked her fingers down my chest.

I watched her eyes as she took me in. I was used to women looking at me in the gym or even going down the street. Even in the military, the chicks I served with favored me. Women usually liked what they saw – toned muscles, six pack abs, no scars.

Well, none on the outside.

My captain told me I intrigued them, which was why they seemed to flock to me. I was a quiet guy – a mystery for them to solve. I didn't know why girls ate that shit up, but he said they did and he was right. As soon as they figured you out – *really* figured you out – they didn't want anything to do with you.

It was part of the reason I preferred hired company.

Bridgett's soft lips molded against mine again, and her tongue played around in my mouth as her hands continued to explore most of my upper body. I got a good grip on her plump ass, pulled her into my lap and down against my waiting cock. Rubbing against her little thong panties felt good – too good. I needed something a little quicker for now.

"How about you blow me first?" I suggested as I pulled back a bit and loosened my belt. "It's been a while, and I want to be able to concentrate."

"Sure," she said.

"Take all that off first," I said with a flick of my finger towards her clothes. I flipped the buttons of my jeans open and slid them down my legs along with my boxers. "Leave the stockings and shoes, though. That's hot."

"Whatever you want," she said with a smile. Her eyes tightened a bit as she looked at my cock, and I knew what she was thinking. I wouldn't push her though, and she smiled up at me again like I didn't scare her.

She faked it all well. I hoped she'd get something out of it, too.

I sat back against the headboard, and Bridgett crawled over between my legs. My fingers ran through her hair as she leaned over and took me in her mouth. Warm and wet – just what I needed. She licked around the head first, and then tried to go down too far. She gagged a little and moved back, refusing to meet my eyes as she tried again.

"Look at me, sweetheart," I said, and she complied. "How long you been doing this?"

"I…um…"

"It's okay," I said. "Tell me."

"Since Monday."

"Shit, are you serious?"

She nodded.

"You want to stop?"

"No," she shook her head. "I gotta make a living."

I looked at her for a long time and wondered why I was even asking her. Since when did I care how much experience a hooker had? Even if she had been turning tricks less than a week, she might have already had more partners than I ever did.

"Go slow," I told her. My hand moved over her cheek, and she nodded slightly before wrapping her lips back around the head of my dick. I spread my arms out across the headboard and let her make the moves. "You don't have to take it all – just use a lot of tongue. That's it…look at me…show me how much you love my cock."

Her dark eyes stayed on mine as she sucked, licked, and ran her hand over what she couldn't get in her mouth. I didn't try to hold back, just let her work on me as my thigh muscles tightened along with my balls. The tingling sensation rose up, circled the base of my dick, and then focused through the tip of my cock as I let out a muted grunt and poured into her throat with a single thrust of my hips.

"Fuck, yeah," I muttered. My hand passed over her hair again as her throat worked to swallow it down. She moved me back and forth in her mouth a couple more times before I placed my hand on her cheek again. "You're good…come here."

I gave her one of the water bottles and watched as she drank half of it down while I got my breathing under control. Maybe the asshole pimp wasn't taking care of her like he should. That shit didn't make sense to me. Why have expensive pieces of merchandise you can sell over and over again and not take care of them?

At least this one wasn't strung out. I hated junkie hookers.

She placed the bottle back on the edge of the nightstand, and I pulled her to my chest. For a minute, I held her to me. Feeling her weight on top of me was kind of nice and made me feel warm and sleepy. Maybe I didn't need the sex as much as I needed the company.

"I'm gonna sleep a bit," I told her. "You can sleep with me if you want, or there's a TV in the other room, cable and everything. There's pizza in the fridge, too."

"I could use a little sleep," she admitted. "I don't usually get much."

"Hard to sleep during the day?"

"Yeah, it is."

I shifted around until I could pull the comforter and the sheets down enough to get our legs underneath the covers and then pulled her back to my chest. She settled her cheek on my shoulder and closed her eyes. My fingers stroked through her smooth hair, and she blew warm breath over my skin.

Sleep came soon, and with the warmth of another body next to mine, it came without thought or dreams.

There was just no substitute for a good hooker.

CHAPTER TWO
Annoying Rival

"That's custom."

Jonathan Ferris tapped the police report on the laptop's screen right above the bullet hole I left where the board member's eye used to be. I wasn't sure how he managed to get into classified information online, but he always had all the same info the Chicago Police Department had in its system. I wasn't sure if the CPD realized how many people ended up with all their classified records, but Jon was the kind of guy who was brought up sharing.

"That's what you always say," I reminded him

"It's always *true*," Nick replied. "I don't *think* I've ever heard of you *actually* missing. Well, *sometimes* you might kill a few *extras*, but who's counting, right?"

Nick Wolfe had a way of putting a lot of emphasis on various words in a sentence for no particular reason. It gave him a hippie-stoner vibe, which wasn't totally inaccurate, but didn't completely fit, either. The guy was a classic chick-magnet, too – both in looks and the ability to get a group of women around him and listen to him tell stories. He'd always leave with at least one of them, sometimes two. He was completely uncockblockable at a club or a bar, but that would be a whole other story all by itself.

He could also get away with shit other people couldn't, like bringing up the reason for my exile without me smashing his face in. I had no idea what he actually did for Rinaldo, but even with all the bullshit, I liked the guy. Everyone liked him. I did narrow my eyes at him, which made him smile and laugh a little.

"Just saying, dude."

I rolled my eyes and looked back at the computer screen.

"You're the fucking master, Evan," Jonathan said, and I thanked him.

It had been a pretty nice hit.

"It's good to know you didn't lose your touch out in the desert, Arden." I turned towards the voice and watched Rinaldo Moretti walk into the plush office where he conducted a lot of his business. He wasn't much to look at, my boss – average height, mostly bald, mid-fifties, a bit of a gut on him – but what he lacked in looks, he made up for in power. The man could make shit happen with a couple taps of his finger.

He was nervous about something today. Even though he walked with confidence and showed nothing in his face, there was something bothering him. The vein near his temple was beating rapidly, and his left hand kept clenching into a fist.

Behind him were two other men – Mario Leone and Terry Kramer. Mario was a huge guy – towering over my six-foot-two frame by a good five inches with enough muscle to deter most anyone from taking a stab at the boss. Of course, that was exactly why he was hired. Terry was a little wiry guy who looked like a dwarf next to the massive pile of muscle. If Mario fell over, Terry would get crushed, and it would suit me just fine if he did, too.

Leone was okay – he would sit down and have a beer with you when he wasn't working and just shoot the shit. Terry was a whole other story. He was an obnoxious kid who rubbed me the wrong way even before he started trying to take my job.

None of them looked unusually concerned about anything – just Rinaldo.

"No, sir," I responded automatically. I gave Mario a nod but ignored Terry completely. I took a long breath in slowly and silently, hoping we weren't going to spend the entire afternoon reminding me of where I had fucked up. I'd already paid my dues as far as I was concerned.

"Good to know because this next one's going to be a little more challenging." He dropped his ass onto one of those big, leather executive chairs and leaned back.

"Whatever you need, sir."

"Show him the picture." He huffed a quiet breath through his nose and glanced away from the desk. He was annoyed with this person he wanted me to kill, no doubt about it.

Leone walked over and dropped a magazine on the desk in front of me. On the front page was a man I recognized immediately – I'd seen him in at least a dozen *Bruce Willis* style action films.

"Brad Ashton," Jonathan said. "I saw him in that terrorist movie with the chick with the boobs."

"Angelina Jolie," I reminded him.

"Yeah – that one."

"He's got round the clock surveillance and never goes anywhere without a guard," Rinaldo said. "Paparazzi follow him everywhere, too. The guy is never alone. He even fucks in pairs."

"Makes him harder to hit," Terry said.

Like I needed his fucking opinion.

"It's gotta be close," Rinaldo said as his eyes turned to me. "In his face, you know? Up close and personal."

"I'm a sniper, sir," I reminded him.

As soon as the words were out of my mouth, I knew I shouldn't have said them. My eyes closed a little longer than a normal blink as I tried to reset and get my head back on straight. If I didn't, it was likely going to get knocked from my shoulders. There was no doubt that most of my work was from afar, but I had done plenty of hits up close and personal, too.

"Whatever, dude," Nick snickered.

Rinaldo glanced at him, and he replied with a toothy grin.

"You tellin' me you don't know how to shoot a handgun?" Rinaldo raised an eyebrow at me as he leaned forward a bit in the chair. "Because I happen to know you've done that once or twice before."

"No, sir," I responded. I hoped the tension I felt in my body wasn't outwardly visible. I didn't think it was – I tended to stand up pretty straight anyway. I didn't miss Rinaldo's jab – the reason I had been sent into temporary exile months ago had to do with putting someone down with my Beretta. Like Nick bringing it up wasn't bad enough.

I had never heard of James Carson prior to killing him, but he was apparently pretty important to his cousin, Miss Fiona Carson. When the wife wasn't around, Fiona happened to be sleeping with Gavino Greco, my boss's primary competition. Her cousin had been a witness to an assassination where Rinaldo had ordered the hit, and I had made it happen. I hadn't known who the guy was; I only knew he had been behind the dumpster when I killed Robert Franco, the idiot who dared dip into Rinaldo's casino profits.

I thought I had cleaned up the scene, but it was a bigger mess than a witness, according to Rinaldo.

"I'll take care of it for ya, boss," Terry piped up. "I took care of plenty for ya while he was on vacation."

Vacation.

Asshole.

I was sorely tempted to show him just how accurate I was with a shorter-ranged firearm.

"That you did, Kramer," Rinaldo said with a nod. "That you did."

I stood there and watched the exchange in silence. Showing any kind of annoyance at this point wasn't going to get me very far. Rinaldo Moretti was watching me and watching me closely. I wasn't going to let that stupid little shit Terry get to me.

"So this one's mine," Terry said with a big, toothy grin on his face.

Rinaldo cocked a half smile at the kid, who beamed back.

Idiot.

Nothing good ever came of that smile.

"Not this time," Moretti said. "I need Mister Arden for this one."

"I'm just as good as him," Terry hissed back. He started to say something else when Mario placed a hand on his shoulder, effectively silencing him.

I tried not to smile as the boss turned back to me.

"The fact is," Rinaldo continued, "he knows I'm gunning for him. Anyone who knows I'm gunning for them knows they can't walk out into daylight, or they're gonna have a bullet in their brains. Now I have you to thank for that, and I'm grateful, but don't give me a line of bullshit. Let's be perfectly clear, now – you *are* familiar with other firearms, are you not?"

"Yes, sir, I am."

"This needs to be done quick, easy, and quiet," he continued. "This isn't your usual where you don't give a fuck who sees you, Arden. Nothing can lead back to my organization. You got me?"

"Yes, sir."

"Now you go collect your short-range, in-your-face weapon of choice and kill that motherfucker."

"Yes, sir."

Everyone was dismissed from the office except for Nick and Mario. I tried to get the fuck out of the building before Terry could catch up with me, but it didn't work out that way. I maneuvered to get a bit ahead of Jonathan to put some pace between me and Terry, but Jonathan was a quick walker.

"You want me to help ya scope him out?" Terry asked as he ran up beside me. He reminded me of those hyper little terrier dogs, and I kind of wanted to kick him.

"No," I replied. I knew exactly where that would end – the little fuck would either get in the way and screw it all up or take the actor guy out himself. Though it would ultimately piss off Rinaldo because it wasn't Terry's assignment, credit was credit.

Actually, he'd probably try to take me out first. The credit would be a lot higher then. Not only would he have eliminated the target, but he would have done it when I couldn't. Just taking me out would give him a reputation that wouldn't be easily matched.

"What the fuck is wrong with you, Arden?" he yapped.

"You're annoying," I replied.

"And you're an asshole!"

"Whatever." I passed Jonathan and shoved the door that led into the stairwell and began clomping down the stairs. As much as I wished Terry would stay where he was, I heard two sets of footsteps behind me.

"You think you can treat everyone like shit," Terry babbled.

"Just some," I countered.

"You think you're better than everyone else," he continued, "just 'cause you were all military hero and shit."

"Not a hero," I muttered under my breath. I quickened my pace as Jonathan moved in a little closer behind me – separating me from the little shit trip-trapping down the stairs in my wake.

"Like it takes a hero to get himself captured."

I stopped in my tracks, just at the bottom of the second landing. Jonathan had to veer to the side to keep from running into me. I turned slowly, my narrowed eyes finding the smirking little fucker standing just a few steps above me.

"Crack in that armor, hey Arden?"

"You shouldn't speak shit you know nothing about," I said. My hands were shaking a little but not enough that anyone would notice except for me. "Mention it again, and maybe I'll go dig a hole and show you what it was like."

Turning on my heel, I quickened my pace down the rest of the stairs.

"Fuck you!" Terry called out as I clomped down the steps and out the back door with Jonathan still beside me. The heavy metal door slammed with a bang.

"You all right, brotha?" Jonathan asked as we walked across the parking lot to his white F150 Ford Pickup.

"I'm good," I replied. "Why?"

He furrowed his brow a bit, looked back towards the closed door, and then shrugged. He knew me pretty well and knew when to change the subject.

"Because since you got back, you've been a little off," he finally said as he pulled a pack of Marlboro's out of his shirt pocket and fished out a cigarette. He shoved it between his lips as he hunted around in his pants pocket for a lighter. "You were gone a while."

I just shrugged as I climbed into the passenger seat. Jonathan tossed his Luke Skywalker style hair out of his eyes as he maneuvered himself into the driver's side.

"I think that would drive me nuts," he said, "sitting in some piece of shit cabin for half a year by myself."

"It was just a little over three months," I corrected. "Not a half year. It wasn't that bad, and I had Odin with me."

"Still…" He whistled low and shook his head. "Three months without pussy would suck balls."

I glanced sideways at him and raised my eyes at his choice of words.

"Just sayin' it would suck," he said with a shrug. He turned the key and rolled down his window to blow smoke back past his shoulder. Reaching forward, he fiddled around with the radio controls until he tuned it to a classic rock station.

"Well, you know me," I said, "I always find a way to get shit done."

"You got blisters on your hand?" he snickered as he put the truck into reverse.

"Nope." The corners of my mouth turned up a bit as visions of that long, dark hair spread over the creamy skin of Lia Antonio's back filled my head. I could almost feel her pussy gripping my cock as I thought about it.

Jonathan blew smoke out the open window, shoved the gear shift back into park, and turned to look at me.

"No way," he exclaimed.

"What?" I asked.

"You were out in the middle of fucking nowhere and you still got laid?"

I smirked.

"Now *that's* custom!"

Jonathan had worked in an auto shop prior to his first stint in prison for dealing. He specialized in tricking out people's cars with all kinds of shit, so anything remotely out of the ordinary was always "custom." It was mostly his code word for anything he thought was worthy of his admiration.

"I need some deets, brotha!"

I rolled my eyes.

"You that interested in what my cock does?" I asked.

"I just don't understand how you manage to get pussy to fall into your lap no matter where you go."

"It's a gift," I replied.

Jonathan shoved the truck back into gear and started backing out.

"So who was she?" he asked.

"Just some chick lost in the desert," I told him. "Her boyfriend, or whatever, was an asshole and dropped her off on the road when they were fighting. She didn't have anywhere to go and it was getting late, so she spent the night riding my cock. That's it."

"Custom."

"Worked for me." I leaned back and let the smoke from his cigarette waft around me. I didn't indulge anymore myself, but I liked getting some second-hand every once in a while. As much as Jon lit up, I probably smoked a couple cigarettes worth any given hour I was with him.

"How was she?"

"Fucking fine!" I responded.

We both had a good laugh until Def Leppard started playing, and Jonathan quickly turned up the volume and started air jammin' at red lights. I stared out the window at the line of people waiting for Garrett's Popcorn and tried not to let thoughts of Lia invade my head too much. If I did, I'd start regretting shit, and I tried not to do that.

Jon followed me up to my apartment, and we immediately started researching Brad Ashton. There was so much shit on him, it was hard to separate the real stuff from the gossipy crap, but we started with the basics.

He was twenty-nine years old, born in Australia, six feet tall, blond hair, and grey eyes. Though he made himself famous with action films, he had his start in the porn industry, and I had to admit some of the footage made me feel a little uncomfortable.

Maybe it was because Jon was watching it with me.

"Do you really have to play more of that?" I asked as he flipped from a scene with one pair of writhing bodies on a bed to a video with two pairs.

"It's pretty good," Jonathan said. "Might have to download a full copy of this one."

I shook my head a little, but my mind was wondering about the possibility of Bridgett spending the night again. I must not have hated the porn too much. I was going to have to take a little trip later.

I'm going to kill a guy I've watched fuck two sorority chicks and a frat boy.

Shaking my head again didn't seem to completely rid my mind of the thought, so I headed to the kitchen and popped open a couple of beers.

"Here's his schedule of appearances," Jon said as he yanked a piece of paper from my printer. "He'll be here in the city three times between now and February."

"Not gonna kill him here," I said. I silently berated myself for saying *gonna*. The nuns would have smacked my mouth for such abuse of the English language. I blamed Jonathan's influence. The "Midwest meets southern twang" of his was addictive. "I think away from here will be better. There are ties to Rinaldo with anything done in Chicago, and I want nothing to look suspicious. Where else is he going to be?"

We went over all the various options and finally decided Atlanta was the place. He'd be there the first week of January, and that was when he was going to die.

Jonathan headed out, and I fed Odin and tossed his rubber bone around for a while. He actually got tired of the game before I did, which reminded me that he wasn't a young pup anymore. He'd be nine in the spring, which was getting up there for a good-sized dog like him.

I rubbed my eyes; it was getting late, and I was tired. After I tossed the beer bottles in the recycling bin and drank one of those protein shakes, I headed off to bed. Odin followed, whining slightly. I gave his head a rub, but he just kept looking at me.

I peeled off my shirt, dropped my jeans, and tossed all of it into the hamper next to the dresser. My watch and keys went in one of those little ceramic bowls for such things, which made them clang against the set of dog tags on a chain coiled up at the bottom of the dish. With a heavy sigh, I lay down in the bed and stared at the ceiling until my eyes couldn't stay open any longer.

On my stomach…unable to bring my knees to my chest to try and right myself. There's something cutting into my wrists – wire or those plastic ties – I'm not sure which. It's pitch black, and I can't even hear anything around me. The sand below me is cold, and I think I might be underground.

Minutes. Hours. Days.

I can't tell the difference. I try to swallow, but I don't even have enough saliva left to do that. I'm going to die of dehydration, and I wonder if it's a blessing.

Footsteps. Loud voices speaking in Arabic. I can't make out enough of the words to make any sense of it. I hear and feel a presence beside me just before I'm grabbed by the neck and forced into a kneeling position. Water is poured over my face, and my mouth opens to receive it before it can choke me…

Sweat was pouring into my eyes as I woke with a start. My breath was coming in short, staccato gulps, and my hands were shaking. Odin was there beside the bed, whining slightly. I should have reached down to him, but I couldn't move.

Why? Why now? I had barely thought about any of it in over a year.

I wiped sweat from my forehead before I shuffled over to the bathroom to wash my face. I stared at myself in the mirror and kind of hated what I saw looking back at me. I was pale, and it made my dark blue eyes stand out in my face like I was in shock or something.

Maybe I was.

I reached up and rubbed at the back of my hair. It was getting to be kind of long for me, and I decided midnight was as good a time as any to give myself a trim. The clippers were in the linen closet, and within a few minutes I had a haircut that would make any Marine officer proud. It was very short around the sides and the back with just a little more on the top.

It also seemed to make my dark blond hair look a lot lighter and kind of reminded me of how it would look in the summer when it got all bleached out in the sun and from the chlorine in the community pool. I shaved my face while I was at it, too. I hated having a face full of itchy scruff.

Odin sneezed behind me, and bits of hair flew up into the air. I brushed some of the hair bits from my shoulders, but I started to itch anyway. Once I cleaned up the mess I made on the floor, I jumped in the shower to get the rest off of my skin.

I found myself out on the balcony staring across the buildings towards Lake Michigan. I was wide awake, and I knew sleep wasn't going to come very easily. It was just a bit past one in the morning, and I didn't have any early morning plans other than some more research and the usual jog with the dog. I thought about ordering a pizza, but all the good places that delivered would be closed.

Some company would be nice.

A few minutes later, I was in the Mazda, heading to a particular street corner.

Her pimp was there, but I didn't see Bridgett. I had been telling myself the whole way over that I was coming out to get *a* hooker, not that *particular* hooker. That didn't seem to stop me from looking for her as soon as I pulled up.

"Mister Arden!" the pimp called towards my open window. His collection of ridiculous gold chains hung down, and I tensed a little. If it scratched my car, I'd kill him. "Pleasure seeing you again. You going to become a regular of mine?"

"Depends," I said noncommittally. "Where's Bridgett?"

"Blowing some dude in the alley," he replied.

I nodded as I ignored the creepy feeling the thought and mental image gave me. She was a hooker, for Christ's sakes. Of course she was blowing a guy in the alley.

"You wanna wait?" the pimp asked. He took a half step back away from the paint job, which helped me relax a bit. "Maybe you wanna taste of Candy over here?"

Another slim brunette sauntered over with her hips swaying. She gave me a big smile and a show of tits as she leaned over the car, practically crawling up on the hood. Long legs, nice shape, cute as hell, but she had a totally flat ass.

Definitely not my type.

"I can wait a minute," I replied with a shrug. Candy pouted and licked her lips at me as she backed up onto the sidewalk again.

After about three minutes, Bridgett appeared from the darkness of the alley behind the liquor store. It was getting to be damn cold out, but that didn't stop her and her coworkers from wearing those skimpy hooker outfits. The cold was making her nipples practically leap right out of her tank top.

"Bridgett!" the pimp yelled out. "Git yer ass over here!"

She walked up to him and handed him a wad of cash. He counted it carefully, jammed his finger under her chin, and said something in a voice too low for me to hear. She shook her head quickly in response, and he took a step back and pointed to my car.

She climbed in and settled into the leather seat.

"All night?" she asked quietly.

"That's how I roll," I answered.

She gave the pimp some hand signal, and I drove away from the curb.

"It's a little late for a good night's sleep," she said.

"What do you mean?" I turned around and started heading back to my apartment.

"Last time you didn't even fuck me," she reminded me. "We just slept."

"You blew me."

"You could have gotten that for a lot less cash."

"Maybe I'll make up for it tonight." I glanced over at her and half grinned.

We didn't say much the rest of the trip back to my apartment. Everything was closed, so we didn't make any detours or anything, either. Odin was waiting by the door when we came in, and she reached out and touched his nose.

Odin sneezed at her before he walked back to his dog bed and flopped down. I snickered as I headed into the kitchen and got myself a beer. I offered one to Bridgett, but she declined.

I wondered if she was actually old enough to drink.

I popped open the bottle and took a long pull from it. Bridgett looked at me, and I was trying hard to figure out her expression. She seemed almost shy, and it wasn't just her general newness to the oldest profession but something else.

Her cheeks suddenly darkened in a blush.

Holy shit.

You have to be kidding me.

She had some kind of crush on me, and now that I was paying attention, it was obvious. Take the girl off the streets where she'd been hurt and treat her nice for a few hours, and suddenly you were some kind of goddamned hero.

"We're just fucking here, Bridgett," I said darkly. I narrowed my eyes and tilted my head a little to the side.

She blinked a few times before licking her lips nervously.

"I...I know that. What do you mean?"

"You know exactly what I mean. You keep that shit up, and I'll pass you over for another bitch. We clear?"

She nodded slowly. I could feel the tension rise in the room, and knew I had taken the whole warning thing overboard. I probably could have blamed it on the lack of sleep, but it still needed to be said. I didn't want her thinking this hookup was going to change into something else.

"Good," I said. I watched her as I drained the beer. "Now get in my bedroom and take your clothes off."

I followed on her heels, glad to see she wasn't wasting any time when she passed through my bedroom doorway. As soon as she was inside, she pulled her top up and over her head and then looked at me over her shoulder with one of those little, secret smiles hookers thought they could get away with, but they couldn't. I smiled back anyway as I moved across the room and sat on the edge of the bed to take off my boots.

"Keep going." I nodded towards her.

I pulled my shirt off as well, and Bridgett took a couple of steps to the side until she was standing right in front of me. She rubbed her hands down her sides and moved her hips as she leaned over a little to unzip her mini skirt.

"You can take the shoes off, too," I said.

Ditching my boots and socks towards the end of the bed, I popped open the buttons on my jeans before I leaned back on my elbows. It was definitely more comfortable that way as I watched Bridgett strip in front on me.

Ultimately, I was still too tired to stand up, but I had to keep up pretenses.

Unlike the rest of me, my cock was all too willing to join in a little late night fun, and I could see Bridgett's eyes move to my crotch a few times as she removed the rest of her clothes.

I took a good look at her for the first time. When she had been at my place before, I really hadn't looked at much more than her ass, which was definitely "custom," as Jonathan would have said. Now I checked out her equally round tits – not *too* big, but nice and fleshy – and curved hips. She was built like a woman, not a twiggy little thing, which I appreciated a lot. She had good skin, pale and perfect.

"You really want the shoes off?" she asked.

I nodded my head, and she removed them before climbing over the top of me and pressing her lips down to mine. I kept myself propped on my elbows and just let her do what she wanted for a few minutes while I kept looking at her.

Long, dark hair and a little patch of matching triangle lower down tickled as she ran her hands up and down my sides. She straddled me lower, kissed down the center of my chest to my stomach, and then got off the edge of the bed. I raised my hips as she pushed my jeans down my legs until she was kneeling in front of me. Her hands caressed my thighs, and I closed my eyes as the warmth of her mouth covered my cock for the second time.

"Fuck, that's nice…" My hand reached down and grabbed her shoulder, encouraging her to come back up and stop sucking me off. I had another idea this time. "Lay on your back."

She did as I said, and I raised a leg up to straddle her this time. I watched her tongue dart over her lips, and I moved up her chest with my dick pointing towards her face. My hands came up her sides and took hold of both tits. My thumbs grazed over the nipples until they stood out nice and hard and then pushed them both together and around my cock.

Bridgett sucked her lower lip into her mouth and bit down on it a little as I started to fuck her tits. Rocking slowly back and forth, I didn't quite go up far enough to touch her mouth with the tip. I probably could have, and she would have given me both the tit fuck and her mouth at once, but the angle wasn't quite right, and I wanted to be done soon.

Moving a little faster, I felt the pressure building in my balls as my thighs trembled a little. I leaned my head back and let out a moan as the first shot coated her skin between her breasts. I looked down as the next one went higher, coating her neck, and the third stream further soaked her tits.

With a final groan, I climbed back off of her. On shaky legs, I quickly went to the bathroom and soaked a washcloth, then took both it and a dry towel to hand to her. As soon as she took them from my hands, I dropped to my back on the bed. I stretched my arms up over head and yawned loudly as she cleaned herself up. Once she was done, she curled up against my side and ran her hand over my chest.

I reached over, twisted my arm a little around hers, and gripped her hip to pull her against me. This effectively cut off her reach to my cock as well, which was going to make it a little easier to get some sleep. My head was getting that foggy feeling again, and I closed my eyes to let myself go.

"You're going to fall asleep on me again, aren't you?" Bridgett said with a bit of a giggle.

I grunted but didn't open my eyes. A moment later, I felt her fingers against my jaw.

"Really?" she asked quietly. "You're going to spend all that money and not even fuck me? Twice now?"

I opened my eyes half way and looked up at her.

"What do you care?" I mumbled. I was starting to feel the warm cover of sleep moving over my body, and making sounds wasn't helping at all. I needed the rest, and she was going to pepper me with questions.

"It doesn't make sense," she said.

I ignored her, figuring that was the best way to get her to shut up. I tucked my head into the pillow and subsequently against her arm as well before I closed my eyes again.

"You paid for me all night last time for a blow job and this time for a tit fuck? Do you really have that much money to throw away? I mean, I figure if you're Moretti's killer then–"

I rolled quickly, covered her body with mine, and placed my hand over her mouth. I felt her fingers grip into my arms, but she wasn't even close to matching my strength and remained immobilized. Completely awake now – unfortunately – I stared down into her eyes with as much menace as I could muster.

"Some things aren't discussed," I said slowly and quietly.

I raised an eyebrow and waited for her to acknowledge what I said. When she nodded quickly, I released her mouth, but the damage was already done. A single tear fell from the corner of her eye. Part of me wanted to apologize, but she had to know she couldn't just open up her mouth and talk about that kind of shit – it didn't matter where we were. Next time we'd be in a bar or someplace, and she'd end up getting us both killed.

Pushing off of her, I landed on my back against the mattress. The ceiling needed to be painted, and I spent a moment wondering if I should put on a fresh coat of your basic ceiling white or maybe try something at little more interesting.

"I'm sorry," I heard from beside me. "If you want to…to just sleep or whatever, that's cool."

Swallowing down whatever tetchiness was still left in me, I nodded and looked at her. Though her eyes were dry now, I knew I had scared her, and that's not what I really wanted to do. She needed to remember what kind of life she was leading and what kind of people ended up around her because of it. She was young, but she couldn't afford to be stupid. If she did, she'd die young, too.

"I…I sleep better with someone here," I finally admitted. "I'm not seeing anyone, so…"

I let my voice trail off in hopes that the whole conversation would go away, but Bridgett was the most inquisitive of streetwalkers.

"You have nightmares?" she asked.

"Sometimes."

"Bad ones?"

My eyes narrowed at her slightly. I didn't want to go in this direction, and I also didn't want to have to throw her out. I nodded once without speaking, but she still didn't take the hint.

"What about?"

"For fuck's sakes," I growled. I resisted the urge to get up and drag her ass back to the street corner but only just barely. "Look, I'm tired, okay? I haven't slept in two days because I have shitty dreams, and the last time you were here, I slept really well, okay? Now can you just shut up for a few hours, or do I have to drag your ass back to your pimp and find a new whore?"

My heart was starting to pound faster, and if this kept up, I wasn't going to be able to sleep no matter who was here. Thankfully, Bridgett finally understood and lay her head down beside mine.

There was just no reason to go into the details.

CHAPTER THREE

Conjured Plan

"So tell me what brings you here, Evan."

I leaned back against the back of the chair and closed my eyes for a minute. Mark Duncan, the military counselor assigned to me after I was discharged and moved to Illinois, seemed to be a patient man. Though we had only spoken once before – the same month I relocated to Chicago – he understood it took a while for me to get going.

He was a short guy with dark hair and glasses. He must have loved what he did because he didn't make enough money to get glasses that actually fit, and the little marks on the side of his face where the frames bore into his skin were red. There were papers all over his desk, and his bookshelf was disorganized to the point of annoying me. There was a picture of a young woman, but it was an old picture. Her hairstyle and clothing screamed the nineties. There weren't any other pictures of her, and I figured she must be an ex since she was too old to be his daughter.

There weren't any family-type pictures, though he was prime age to be married with a couple of kids. There were other pictures on his desk and on the window sill behind his chair, but they consisted of what looked to be a build site for a new house and a huge group of people holding tools. There were also pictures of groups of kids holding banners that showcased various walk-a-thons and similar functions.

"I'm having dreams," I told him.

He scribbled on his notepad, which made me want to roll my eyes, but I managed to refrain.

"Bad ones?"

"Not awful," I said. "Not like I've had in the past when they put me on meds. It's just that I haven't had any like that in a couple years, and they're keeping me up at night. I don't know why they're coming back."

"Can you tell me about them?"

"I…uh…"

Fuck.

I should have realized he was going to want me to talk about them. Talking about the dreams meant talking about what happened in the desert, and I didn't want to go there. All I really wanted to do was get some sleep, and this option seemed to be the most expeditious.

"Just…just about the past," I finally said. "I just want to know why they're back. Why now, when I haven't really thought about any of that crap for a long time?"

"If you don't tell me what they were about, I'm not sure how much help I'm going to be," he urged softly.

With my eyes closed, I went through some of the deep breathing shit the first counselor taught me to do when I had panic attacks. I didn't get those any more – not since the first year – but the breathing still helped sometimes when my brain went into overdrive.

"I'm…I'm in the hole."

"Where you were kept prisoner?"

"Yeah." I swallowed a couple of times. "I'm just waking up, like I did every day when it got hot. I kept trying to spit sand out of my mouth, but I never could, you know? There was always more of it."

I swallowed hard, but the dryness in my throat made it feel like I was swallowing sand again. I could almost feel it scratching my larynx.

"Fuck."

"Where are you now, Evan?"

"Chicago," I said quickly. "I'm not there. I know that."

"Can you go on?"

"Yeah." I leaned forward, put my head in my hands, and took a minute to center again. "There isn't much more, really. I'm just in the hole, waking up over and over again, and trying not to eat the fucking dirt. It made me cough, and it would get in my lungs, too."

"You haven't told me much about what happened there," Mark said.

"Not something I like to talk about." I hoped my succinct words and terse voice would dissuade him, but he was a fucking counselor, so that wasn't going to happen.

"It was a very significant life event, Evan. You were a prisoner of war for eighteen months. Don't you think that warrants some discussion?"

"I talked about it with the last guy," I reminded him. "The one in the hospital – in Virginia. He cleared me."

"He cleared you from the psychiatric hospital," Mark clarified.

"Yeah," I responded as I looked into his eyes, "where I was held for observation only, evaluated, declared unfit for further duty, but otherwise unharmed."

"And when was the last time you talked to..." he glanced down at the file in his hands, "...Doctor Hartford?"

"Before I moved here."

"Before you were discharged?"

"Around the same time," I said. "He's the guy who discharged me."

"With a diagnosis of PTSD."

"Look," I said, "I know all this, and we went through all this shit when I saw you the first time. Do we really need to do it again? I was really just hoping you could tell me if there's some kind of sleeping pill or whatever I ought to be taking."

Mark looked over my file, glanced up at me, and then back to the file again. He adjusted his ill-fitting sports jacket before settling back into his chair with one leg crossed over the other.

"I'm a psychologist," Mark said, "not a psychiatrist. I can't prescribe medication, though I can make a recommendation to your regular doctor. Honestly, I think you'd be better off if we just talked for a bit. It was recommended that you visit with me at least every other week after you moved here two years ago, but this is only the second time you've been here."

"I don't usually need it."

"But you do now."

I shrugged and leaned back against the chair. I glanced at the couch, and though lying down did sound good, I had never felt comfortable on a shrink's couch. It was just too cliché. I was glad he had the high-backed chair as an option because Hartford never had.

"I just want to get some decent sleep without..."

"Without what?" he asked when I stopped talking.

I took a long breath. I was so off my game, I was going to fuck up at my job which was completely unacceptable. I needed sleep to focus, and I couldn't seem to get any rest without Bridgett, the newbie hooker, in my bed. That was about as fucked up as some of the shit I went through in the Middle East.

Well, no, it wasn't, but it was still fucked up.

"I just need some sleep," I finally said. "I really think if I just got a couple nights of decent sleep, I'd be fine."

"How about I make you a deal?" Mark said. "You tell me a little more about your time in the desert, and I'll talk to your doctor about the possibility of getting a prescription for sleeping pills."

"I don't have a doctor," I admitted.

He eyed me again, wrote something down on his notepad, and then looked back up.

"Taking care of yourself isn't much of a priority for you, is it?" Mark leaned back a bit in his rolling desk chair. He put the end of his pen in the corner of his mouth and chewed on it a bit. I wondered if he was a smoker because it reminded me of Jonathan and how he would play around with anything even slightly cigarette shaped.

I checked out his fingers and noticed slight yellowing. Inhaling slowly, I detected the slight scent of tobacco smoke in the office. He didn't smoke in here – it wasn't strong enough for that – but the scent was on his clothes.

I looked up at him through narrowed eyes.

"It's a little hectic at work," I snapped. "The place doesn't offer health care."

Quite the opposite, really.

"There are still some basics you should be considering. When you were in the Marines, you had regular physicals. Don't you think that's important now?"

"I'm not sick," I stated.

"Sickness is relative," Mark replied. "You are here for a reason, just like you might go to an urgent care facility if you had a cold you just couldn't shake."

"I'm not sick," I repeated, "and I don't go to the ER for a fucking cold. I know what I was diagnosed with, and I know I didn't go and get every single checkbox checked that I was supposed to after discharge, but I also didn't see the point. I wasn't getting severance since I didn't have six years of active service. Hartford gave me the diagnosis just to make sure I could still see him after I left the hospital."

"And did you?"

"No."

"Why not?"

I sighed.

"This is totally irrelevant," I said. "I didn't come here for this."

"Your health is exactly why you are here," he countered.

"Just forget it." I stood and began to walk to the other side of the room.

"I'd like you to stay," Mark called out. He stood up and took a couple of steps towards me, which emphasized a slight limp. When I glanced down, I could see he wore a shoe with a thicker heel and sole on his right foot. "There's only twenty minutes left in the session. You can stick it out that long, can't you? I really would like to talk to you some more."

"Morbid curiosity?" I sneered.

"No," he replied sincerely. "I'm concerned about you."

"I don't want anyone writing a fucking book about it, all right?"

"All right," Mark replied through narrowed eyes. "What makes you say that?"

Tensing a little, I tried to keep myself from actually balling my hands into fists. Whenever I thought about Hartford and his ideas, I wanted to punch something.

"Hartford wanted to write a book."

"Ah." Mark shifted in his seat. "Well, I'm not much of a writer, and I really just want to know how you are doing now, so can we finish the session? I mean, you already paid for it."

Forcing myself not to roll my eyes, I sat back down in the chair and looked at him.

"What do you want to know?" I asked.

"All I really know is the part that is a matter of public record," Mark said. "Anything you want to tell me that isn't still classified would be a good place to start. If you'd rather talk about the known stuff, that's fine, too. It's up to you."

There was a lot that was still classified as far as I knew. It wasn't like there was anyone coming out here to debrief me of any changes, of course. Regardless, it was best to go with the things that could be found by anyone who did some digging.

"You see the video tape?" I asked. An involuntary cold shiver went down my back, and my stomach tightened up.

"I have," he admitted. "I watched it again when you were assigned to me, but I had seen it on the news before then."

"That guy – that writer guy," I said. Inside my head, tiny little explosions began to commence in the center of my skull. My hands clenched without my permission, and my mind fought to only say the words, not actually see the pictures. "You know the one? When they had us all on our knees in front of the camera – right after the bags were taken off our heads – he was on my left."

"I know who you mean."

"He kept saying he had a wife and kids," I remembered. "He kept begging them and talking about his two little girls."

I hesitated. Most of this was on the tape – the one they played over and over and over again. There were probably five hundred copies of it up on YouTube. Most of it, but not all of it. There was a whole bunch of it before that part that never got out of the government's hands.

"Before they had us on camera, when the guy was talking about his kids – there was one of them – one of the insurgents – he said someone had to die, and I told them to just shoot me instead of the writer guy because I didn't have a family. It didn't make any difference though. They shot him anyway."

Pain in my lungs made me stop speaking for a second. They were trying to go into overdrive or something, and it took all my concentration to stop myself from hyperventilating. My fingers gripped onto my knees in an attempt to stop shaking, but at least my voice remained steady.

"Sometimes I think he got off easy," I said. "Thinking that sometimes makes it hard to sleep, too."

"That's a change in your thinking," Mark said. "At least, as far as what you talked about when you were here before. There's nothing about the video in Doctor Hartford's notes."

"Maybe it's still classified and no one remembered to tell me." I shrugged. "If you see any MPs coming up the driveway, give me a chance to run, okay?"

I laughed, but he didn't smile, and I couldn't really hear the humor in my voice, either.

"It was on the news a lot."

"I was still in Saudi Arabia when it broke out," I said, "then Germany, and then the hospital in Virginia. I didn't see it for a couple of months – not until they were discharging me. It was a year old by then, anyway. It's not like I had paparazzi following me or anything when I got back. Instead, I had freaking MPs. The whole media circus didn't have any effect on me."

"You think something like that just goes away after a year?" Mark asked.

"No," I said, "but it wasn't the worst anyway."

"What was?" he asked quietly, but I shook my head. He must have realized he wasn't getting any of that because he changed tactics.

"Did you dream about that time?" he asked. "Did you dream about the video?"

"No," I said, "just the hole."

"Your focus when we first met was on the others who were with you when you were captured. Your dreams then revolved around feelings of guilt – that you should have been able to do something to save them."

"Yeah." I cleared my throat, and my head began to pound a little under the effort of not remembering. "Not those dreams. None like that this time."

"You still blame yourself," he observed.

"I fucked up."

"You were ambushed."

"I was the one tasked with not letting that happen," I said. "I was their officer. I was in charge. I fucked up, and they died."

"Do you expect yourself to be omnipotent?"

"Yes."

"Evan," Mark sighed, "you know that isn't reasonable."

"I don't give a shit about reasonable," I said. "It's what I should have done. They were counting on me."

"I have the files," he reminded me. "Full investigation. You were found to be completely without…"

"I don't give a shit about what they said!" I snapped.

Mark's eyes went wide for just a half-second before his carefully constructed therapist's mask came back into play. He couldn't completely hide his shock from me. I could almost hear little gears clicking in his head as he considered this new information. He wrote on his notepad while his eyes stayed on me. I could just imagine the words on the page.

Evan Arden does actually have an emotion in there somewhere.

"Sorry," I muttered. "I guess I'm a little on edge. Work has been a little hectic, and with the nightmares…well, I'm not sleeping much, like I said. Very sorry for my outburst, sir."

Mark stared at me for a moment, undoubtedly wondering what he could say to make me explode again.

"What you went through was horrific, Evan," Mark finally said.

Like I needed to be reminded.

"You've come a long way since then, haven't you? You still work at the gym?"

"Not right now," I said. "I took a little extended vacation. Just got back into town a month ago."

"So where are you working?"

"Nowhere at the moment."

"You just said work had been a little hectic."

Shit.

"I…ah…" Damnit! What the hell was wrong with me? I never made such stupid mistakes. "I don't have a real job. I've just been helping out a friend."

"Evan, I can't help you if you keep things from me. You have to trust me if this is going to work. You know whatever is going on, you are completely protected by doctor-patient privilege. Unless you tell me you're going to hurt yourself or someone else, it will all be totally confidential."

Well, that was the problem there, wasn't it?

"It's just...not completely on the up and up," I said as I tried to buy a little time for a plausible story. I was falling into a pit of lies, and I needed something simple so I could keep it straight. I had already said far more than I had planned to say.

"Doing what?" he pressed. He wasn't going to let this go until I gave him something he would take to be me opening up – trusting him more. What I had said before was in the files – he could have read it already. He needed something new.

The story actually came pretty quickly.

"Well, it's just..." I hesitated and rubbed my fingers in my eyes. I was surely the perfect picture of angst. "It's not totally legitimate, you know? I'm doing some roofing work for this guy's brother. Strictly cash, all under the table, you know?"

"Yes, I know." He did a wonderful job of not showing his disappointment. I was just pleased he bought it.

"You're not pissed?" I asked, supposedly surprised.

"Not at all," he said. "I can't say I think it is the best thing for you because legitimate work will always be in your best interest, but I'm not *pissed*, as you put it."

"My Marine buddies would have a fit," I said. It was the truth, or at least would have been if I had any Marine buddies. "Everything has to be on the up-and-up, you know? It's a matter of pride."

"And does doing that kind of work hurt your pride?"

"Yeah, a little," I admitted with a shrug. In my mind, I considered what I actually did to make my illegitimate cash. "I know it is ultimately illegal and immoral, but if I don't do it, someone else will. The gym wouldn't hire me back since I didn't exactly tell them I was going to be gone for a while."

"So where did you go on your trip?"

"Arizona."

"You went to the *desert* on vacation?"

I looked up at him, and we just stared at each other for a minute.

"Yeah…um…I guess I did."

"And you're wondering why the dreams came back?"

"Well, now that you put it like that…"

I leaned forward and rested my forearms over my knees. The throw rug in Mark's office really wasn't all that interesting, but I stared at the blue, swirly patterns in it anyway.

"Did your vacation remind you of the Middle East?"

"I didn't really think about it while I was there," I admitted. "I mean – it wasn't the same at all. Just a little cabin, me and the dog… it never even crossed my mind while I was there."

"What did you do while you were there?"

"Nothing," I said. It was accurate enough.

"Sounds like an exciting vacation."

I glanced up and raised an eyebrow at the sarcasm, but Mark wasn't apologetic.

"I wasn't looking for any excitement," I said. "I've had enough excitement in my life. I just hung out in the cabin. I didn't go anywhere or do anything, really."

"Did anything significant happen while you were in Arizona?"

My eyes dropped back to the rug, and my tongue darted over my lips. I could still taste her there, the brunette beauty who stumbled across my path in the middle of nowhere, spent the night in my bed, and then disappeared from my life.

Lia.

Did she ever go back to that rickety old cabin? Did she call my name, wander inside, and find the lame-ass excuse for a note I left her?

Would I ever know?

"No," I finally said. "Nothing happened while I was there."

Much like the other times I had visited a counselor before I had been discharged, I was left feeling empty inside, more unsure than I had been before I walked into the office, and in need of a lot of distractions to keep my mind from dwelling on whatever was said. Keeping myself occupied usually came in one of three forms: throwing myself into exercise, spending all my free time with a hooker in my bed, or focusing on my work.

Sometimes doing all three was the only way to keep my mind off of whatever was bothering me. When I wasn't even sure what was quite literally keeping me up nights, even that didn't help. For the moment, my best distraction was work, which meant digging into my target's life.

Brad Ashton was not an easy guy to get close to, that was for sure.

The whole Hollywood scene sucked, whether you were in LA, New York, or downtown Chicago. Red carpet events weren't overly common in the area, but I guess when you're into a mob boss for a shitload of gambling money, you do what you need to do.

The premier of Ashton's new movie was all over the place, and this was just the Chicago leg of the tour. I knew I wasn't going to get close enough to him tonight – not with all the insanity going on at the AMC River East 21. There had to be at least ten thousand people there, and every one of them was trying to get up close and personal with the dude. The vast majority were women, mostly in their mid-forties, and mostly crazy.

They had to be.

I mean, some of them were actually carrying cardboard cutouts of the guy and trying to get him to sign his own face.

That shit's weird.

There were at least two dozen people acting as a human shield at any given moment. They were all decked out in basic B-movie secret service attire – black suits, receivers in their ears, sunglasses regardless of the weather. They were pretty comical to watch.

As far as my cover went, they were going to be my best chance to get to him.

I heard Ashton was staying at the Embassy right next door, so I made myself comfortable in the bar there and sipped club soda while a scotch sat untouched next to me. It was a long while before the noise of screaming females alerted me to the star's arrival. He was escorted by the caricature guards to the bank of exclusive elevators and disappeared.

Just a little longer.

A few more patrons were hanging out and watching various sports on the large screens around the bar, but no one paid any attention to me except for the bartender. The next time he came around, I ditched the soda and started sipping the scotch.

Two guys in black suits, sans ties, and unbuttoned white shirts came out of the same elevator where Ashton had disappeared and headed towards the bar. Not surprisingly, they opted for a bar-side seat instead of a table.

I watched from the end of the bar.

They were both in their mid twenties, which was convenient. As they talked, I picked up that one was named Jim, but no name was mentioned for the other. They drank cheap beer in bottles and watched football until closing time but didn't talk about work. Jim was apparently a Raiders fan.

They sat reasonably close like they knew each other, but not close enough that they might accidentally touch one another in passing. They both had short hair but not military cut like mine, just neatly short. There were little marks around their right ears where the receivers had pinched them.

They were career guys, not just hired for this event. They would go with Ashton when he left Chicago, which was exactly what I needed. I kept my head down, turned my body away as they passed me, and finished my scotch before heading home.

The next day was a television appearance for the popular actor and then back to the same hotel for some beauty sleep before he flew out to LA. The same two guys came down to the bar again the next night. I sat in the same spot as well, but this time I was wearing a Raider's jersey.

Fortune was on my side, and after the first drink, Jim's buddy called it a night, but Jim didn't seem ready to turn in just yet. It didn't take long for him to approach me and start talking football.

Too easy.

"Raider's fan, huh?"

"Like anybody with a lick of sense," I replied. "Best team in the fucking world!"

I held up my glass of beer and clinked it against his bottle. The beer was still light, same as his, but just different enough not to appear suspicious. This guy knew security, and I couldn't be that obvious. Even wearing his team's jersey on a day when they weren't playing was a little risky.

"Damn straight!" Jim replied. "I'm Jim Conner – mind if I join you?"

"Marshall Miller," I said as I shook his hand. "You staying here at the hotel?"

"Yeah, I'll be heading out in the morning. I work security, and my boss is staying here."

"That's cool," I replied. "I hear the rooms here are really nice."

"You aren't a guest?"

"Nah," I said. I wiped the back of my arm across my mouth. "I just like the bar. Other sports bars around have kind of a crappy crowd, you know?"

"I do," he agreed.

I made a point of scooting my chair a bit so he could sit down without going all homophobic on me or anything. Sports guys could get kind of uptight sometimes, and I didn't want something that simple to blow my chances. We talked about the team's performance over the season and their chances for the Super Bowl and then went on to politics.

I argued with him about one of the viewpoints expressed on the nightly newscast. I took it just to the precipice of pissing him off and then dropped back down. We eyed each other cautiously for a moment before touching our drinks together once more in a truce sort of toast.

It was all about as perfect as it could be until he insisted on shots. I probably should have known better – really wasn't much of a drinker. I'd have a drink or two, yes, but that was usually it. Being out of control wasn't my favorite feeling, but sometimes the job called on you to do shit you didn't want to do.

"Did you play?" I asked Jim as I tipped back the third.

"Nah," he said. "I love the game, but I was never good enough to play more than JV. You?"

"In college, yeah," I said with a frat-boy grin. "Tight end freshman and sophomore years and then screwed up my knee. There went my scholarship. I couldn't keep up with everything after surgery, and I never was the same again."

"That sucks, man," Jim said. As some sort of celebration-slash-condolences he bought the next shot, which we both downed too quickly to count, so we had another.

"I always thought I'd play for the Raiders someday," I mused. "I guess since that didn't happen...well...you know. Life and shit."

"I do know that," Jim agreed.

I didn't really think he had any idea what he was agreeing with, but it didn't really matter. We did another shot, and my head was getting a little fuzzy. I didn't drink often, and it was hitting me a little harder than I expected.

"I got laid off a week ago," I told him. "I was a mall cop, if you can believe it. It was kind of a crappy job – mostly chasing teenaged shoplifters – but it paid the bills."

"Have you been looking for something else?" Jim asked.

"Looking, sure," I responded. I waved down the bartender for two more shots since it was my turn to buy them. "Finding is a whole other thing. I like the security stuff, though."

We did a couple more shots, talked more football shit, and bitched about the economy until the hotel bartender finally tossed us out. Jim and I shook hands, and he wished me the best of luck. I jotted my cell number down on the back of one of the cardboard coasters used at the bar and asked him to call me if he heard of any work.

Once Jim was out of sight, I pushed my way through the revolving doors and hailed down a cab to take my drunk ass home. I hadn't actually planned on drinking as much as I did – I didn't like the out of control feeling of intoxication – but it seemed to have served its purpose as far as "bonding" with Jim was concerned.

I stumbled into my apartment and nearly fell over Odin twice as I attached his leash and took him out the back door. My head was swimming, and I had such a rough time just getting Odin outside in the first place that I decided to forgo the leash law and just dropped the people-end of the thing. Odin never wandered off anyway, and it allowed me time to lean against the wall of the building and debate the merits of puking in the bushes versus puking on the rocks.

Splatter was bad, so I maneuvered a little closer to the bushes.

The dog went about his business, watered down a couple of sticks that were likely going to be bushes in the spring, and then took a shit next to the sidewalk. That's when I realized I hadn't brought any doggie bags down with me.

There was no way in hell I was going to make it all the way back up to the apartment and then down again to clean up shit. It was going to have to wait until morning, and whatever neighbor who was out at this time of night to complain could suck my cock.

I whistled, and Odin lumbered up next to me. I checked around to see if anyone had noticed my dog-owner's ultimate sin, but there wasn't anyone around. Just as I was picking up the end of his leash to take him back inside, Odin decided there was something seriously interesting about the "flower bed" recently constructed in the park. There weren't any actual flowers or even any dirt – just a lot of slate rocks. I was actually considering puking on them, but Odin was more interested in what was down around the brick base. I sighed and let him continue on – it was easier than moving, anyway.

Odin suddenly stopped sniffing at the ground and let out a growl.

I looked up through blurry eyes at the two kids who were walking across the grass of Lake Shore East Park, coming from between the buildings on East Randolph Street. It really was too late for them to be doing anything legal, and the way they looked up at me and nudged each other was so obvious, it was almost pathetic.

At least, it would have been pathetic under other circumstances.

Normally this situation wouldn't have concerned me. Two punk teenagers didn't tend to be much of a challenge, but I was drunk. Aside from drunk, I was also unarmed and feeling pretty damn stupid to boot.

The two kids moved off to one side of the walkway where the light wasn't as good, but I could still see them pretty well. One had dark hair and a pretty beefy build, and the other was smaller, thinner, and had red hair in a greasy mop on the top of his head falling over into one eye.

The dark-haired one reached around to the back of his jeans and pulled out something shiny and sharp looking. Whatever doubts I might have had before about motives evaporated.

Odin growled again before he took a couple steps to move himself between me and the two teen boys. I put an end to that immediately because the last thing I needed was for the dog to get knifed. I wasn't in any shape to drive him to the vet. I cut him off with my legs, forcing his bulk behind my knees and partially into the rock garden.

"How about you give me your wallet," the kid on the right said. "Maybe then I'll decide not to leave you and the pooch bleeding in the street."

I debated telling him that the street was a good hundred yards away but decided against it. The other dude snickered, and I just shook my head a little. That action caused enough vapor trails to make me stop moving immediately. Taking a step back, I almost tripped over the damn dog again.

"The dude's fucked up," the red-haired kid said. I couldn't help but look at his hair and remember David Hasselhoff in *Piranha 3-DD*. He had played himself in the ridiculously campy horror movie Jonathan once made me watch. In the movie, he kept going off on a little red-headed kid who was too stupid to live through to the end. He kept calling him by the same nickname throughout – *little ginger moron.*

I heard myself snicker.

"You think this is funny?" the darker kid asked.

"Now that I think about it, yeah," I answered. "You gonna knife me and the dog here in the park and then drag us over to the street? What exactly does that accomplish for ya?"

My vision blurred again, and the next thing I knew, there was a sharp pain in my side and I dropped to my knees on the cement as Odin let out a short bark.

There was just no way this night could get worse.

CHAPTER FOUR
Patient Research

I landed on the ground, not because of the hit – it wasn't that hard, though somewhere in the back of my mind, I thought a rib might be bruised – but because my body decided it was just the right time to get rid of the alcohol in my system.

Fortitude only goes so far, and I wasn't able to hold it in any longer.

My mind tried to count the number of shots I must have done with Jim, the security guy, as I retched into the shrubs near the edge of the park. The commotion going on around me barely made sense as I fertilized the rock garden and reminded myself over and over again why I didn't make a habit of drinking too much.

I hated puking.

Just hated it.

Even when I was a kid, the very notion of puking was abhorrent. The slightest feeling of nausea had been enough to nearly send me into a panic attack, and if I had an actual stomach bug, I would cry and scream between stomach heaves. I honestly thought major organs or other important bits of my insides would come out if I threw up too much. I remembered the feeling of terror and helplessness as I knelt over the grimy porcelain bowl at the convent and tried to keep my insides actually on the inside of me.

There was one nun who would smack me and tell me to stop being such a baby; I think I had been about four at that time. Needless to say, that didn't help me get over my fear of vomiting, and though adulthood had given me a more realistic perspective on the whole thing, I still hated it with a passion.

By the time I was starting to get a bit of control back, everything seemed to have quieted down. It didn't make any sense at all, but the commotion that had been all around me as I was sick had vanished. The scent from the ground below me was nearly enough to make me puke again, so I started pushing myself backwards and onto the walkway – trying to get away from the stench in hopes of saving myself. My knees scraped the rough asphalt, and I cringed as I finally regained enough sense to look around me.

Odin sat next to me, wagging his tail and lolling his tongue to one side.

Some guard dog.

He tried to lick my face, which was just disgusting. I pushed him away as a pair of feet came into view right in front of me. Dirty tennis shoes and bright white socks over hairy calves bounced around in my vision as my head spun in a steady circle. I knew I needed to lift my head to see who it was, but I didn't have quite enough muscle control.

"You look like shit," a familiar voice said.

My fingers rubbed into my eyes to try to un-blur my vision while the other hand wiped a sleeve across my mouth. It took a minute, but I was finally able to look around with some clarity only to find both the kids who had come after me were gone. In their place, Terry Kramer was grinning down at me.

"What the…" I shook my head, earning me more woozy feelings in my head and stomach. Terry blurred in and out of existence while I tried to keep myself from puking again. With herculean effort, I swallowed back bile and willed myself not to be sick as I looked up at Terry. "What are you doing here?"

"Saving your ass," he replied with a big grin.

I looked around, but I didn't see the two kids anywhere. There was a little switchblade-style knife lying on the walkway next to the grass a couple of yards away, but no one around to wield it. Looking over the park, I saw no signs of anyone walking around, so they must have gone around the front of the building. It didn't make sense – they had come from the park.

"Great timing I got, huh?" Terry said as I forced myself back onto my feet.

Wobbling slightly, I reached down to Odin's neck and grabbed a hold of his collar. My fingers worked their way around to the edge to the leash, and I wrapped my hand around it. He wasn't going anywhere, but I needed something to help ground me. I kind of needed him to help get me off the ground, too.

With shaking knees and Odin as leverage, I managed to stand up but continued to stare at the concrete as it spun around in my vision. I had to focus. I had to get the shit out of my system, so my body would stop revolting against me.

I turned towards the decorative pile of stones and puked again.

"Oh, man!" Terry exclaimed. He took several steps backwards to avoid the splatter. "You're in bad shape!"

Responding to him would have been pointless, not to mention impossible given the current situation, so I didn't. Besides, I had the feeling opening my mouth again would cause problems.

"You're really lucky I was walking by," Terry said. "Those kids might have given you some hurt."

A lot of potential responses bopped around in my head like a *Teen Beat* celebrity, some with words and others with actions. At least one response included my knuckles. I might have tried to say something, but I really was a little afraid that if I opened my mouth, I was going to puke again.

I needed to brush my teeth and drink half a bottle of mouthwash.

"Where you going?" Terry asked as I picked up Odin's leash and started back towards the building.

I pointed at the door of the apartments and then moved up to swipe the security badge you needed to get in late at night. Terry stayed at my heels, but when he started to walk in with me, I put a hand out to his chest and stopped him.

"What the fuck?" he said. "I just saved your life, and you don't even let me in to wash my hands or something?"

"Not exactly in the mood for company," I said.

"I just saved your ass!"

There were very few things that annoyed me more than someone who fished for compliments. Whether it was a chick wanting me to tell her she didn't look fat in the fucking dress, a server batting her eyelashes for a bigger tip, or a punk wannabe thinking I needed to thank him for hanging around my apartment at an opportune time, I found the very act pathetic and undeserving of praise.

"What the fuck are you doing around here anyway?" I asked. Now that my mind was going in that particular direction, I did find it odd. I'd never seen Terry around this area before. "You don't live anywhere near here."

"I was down at Sweetwater's watching the game and having a beer," he said. "I needed to walk and clear up my head, so I cut through the park – figured I'd take the Red Line – it's the only one running this time of night."

The places he was talking about were close, at least. I shook my still fuzzy head and waved a hand at him.

"Go home," I said. "I'm going to bed."

The door shut behind me, and I didn't look back to see whatever annoyed expression might have been on his face. Instead, I let Odin lead me to the elevator and then down the hall to the apartment. I didn't even make it to the bed, but just the few steps it took to get to the couch and pass out.

As the room spun around and around and consciousness started to leave me, I realized the walk from Sweetwater Tavern and Grille to the Red Line train was the opposite direction from my apartment. There was no way a Chicago native like Terry would have walked the wrong direction to get to the L.

He lied to me.

Most people probably thought my line of work was always dangerous and exciting. It could be, I supposed, but most of it was fucking dull. There was a lot more research than target practice or killing – that was for sure.

I Googled. I clicked. I hovered the cursor over balloon links to other sites. I read celebrity gossip websites and websites that debunked various celebrity gossip websites. Ashton was represented in every one of them, of course. Women couldn't get enough of him, gay dudes couldn't get enough of him, and straight ones put up with it because their women came home horny and ready to blow them.

I couldn't seem to find any pictures of Ashton in compromising situations with any of the women, though. No scandalous love affairs with senators' daughters or the co-star from his last movie. No groupies getting groped at parties or secret rendezvous in shady hotels with cute little American Idol starlets.

If anything, he seemed more likely to hang out with the starlet's brother.

Interesting.

He wasn't openly out of the closet, but he hadn't denied anything, either. I was perfectly straight, but if he wasn't…well, it was something I could possibly use to my advantage. Whatever got the job done, got me back on my regular pay and off of Rinaldo's shit list worked for me.

The whole *watching every word I said* thing was getting old. I didn't mind being overly polite to the boss – I was used to calling people above me *sir*, so it came pretty naturally anyway. Still, I felt like he was always waiting for me to screw up again, and I hated feeling like I was being evaluated all the time, especially when he compared me to a second-rate little shit.

There was the added little tickle in the back of my head that told me I was going to have to kill Terry Kramer.

He was in my thoughts a lot as I lay on my stomach at the local shooting range with my rifle up against my shoulder. With a twelve round magazine instead of a ten, I made multiple holes in the center of the target's forehead.

"Nice shootin'."

"You ain't supposed ta smoke in here," I told Jonathan. I cringed as I realized his accent was being extra contagious today.

He laughed out loud and made a grand gesture as he looked around for some stupid motherfucker to argue with him about it. I rolled my eyes and squeezed the trigger again. I was pretty sure Terry's face would look pretty nice with a little round hole between the eyes.

At least thoughts of killing him were keeping my mind occupied. It seemed every time I wasn't thinking about killing someone, thoughts of a brunette riding my cock in a hot, stuffy cabin in the middle of the desert kept coming back into my mind.

Terry Kramer's little appearance at my apartment building at three in the morning hadn't been a coincidence. He had spent his whole life in Chicago and wouldn't have gone the wrong direction from a bar to the train, no matter how much he had to drink. Aside from that, he had been perfectly sober enough to lie to my face about why he was there. If he just happened to be at my apartment as two thugs decided to take advantage of a drunken idiot, there were only a couple of ways that was possible. I never considered coincidences to be possibilities.

One, he had been following me.

Two, he hung out around my apartment a lot but kept out of my sights.

Three, he arranged for the thugs to be there.

For a dozen reasons, I was going to go with all of the above.

Various thoughts, considerations, and scenarios occurred to me as I continued researching Brad Ashton's movements via the internet. Most of the thoughts started with Terry being a little too power hungry for his own good and ended with a bullet in his brain.

First things first, though – Terry wasn't on my kill list. It wasn't that he had to be on an official list approved by the boss, but if I went off on a tangent before hitting my target, Rinaldo wouldn't be overly pleased about it. I needed to take care of Ashton, which meant I needed to figure out everything I could about his Atlanta trip.

I took a few more shots, packed up my rifle, and sat down in the lobby area with Jonathan and Nick. No surprise at all, Nick had found the one and only woman at the shooting range and was telling her some bullshit story about being a makeup artist who specialized in painting women's boobs.

She was totally buying it, too.

"You wanna hit the bars tonight?" Jonathan asked. "Looks like I'm gonna lose lover boy over there early."

"Nah, I still got work to do."

"You got a big job," he agreed. "Terry keeps asking me about it."

"That little fucker needs to stay the hell away from me," I muttered.

"He does push yer buttons, don't he?"

"Doesn't," I corrected.

"Wha?"

"Nothing," I replied. "I'm outta here. Gotta let the dog out."

"Sweetwater later?"

"Yeah, okay," I said. "I'll meet ya there."

"Want a ride?"

"Nah, I'll take the L."

"You're the only fucker I know who has a choice and still takes the fuckin' trains."

I gave him a wave and a shrug as I headed off. Nick was already feeling up the chick's tits, saying something about how he thought he could paint her whole chest as a butterfly or something. I wondered what he did when the chicks he conned called him out.

Maybe they never did.

Maybe he really could paint a titty-fly.

With my rifle in a bag up on my shoulder, I moved through the turnstile and jumped on the next Red Line train. I had a ways to go before my stop, and I found myself a seat near the back of a car, facing forwards. I hated it when there were only backwards-facing seats available. Sideways was all right, but riding backwards made me want to puke.

I really did hate that feeling.

Two nuns in traditional garb got on the train at the next stop, and I watched them carefully. I had been raised by nuns, and though most of them were pretty decent, the ones in power were just as corrupt as the powerful in any organization. It was a lesson I had learned firsthand at a very early age.

"You are turning into a charming young man, Master Arden."

"Thank you, Mother Superior," I reply with a smile. I feel no love for this particular woman, but I have a plan I intend to see carried out. "You know I have so many questions for you..."

It had taken months, but I had eventually worn her down. Found her collection of sex toys and ultimately convinced her to let me out of that hellhole as an emancipated teen. It was either that or I tell everyone about the Harley-themed vibrator in her top dresser drawer.

The thing was totally frightening.

These nuns didn't even sit down but got off the L at the very next stop and went on their way. Having them off the train made it easier to think of something else. I watched them walk off, which was when my eyes spotted something round and shiny down by the door.

A quarter.

Though I rarely admitted such things to myself, I had been doing a decent job of keeping a certain abandoned-in-the-desert brunette out of my thoughts. As long as I kept myself busy, I was fine, but every time I saw a fucking quarter, it was like it all came rushing back to me.

"Not going to do it," I told myself as the urge to pick up the coin washed over me.

A couple of college kids glanced at me and quickly looked away again.

Fucking awesome. Now I was talking to myself right in front of other people. I stood up and got off the train at the next stop, walked twelve blocks, and then hopped on a bus instead. By the time I got back to my place, Odin was looking like he might actually piss on the carpet.

"Sorry," I muttered. "I can't even blame work this time – I was just fucking around."

He sneezed once and then stood by the door as I grabbed his leash. I took him out, then spent a few minutes rubbing his head before I left to meet Jonathan at the bar.

Sweetwater Bar and Grill wasn't my kind of place at all – big sports bar with a hundred TVs all around and guys with baseball caps serving your drinks. It was packed both with tourists and locals pretty much ninety percent of the time, which meant the bartenders never really had a chance to talk with anyone. They were quick with the drinks, but the place was just too crowded.

Jonathan loved it, but he was seriously into football.

It was the most convenient drinking place to my apartment, though, so I was there often enough. I recognized the bartenders immediately – a girl I liked and a guy I hated. I couldn't remember the dude's name. I knew since the day the place opened he was far too busy to do anything other than smile politely and make sure whatever you asked for was poured efficiently.

Okay, so that was basically his job, but I liked a little more effort.

The chick was dark-skinned and had a huge mound of braids all over the place. I couldn't remember her name – only that it started with a "T." She was a lot friendlier than the guy, and her smiles more genuine, but it was still the same "I'm too busy" vibe I got from the rest of them.

It was also a total meat-market.

Jonathan got up to smoke on the porch, and I held onto our ill-gotten table.

"Hi there!"

I only glanced at the girl as she sidled up to the booth where I sat. There was a huge line at the door, and I had seen her come in as I was entering. Of course, Jonathan had used some app he wrote on his phone to hack into the waiting list, and his name was up front as soon as a table became available, so we didn't stand at the door for very long.

She peeked over the back of the booth, probably making eye contact with the blonde who came in with her before focusing back on me. Her red-lipped smile only annoyed me as she moved closer, leaned over, and made the tops of her boobs stick out of her shirt a little more.

"Watching the game?"

"Not a fan," I answered. I picked up the pint glass of whatever microbrew had been on tap and took a sip.

"What *do* you like?" She tried to give me what I assumed was her version of bedroom eyes, but I just couldn't be bothered. I wasn't looking to get laid tonight. If I was, and it was going to be her, I'd end up having to buy her drinks all night and spend nearly as much as I did with Bridgett.

"Go wait for your own table," I muttered just as Jonathan was getting back. The girl glared at me before stomping off.

"Hey, dude – she might have had a friend!"

"So?" I countered.

"Even Nick would have helped me out there, bro!"

"Nick would have gone home with her *and* her friend."

"Point taken." Jonathan sighed, leaned back in the booth, and tapped his fingers on the table top rhythmically to the beat of whatever song was playing. "Didn't your mama teach you to be nice to girls?

"I don't even know who *my mama* is," I said as I tipped back my beer.

Jonathan laughed for a moment, and then looked at my face and the laugh died.

"Dude – are you serious?"

"No clue," I replied. "Never met her. Don't even have a name."

"Man, I'm sorry," he said. "I had no idea, brother."

"It's okay."

The server came back and set his chocolate milk down on the table, and I snickered a bit.

Jonathan loved chocolate milk; he couldn't get enough of the stuff. He'd move over to booze soon enough, but he always started the night with a big glass of chocolate milk, usually ordered off a restaurant's kids' menu.

"So who raised ya?" Jon asked. "Your dad?"

"Nope. Never met him either."

"So who then?" he pressed a bit. "I mean, if ya don't mind my asking – I ain't tryin' to pry or whatever."

I sipped, considered, and then downed my beer.

"I was raised in a convent."

"With a bunch of nuns?" Jonathan laughed loudly. "Are you serious?"

"Why do you ask me that?" I looked over at him as I drained the rest of the beer. "When do I bullshit you?"

"I get ya," Jon said with a nod. "I just didn't know."

He pulled another cigarette out and lit it right there in the bar. I raised an eyebrow.

"If they bitch, you'll be able to order another beer."

I shook my head slowly and stared at the top of the table. I inhaled deeply, and wondered if taking up smoking again might help me sleep.

"So what was that like?" Jon asked.

I considered for a moment again and figured what the hell? My shrink was only interested in the war shit and had yet to get around to the "tell me about your childhood" shit. He was far more interested in how I was tortured as a prisoner.

I was still pretty sure the fucker was writing a book.

"Pretty fucked-up," I answered honestly. "I was the only guy there except for the one priest who came by every Sunday for Mass."

"Seriously?"

I rolled my eyes at the word.

"Sorry, bro, it's just habit. So how'd you end up there?"

"No one would ever really tell me," I answered. "When I got older, I figured it was one of the nuns, and they just didn't want me to know which one. I tried to figure out who it might be, which is when I started watching everyone around me really carefully. I thought if I could read their body language, I'd be able to figure out which one was my mom."

"Did you figger it out?"

"Never did," I said. "Learned a lot of other shit."

I laughed.

"There was a girl there named Marie." I recalled the heart-shaped face of the redhead. "She was a couple years older than me, and she'd been sneaking out of the convent at night to meet up with some guy. I found out, and she offered to fuck me to keep quiet."

"Did you take her up on it?"

"That's how I lost my virginity!" I exclaimed with a grin.

"Ha! Ha!" Jon laughed. "That's custom!"

I finished up my beer, and Jon clacked his fingernails against his chocolate milk glass.

"I might be able to find out," Jonathan said quietly. "I mean, they gotta have a birth certificate on file somewhere, right?"

"I have documents signed by the Mother Superior as my legal guardian according to the State of Ohio," I told him.

"What's the date on it?"

I glanced up at him and narrowed my eyes.

"My birth date," I said. "May fourteen."

"Are you sure?"

The server interrupted us at that point, and we ordered a round of the same microbrew. I rubbed the heels of my hands into my eyes and thought about it. The idea that the date I had always assumed was my birthday might not be what I thought it was pissed me off.

I had to know.

"Okay," I said, "see what you can dig up."

"No worries, bro," he replied. "I'll see what I can find on the interwebs."

When we parted ways, I slowly walked between the buildings to get back to my apartment. I passed the drunks and the tourists without a glance, my head focused on two different memories.

One was the time I flat out asked Mother Superior if she knew who my parents were, and the look on her face told me she did, even as she lied about it. I reminded her about that particular commandment, which earned me a full day of prayer to reflect on my sins.

The other memory was Lia.

Again.

Her body, her voice, her eyes when she glanced back at me before boarding a bus to Phoenix – it was stuck in my head on repeat as I reached my apartment and took Odin out for a late-night walk. She was stuck in my head when I lay down to sleep as well, but the dreams I had were of a different sort.

The girl is young, maybe seven or eight years old, and she's wearing a long robe, but isn't yet old enough to be required to wear the hijab, the traditional women's scarf, around her head. She watches me from a dark corner as I struggle with the ropes around my wrists.

It's taken hours to shake the bag from my head, and my eyes are still adjusting to the light.

"Salam," I croak from my dry throat.

The girl's eyes widen, but she doesn't come closer or reply. I'm not sure what I would do if she did say something back – I only know about a dozen Arabic words, and I'm not about to embark on a long conversation. I focus on her eyes, but she keeps looking away. I nod towards a large barrel.

"Ma?"

Her eyes dart off to the side to the barrel of what might be water, but she doesn't move. We go back and forth for several minutes, and she finally goes a little closer to the barrel as she watches me. She reaches for a little cup, dunks it inside, and comes back with her fingers dripping water.

"That's it," I whisper. "Ma...min Fadlak."

She gives me an odd look, and I realize I've addressed her as a man, but I can't remember how to say "please" to a female, and I think she has the idea anyway. My pronunciation is presumably atrocious either way.

She takes three steps towards me before a man comes around the corner, immediately begins to scream at her, and she drops the cup into the dry sand. The precious water is soaked up by the sand immediately.

I woke in a cold sweat feeling thirsty. After stumbling into the kitchen for water, I was completely unable to get back to sleep at all. The girl's eyes as the man surprised her, picked her up, and carried her out of my sight made my heart pound in my chest.

My memories of her were clear, though I never saw the girl in the compound again. I had no idea what happened to her or what kind of trouble she might have been in for trying to help me. I'd caused so many others, at that point, to die on my watch. I never found out if I had attributed to her undoing as well.

The idea haunted my thoughts regularly. What if she was punished for doing what I asked her to do? What would her punishment have been?

Further memories – ropes, chains, fists, knees – flooded my head until I felt sick.

I tossed and turned, dozed just long enough to taste dry sand in my mouth, and got back up again. I took a piss and came out to find Odin standing there, looking up at me and wagging his tail. I took a step closer to him and reached out my hand to scratch his head.

Odin took the affection, then turned and headed back into the main room of the apartment. I followed, assuming he was going to want to go out, but he didn't. He stopped, looked at me, then went over to his dog bed near the window. He lay down and placed his head on his paws.

"You think I ought to just sleep with you?" I asked him.

His tail answered me by thumping against the carpet. I went back into the bedroom, grabbed my pillow, and then came back to the living room again. With the pillow held to my chest, I looked down at Odin.

"This is ridiculous," I said.

Odin's tail thumped.

"It's not going to work."

More thumping.

Sighing heavily, I lowered myself to the floor and put my pillow down next to Odin's bed. I lay down on my stomach with my arms on top of the pillow and looked over at him.

His eyes shone brightly in the nighttime city lights reflected from the window, and he panted, which always made him look like he was smiling. He reached out with his tongue and licked my arm before putting his head back down on his paws.

"That's gross," I told him as I closed my eyes.

Sleep came eventually. It wasn't great, and I still had nightmares, but when I woke, Odin was there, watching me and thumping his tail.

I spent the next six weeks in my apartment researching. I took Odin out for walks, but December brought winter and the weather at the edge of the lake sucked, so neither of us wanted to be out there too long. The rest of the time he would just lay across my feet until they went numb, and I would have to throw his rubber bone to get him to move.

Sleep was still something of an issue.

On a good night I would maybe get three or four hours, but it wasn't usually consecutive. The dreams weren't any worse – in fact, they were almost exactly the same every time – but they still woke me up and kept me from going back to sleep. Not sleeping consistently was taking its toll on my ability to think clearly, research thoroughly, and generally pissed me off.

It was the not knowing why the dreams had suddenly returned which was going to drive me crazy.

Mark's idea that my trek to the Arizona desert reminded me of Iraq wasn't a bad idea; I just didn't buy into it. I didn't have nightmares while I was there – I didn't remember a single dream until after I had returned. Maybe there was a connection, but I didn't think it was the climate.

Lia.

As soon as the name entered my head, I refused to think about her. I would not dwell on the woman who wandered into my sights and made me feel something for the first time in ages. There wasn't any point; no good would ever come of it, and I simply refused to consider her.

How well was that working?

I stood up from the desk that housed my computer, stomped to the kitchen, and started pulling out frozen fruit. I added half a banana, some pineapple juice, and some flax seed to the blender before turning it on and cringing as the noise invaded my ears. I poured the smoothie into a glass, added a straw, and downed it while my fingers tapped against the counter. Odin walked up, sat down at my feet, and eyed me impatiently.

"What?" I snapped at him and then immediately felt bad about it when he looked so happy about me giving him a little attention, even if it was gruff. I'd been ignoring him a lot lately as I dived into the internet.

Odin stood, wagged his tail at me, and then walked around in a circle a couple of times before knocking into my hand with his head. I rubbed the velvety spot on top of his nose, and his tail wagged harder.

"Fine," I muttered. I grabbed his leash from the hook near the door and headed outside.

Lake Shore East Park was right behind my apartment building. It had a decent-sized dog run, lots of grass and trees, which Odin enjoyed, and was usually less crowded than Navy Pier. There was always a pile of kids at the playground, but we stayed away from that area. Odin had never really been around kids, and though he was quite well-behaved under normal circumstances, you just never knew what a kid might do. If Odin got agitated and snapped at someone…well, that would draw way too much attention to me.

Besides, I liked Odin. If he bit someone, and they told me I had to put him down…well, that wouldn't go over well. I imagined there would be a lot of dead bodies around, but none of them his. At least, not until someone managed to take me out.

They would, too. Nice little park like this, surrounded by high-rises – there were plenty of places for snipers to hide out and strike without ever being seen. It was part of the reason I chose to live in the area. That and the dog-run.

We traversed all of Odin's favorite trails, circled the whole park, and paused to rest while I checked out the specials at III Forks. I hadn't been out to a restaurant for a while and wondered if Bridgett would like to go out for dinner sometime. I could call the pimp up early on and tell him to dress her up for me in something a little classier than thigh-high stockings and see through tops. Hell, I could get her a dress myself and then she could keep it.

I nodded to myself and decided to do it. That would be better anyway, since pimps were assholes and he'd probably just take the cost of a dress out of her cut of my money.

I wondered how Lia would look all dressed up for a night on the town but shook the thoughts away again. Thinking about it definitely didn't help, and I had a reason to consider Bridgett instead.

My mind wandered to her body and dwelled on the curves of her tits and her ass. My hands remembered the feeling of her, and I decided she was probably about a size eight. I recalled just exactly how much I needed to bend over to kiss her and figured she was five-six.

That ought to be enough information to get a dress picked out for her.

"Come on," I said to Odin, and we started back home. I cringed a bit as the door of the parking garage exit across the street from the dog run opened, blaring out a warning signal that echoed through the otherwise peaceful park. It was a fairly recent addition to the area, and the noise always pissed me off, public safety be damned.

We crossed the street and headed over the grass towards my building. As we did, thoughts of obnoxious noises, dinners out, and hookers left my head as my target took over my mind. The more I considered it, the more I knew this job was exactly as described – fucking difficult.

I needed to do more recon.

As soon as we were back inside and Odin's leash was put away, I walked back to the computer, pulled up Ashton's official schedule, and called Jonathan.

"I need a plane ticket to New York."

"Chasing what's-his-name?"

"Yep."

"Hold on."

A few moments later, Jonathan provided me with an online account number and all the credentials I needed to get a plane ticket. Ten minutes after that, the dog sitter was arranged. Within a half hour, I was throwing shit into a bag and calling a cab.

New York wasn't my favorite place, but Manhattan did give me a lot of options as far as rooftops went. People didn't really pay any attention to who you were, either, which made it a good place to be when you were looking to kill people.

The food was pretty good, too.

From the top floor of a hotel and through binoculars, I crouched down on a balcony and watched the crowd around Brad Ashton and his security crew. There were others there, of course – media people for the most part, but a few fans and other celebrities as well. Some chick who was bouncing up and down like she was on a fucking pogo stick was obviously annoying Ashton. His jaw tightened when he turned to her, and his shoulders would go stiff when she spoke or reached out to touch his arm. He was still smiling and putting up with her, so I could only guess she won some kind of contest.

Those things should be fixed.

I put the binoculars down for a moment and grabbed a sandwich off the room service tray. I chewed while contemplating which of the four guys around Ashton needed to die. Jim was out of the question, so that left one of the other three. They were all in my field of vision, which meant blocking Ashton. I had originally hoped I would get lucky, but found out soon enough Rinaldo knew what he was talking about – picking off Brad Ashton from a distance wasn't going to work. They were all over him all of the time.

Besides, if I killed one of the guards right in front of Ashton, he'd be just a bit on the suspicious side. He'd increase security to the point where I wouldn't be able to get close enough, and that just wasn't acceptable. I needed to go with a lot more subtlety.

As I used my binoculars to scan around me, I could see various security people placed on at least two rooftops and likely on top of the building where I perched as well. They alternated looking around at the ground floor and checking out the skyline. Ashton knew he was a target, no doubt about it – even this far from Chicago. With him on the alert, I was going to have to do a lot more waiting. I didn't really mind the waiting too much. If it all worked out, it would be well worth it, and I was used to being patient.

I followed his tour for two days in New York and then another day in Boston. From there he went to Orlando, which was a nice change of pace from the winter weather up north, and he finally boarded a plane back to LA. That's when I returned to Chicago to study my notes.

There were some definite trends I could use to my advantage.

Once Brad Ashton was in the safety of his hotel, the security guys were free to do what they liked, more or less. Mostly that involved the bar and football, though talk of the upcoming basketball season was also prevalent. There was one guy who always stayed behind, but he seemed to be more of a PR guy or agent, not a security guy. He was probably just a manager with a thing for the little earpieces.

I knew which one I was going to kill.

Henry Jefferson. He joined the group about six months ago, which made him the least senior, the least tight with the group, and the least likely anyone would go looking for when he disappeared.

He also lived alone, didn't seem to have a lot of close friends, and would probably go a few days before anyone missed him.

In a week they would be in Cleveland, which was just about the right distance. The timing was also perfect – right before the holidays, a time when everyone would be busy with other concerns, which could buy me a little more time before his death was discovered. Three days after New Year's they would head for Atlanta, which was where I planned to end Ashton.

Up close and personal.

Probably more personal than I cared to be, but I had to do what I had to do.

I hung out on a bench in the lobby of the Ritz-Carlton in Cleveland. The bench was off to the side – near the gift shop – and an unlikely place for Jim or anyone else to notice me. I hadn't gotten an actual room since I didn't plan on staying long. I only needed to do a quick job and then get back on the road as early as possible. I wanted to be home before midnight.

I hadn't picked up Bridgett recently, and I was in the mood to fuck.

Patiently waiting, I watched various people go by. Families on vacation, college-aged couples with Rock and Roll Hall of Fame T-shirts, and uncountable businessmen and women wandered through the lobby on their way to the elevator, the lounge, or to inquire at the front desk about their valet parking voucher.

None of them seemed to notice me in my business-casual Dockers and navy button down. I blended in, sat back, sipped at a bottle of Evian, and waited.

There he was.

Like he had most days, Henry Jefferson came back to the hotel around lunchtime to sleep. His was the overnight detail, and his shift officially ended at nine o'clock in the morning. He would go find a place for breakfast before going back to the hotel to sleep.

I stood and followed him into the elevator.

As he tapped his finger against the round button with the number seven on it, he blew out a long breath and grumbled. Taking a step back, he gave way for me to hit my own number, but I just smiled slightly and nodded at the already indicated floor.

There was something definitely off about his behavior.

Every time I had observed him before, he had the typical calm and quiet demeanor of a career security guy. He kept his hands behind his back except when he needed to put one of them up to his ear piece to look super cool. His suits were tailored, his shoes shined, and though it wasn't in his history, he probably would have made a decent Marine.

Jefferson was either really tired or agitated. He rubbed at the corner of his eye once, sighed twice between the first and seventh floors, and stared at the elevator door as if he was expecting it to try to clamp down on his arm. He tapped his toe a lot, and his hands kept gripping into fists.

Something had pissed him off. Not part of my plan but rather handy. If I had the good fortune enough for him to have had some kind of incident either at work or with a coworker, my plan was going to be even smoother than originally intended. There was nothing better than a convenient patsy.

The elevator chime went off, the doors opened, and despite the glare, Jefferson's arm wasn't captured by the machine. I still smiled a bit at the mental imagery and followed him quietly out of the car. He glanced over his shoulder once but didn't pay any attention to me afterwards, so I stayed fairly close.

Some security guard.

Maybe he wouldn't have made a decent marine after all.

I glanced up and down the hall and was pleased to see there was nothing but a single maid's cart at the far end of the hallway. There wasn't even a maid standing near it. Jefferson's room was right off the elevator, far from the room where the cart was standing. He slid his key card in the slot and stepped through the door.

I was right behind him and followed him swiftly through the doorway. I stood just inside, listened for the click as the door closed behind me, and followed up with a bullet in the back of his head before he even had a chance to realize I was in the room with him.

The whole thing took about six seconds.

I loved silencers.

Grabbing the body quickly, I moved it around the corner of the bed to conceal it a little better before the blood started seeping into the carpet. I failed to be quick enough to avoid a mess, but it would be minimal. Kneeling down next to the body, my gloved hands went through his pockets and came up with his wallet. I pulled out a credit card and used the on-line app provided by the hotel to extend his stay an extra week.

That could buy me a little extra time or not, I didn't really care. I hoped by the time he was discovered, I would be completely done with this whole assignment, but if he was found earlier, I didn't think it would change much.

I stepped over by the door and looked into the room to see if I had hidden him well enough. Of course, anyone who peeked inside was going to see a decent amount of blood and brains on the floor, but it was slightly better than a body.

I put the *Do Not Disturb* sign on the door as I left.

Interstate 80 wasn't too crowded, and I made it back home in record time. A half hour later, Bridgett was in the car with me and headed back to my apartment. Ten minutes after we arrived, she was giving me head, and I was finally starting to relax a little.

That night I got some real sleep. It was a good thing, too, because the call came a lot sooner than I expected.

"Hey there, Marshall!"

"Who's this?" I asked, knowing full well who had called this particular cell phone number. There was only one person who had it.

"Jim Conner," he said. "We met at the Embassy and talked football."

"Raiders fan, right?"

"Yeah! That's me!"

We both laughed a bit.

"So did you ever find another job?" he asked.

"Not yet," I answered with a convincing sigh. "I had an interview a couple days ago, but it wasn't very promising."

"Are you still interested in some security work?"

"It would be my preference," I said. "This last one I applied for was more usher than guard."

"Well, I couldn't really talk too much about it before," Jim said, "but I might have an opportunity for you."

"Really?" I smiled as I leaned back in my chair.

"Yeah," he said. "I work for Brad Ashton – you know, the actor?"

"Yeah, I know him. Well, I know who he is, anyway."

"As it turns out, we need a replacement security guy for an event coming up, and when he asked if we knew anyone, I remembered talking to you about needing a job. It's not quite in time for the holidays, but you could start the first week of January. You interested?"

Too fucking easy.

All right, it wasn't – there was a lot of work to make it happen, but it always felt good when it all came together perfectly.

Before I hung up the phone, I had a job lined up in Atlanta for just after the first.

There was just no way it could have gone more smoothly.

CHAPTER FIVE
Tense Situation

"Ten minutes."

"On my way." I dropped my cell phone into my pocket, grabbed my Beretta, and shoved it into the side holster under my jacket. Three minutes later I was in the car and heading to Moretti's office for an impromptu meeting that was suspicious to say the least.

In fact, he sounded a little panicked, and the boss never panicked.

It was the day after Christmas, and Rinaldo had just received a tip that Gavino Greco and three of his goons were on their way to his office. Mario Leone had been unexpectedly called away on personal business across town, and there was no way he would get back in time. I was close, though I was going to have to hurry.

My tires screeched as I rounded the corner, ditched the car – door still open – at the back entrance to Rinaldo's office building, and rushed inside. I took the stairs two at a time, and drew my gun out as I got to the fourth floor.

I paused, took a calming breath, and then quickly opened the door to the hallway.

Left.

Right.

Left again.

There was no one in the hall and no one besides me on the stairs. The elevator showed all cars on the first floor except for one, which was on the sixth. I listened intently, but the only sound was the usual noise from the heating ducts.

Walking backwards a few steps, I kept my weapon raised as I made my way to Rinaldo's office. It was empty, but there was sound coming from the back of the room near the rear door, which was closed. I'd never been through it but always thought it was just a personal room for Rinaldo in case he ever needed a shower or a nap.

With silent feet I moved to one side of the door. I was about to knock on it, but it started to open slowly before I got the chance. The first thing I saw was the barrel of a gun, and my hand flew up on instinct.

The gun flew into the air, landed on the desk, and then bounced to the ground again. I grabbed the wrist that had wielded the weapon, twisted it, and shoved the body it was attached to against the far side of the door.

Which is when I realized it was my boss.

"Shit!" I jumped back, released him, and tried to come up with something brilliant to say. "I'm sorry, sir, I didn't know–"

"Shut up," Rinaldo said. He reached over and rubbed his shoulder and wrist a little before he retrieved his gun and shoved it into the holster concealed by his jacket. "You got here quick."

"You said ten minutes," I reminded him.

"That was more like four."

"I figured ten was more of a maximum."

He laughed.

"I always liked you, Evan." Rinaldo clasped his hand on my shoulder as he started to say something else, but I heard the distinctive ring of the elevator.

"Sir," I nodded towards the door.

"Can you cover this?" he asked quietly. I glanced at the monitors which displayed the view from the security cameras back in the corner of the office. There were four of them, Gavino Greco included.

Greco was a man I had met on only a few occasions yet knew extremely well. His family had been around for a long time – back to the Capone days – and he had a lot more support overall in the mob world than my employer. Rinaldo Moretti had only arrived in Chicago about twenty years ago but had made quite a name for himself in a relatively short amount of time. He came from a well respected crime family back in the old country, as they say.

"This is a problem, Arden," Rinaldo said as the four men moved swiftly down the hallway.

"I've got it," I replied, hoping I sounded confident.

I felt confident…for the most part.

I usually did.

Of course, a lot of that stemmed from truly not giving a shit if I lived or died. The worst thing that could happen would be disappointing Moretti. Considering there was likely only two ways out of this – winning or dying – I wasn't too nervous. If I disappointed him, neither one of us was likely to be around long enough to regret it.

Rinaldo nodded, placed his trust in me, and sat down in his high-backed leather chair. He rotated his shoulders and adjusted his jacket before placing his folded hands on the desk in front of him. I took the place to his right, since it would be easier for me to cover him from that area, and stood at attention with my hands behind my back.

"Greco, my old friend!" Rinaldo said with an overly enthusiastic smile. "You are all the way across town, *out of your territories*, and unexpected. I hope you bring me good news!"

I resisted the urge to glance sideways at my boss to get a better understanding of his words, and decided my eyes were best kept on my opponents.

My targets.

My potential victims.

Of the three surrounding Greco, I only knew one. His name was Craig Flannigan, and he used to be a gun runner in one of the smaller operations before Greco wiped them out. Flannigan was thought to have been the informant amongst the gun runners that made the hit easy for Greco. He was tall, redheaded, and had a thick beard to match his thick Irish accent.

The other two were dark-haired and dark-eyed with big muscles bulging out of their tailored suits. They could very well have been twins, but one had a scar across his cheek, and the other had a mustache. They didn't speak but flanked their boss closely with their hands placed near their shoulder holsters. These two were Italian-descended and likely related to Greco in some way. Flannigan would rat them all out if the money was right or his life depended on it, but not these two. They would give their lives for Greco if it was necessary.

Loyal men.

Flannigan stood directly in front of me, blocking his boss from the known hit man. It was defensive, and though it made sense on some level, it showed weakness. It put a man between me and my target, blocking him from me, yes – but also providing me with a shield if I needed it. Flannigan wasn't even looking at me, so he obviously didn't consider me a major threat – not when they had numbers on their side.

He wasn't prepared for me to be here, and it didn't fit whatever plan they had. He wasn't a bright guy, and impromptu wasn't his forte. This gave me a significant advantage.

"I bring news, old friend," Greco said. He didn't bother to hide the menace in his voice, which wasn't a good sign at all. It meant he had already made a decision and there would be no pleasant negotiating before he intended to carry out his plans. "I do not consider it *good*."

"Do tell," Rinaldo said as he leaned forward on his desk.

I wanted to tell him to lean back – he would be able to drop to the floor much faster if necessary – but of course I couldn't.

"A shipment of heroin," Greco said, "a shipment with my hands already around it has gone missing from my docks. It is the third time in two months."

"Unfortunate," Moretti agreed. "Do you think these thefts of your property are connected?"

"I do," he said. "I think they are connected to you."

"That is quite an accusation," Rinaldo snarled. "You speak without thought."

"I speak with evidence!" Greco growled back. "Your own man found at the site with some of the goods still on his hands!"

"A mistake," Rinaldo said. "Why would I do such a thing and spark war with my ally, hmm?"

"Because your supplier has been hit twice by the feds now, and you are losing money!"

"Why do you say this?" Rinaldo's voice went calm, and he sat back in his seat, thankfully.

I tensed as Greco leaned forward slightly and placed his right hand on Rinaldo's desk.

"Because your own man told me."

"What man is this?" Rinaldo asked. "I would like to know who is claiming to be in my employ under such circumstances. Perhaps he had a Russian accent you failed to notice?"

The dig was definitely felt. Greco's eyes narrowed slightly, and his hand clenched into a fist at the mention of the Russian spy who infiltrated his organization last year and killed one of his sons during a drug deal.

"There is only one mistake this time," Greco said quietly, "and that mistake is yours."

It was Flannigan who acted when Greco tapped his thick finger on the desk – a prearranged sign.

I moved without thought.

Flannigan was going for his gun inside his jacket, and I wasn't going to be able to both outdraw him like an old western and protect my boss at the same time. Instead, I went with a more melee approach.

My hand moved out, knuckles forward, and collided with the center of his neck. The choking, raspy sound that emerged from his mouth was accompanied by bulging eyes and a rapidly reddening face. He dropped to the ground, and I kicked out at him while drawing my weapon from the back of my pants at the same time.

I didn't bother with the other two men – there wasn't time to actually shoot anyone. Their weapons were already out and aimed at me. I had to go with a more tactical approach, which meant pointing the barrel of the Beretta at Greco's face.

Flannigan heaved in a breath, and in my peripheral vision I could see him drawing his weapon and pointing it towards my head. This wasn't part of their plan, though, and he didn't know what to do next.

With three guns pointed at various parts of my body, I remained completely still. My heart was pounding in my chest, and adrenalin coursed through my system, but I refused to let it show in my face or in the steady way I held my Beretta right between Gavino Greco's eyes.

"You know you die if you pull that trigger," he said quietly. The calm of his voice didn't match the slight tremor in his fingertips, nor the tiny bead of sweat forming at his hairline.

"Yes, sir," I replied.

"So why don't I just have them fire?" Greco said with a sly little smile. "You'll be dead before you can retaliate, and your boss there will follow you into the afterlife shortly."

"No, sir," I said. "If I get hit, even with an instant kill, my finger's already tight against the trigger. With the angle and the trauma to my system, my finger will pull back in reflex. Yeah, I'll be dead, but I'll take you with me. Whatever happens after that… well, honestly? I don't give a shit."

Our eyes remained locked with each other. I could see the man's eyes as they looked for lies within my face, but he could find nothing. He obviously played more cards than he watched the Discovery channel, and I could see him ask himself – was I holding aces or deuces? Was my knowledge of physiology accurate?

He had no idea, but he was self-centered enough to not take the chance.

"A misunderstanding," he said softly. "I'm sure the Russians must have been behind it."

"Let's put it behind us then, shall we?" Rinaldo's voice floated from my right, but I could hear the odd tenor in the sound. He still wasn't sure – he didn't know if we had won or not, but I knew we had.

Just the battle, not the war. This was far from over.

"Put those down, boys," Greco said. "We don't want to be late for dinner."

Three guns dropped towards the ground, but I didn't alter my position at all. Even as all four of them backed out of the office, turned and raced for the elevator, the business end of my Beretta stayed trained to his face.

I did not take chances.

Never again.

I stood still as my heart pounded, and the adrenaline in my system started to sour. My eyes stayed locked on the hallway, daring one of them to try to come back. The lighted numbers at the top of the elevator showed their descent back to the first floor, and I still watched to make sure none of the elevators started to rise again. When they didn't, I listened for the echo of footsteps on the stairwell.

"I think they're gone," Rinaldo said.

I didn't move.

"Arden, they're not coming back. Look at the security cameras."

My fingers twitched on the handle of the gun, and my index finger flexed slightly.

"Evan."

"Just making sure," I said simply.

"Well, I'm pretty sure."

I nodded, took a step back, and lowered my weapon. When my eyes turned to the monitors, I could see them in a long, black car leaving the parking lot.

"They knew you were going to be alone," I said.

"Yes, I think that's correct."

"Who knew Mario was across town?" I asked.

"A handful," Rinaldo replied. "There were six others besides Mario and myself in the room when he had to leave. All loyal men, though."

I looked over at him and raised an eyebrow.

"One of them isn't."

He nodded.

"Apparently."

Rinaldo went through the list of people who knew about Mario's sudden absence, and it didn't make me feel any better at all. Two were family in the quite literal sense. Another pair dealt with some of the side businesses – money laundering, mostly. Jonathan and Terry were also on the list

I couldn't consider either one as definitely innocent or definitely guilty – I was too biased against both of them, just in different directions. If I found out about Jonathan being treacherous, I'd have to kill him. On the other hand, I wanted to find out Terry was a rat because he was annoying and I wanted him dead, anyway. I'd shoot first, never bother to ask any questions, and then get burned later if I was wrong.

It was probably best I didn't get involved in this one.

"I need you to do a little side job for me," Rinaldo said.

He must have been reading my mind, but not in a way I considered favorable.

"What about Ashton?"

"When do you plan to take him out?"

"In Atlanta," I said. "He'll be there next week.

"Ashton can wait," Rinaldo said. "I need this sooner."

Shit.

His mind was set, and there was no way I was going to change it.

"Whatever you say, sir."

"Do some spying, do some watching – all that shit you're extra good at. What do you call it? Recon?"

I nodded.

"I need your top three picks," he said. "The top three guys you think might have said something to Greco. I want to know why they're your top picks, and then we're going to bring them all together for a little party."

"What about family?" I asked quietly.

Rinaldo's eyes darkened.

"Your top three picks," he repeated. "I don't care whose cunt they've been in *or* come out of, you understand?"

"Yes, sir," I said.

He turned towards me and placed a hand on my shoulder.

"I can't let this go, Evan," he said. "I need some closure on this one. I can't take out Greco. I'm not positioned to do that just yet, but I need this – I need this fixed."

"Yes, sir," I replied. "I understand."

"You will do this for me?"

"Yes, sir."

"Now?"

"Now?" I repeated. The look in his eyes didn't indicate he was going with the equivalent of *sometime soon*. "As in, right this moment, sir?"

"Find the rat scurrying around in my business, Evan. Find him and bring him to me. I don't care about his relationships or how long he's been here; I need to know who he is."

"Three top men?"

"You bring them to me," he said. "I'll make sure I get the right one."

"Today?"

"Right now."

I swallowed, and my still tense body tried to relax enough to think. If this wasn't a test, I didn't know what was. This was it though – this was the real way I got back into his graces. I could read between the lines, too. *Don't fuck up, Arden. Not again.*

"I will be counting on you, then, Mister Arden."

I nodded, turned, and left the office.

There was a lot of work to do if I was going to have any chance at coming up with the right three people as quickly as he wanted them. I also still wanted to make the hit on Ashton in Atlanta – I'd already done so much work to get ready for that, and changing the hit to another place was going to make it ten times harder. I'd practically have to start over again, and I hated to waste work.

I had to move fast, but I had to be careful, too. Bringing in the wrong people would be just as dangerous and career-ending as being late. I had to know I was right, which means I had to go the fastest route possible.

First and foremost – alibis.

Usually I would use Jonathan Ferris and his computer skills for such work, but I was going to have to do this one on my own. It wasn't my strong point, but I had resources people didn't know about.

I walked into Walgreens and picked up a pre-paid cell phone which I paid for in cash. I examined the packaging as I headed back outside. As soon as I stepped out of the revolving door, I had to jump back against the building to avoid some guy doing a duck-walk down the sidewalk. He had a cup of something in his hands, which were clasped behind his back. With every step he took, the liquid sloshed out of the cup and onto the cement. A nearly burnt-out cigarette stuck between his lips completed the scene.

I shook my head and tried not to laugh as I dumped the phone's packaging into the trash, activated it, and dialed a number from memory.

"Hey Eddie-boy," I said into the phone. "It's Arden."

"How goes, LT?"

"I'm retired, asshole," I reminded him.

"You'll always be my lieutenant."

I honestly wished he wouldn't say that.

Edward McHenry, or Eddie-boy as everyone called him, was the communications guy during the first mission I commanded and the only mission I commanded that turned out favorably. We bonded just because we both grew up in southwestern Ohio, and his was the first friendly face I saw after I was brought back from the desert.

"Well, how about you do your *friend* a little favor?"

"Anything you want, LT," Eddie-boy said.

"Phone records," I said. "From the past week from six different people. Just numbers and shit will do, but if you got VOIP logs, that would be awesome."

"Give me the numbers," Eddie-boy said.

I rattled off the phone numbers.

"I need this quick," I told him. "Super quick."

"You paying super much?" Eddie-boy asked with a laugh.

"What happened to all that 'oh, my lieutenant, my lieutenant' shit?" I asked.

"You should have gone for the promotion, war hero," Eddie-boy responded. "It just doesn't flow like *captain* does."

I sighed.

"Wire transfer?"

"Naturally."

"On its way," I said. "Half now, half when your information proves good. Double if you get it in the next hour."

"Yes, sir!"

I could practically see him saluting.

It cost a shitload of money, but the information received fifty-two minutes later was definitely worth it.

I checked out Jonathan first and was glad to see that he ordered a pizza on his way out of Rinaldo's office and spent the next three hours exactly where I would have expected – on the internet, watching porn. I scrolled through the other numbers he'd dialed and other areas his GPS had tracked him, but found nothing the least bit suspicious, and I was glad.

I took a deep breath and happened to glance up at a shop window across from Millennium Park. In the window was a "Save Ferris" T-shirt from the *Ferris Bueller's Day Off* movie. Jonathan always took shit for his last name because of it, but I couldn't resist the irony, so I popped inside and bought him one. His birthday was coming up.

For better or worse, Terry was also clean. I had full speech-to-text logs on him going back a month, which was actually kind of handy. He'd gone from the Moretti household to some shit bar by Dearborn Park and hung out with two friends he called along the way. They were still there – or at least his GPS equipped phone was. I wasn't going to have time to go through all his logs until later, but it would be convenient if I ever needed anything on him.

The third one I checked was Steven Hobbs. He did a lot of the grunt work when it came to siphoning funds from the world of electronic payments and turning it into cash that could be used anywhere. The man probably had three hundred bank accounts, credit card accounts, and ACH routing numbers in his pocket at any given time. He was paid well for his services, though he could probably just pay himself any time he wanted.

There weren't any phone logs, but there was one call that looked a little strange. Someone called him from a payphone across town – not an area of town where my boss' people were usually to be found. It didn't make him a rat, but he went to the top of my list.

I went through the family next with a bit of trepidation. Bad news to a family like the Moretti's was likely to go from no Christmas card next year to an all out war in just a couple of minutes if the wrong words were said. The last thing I wanted to be was the catalyst for a family war. Fault or not, I'd be one of the first casualties.

The two in question were second or third cousins to Rinaldo and not close in the family business. Close enough to not be stupid, I would have hoped, but they didn't have their fingers in all the little pies Moretti had going. They had been at the house to see Luisa – Rinaldo's fair daughter. Like Jonathan, she had a birthday coming up apparently, and they were all planning a cruise somewhere in the Mediterranean.

I made a mental note to come up with a suitable gift.

All the family members checked out, too.

Even Steven Hobbs' boss checked out, which left me – interestingly enough – just the one real suspect. I wondered if I might actually get that lucky that quickly. It was possible.

I needed more intel.

I called Eddie-boy back and got Hobbs' location – a bar over on North Michigan Avenue – and quickly made my way over there. I recognized the guy at the end of the bar when I walked in, but he didn't look up or notice me.

Hobbs was a chunky guy, mid-thirties with bad skin and greasy hair. He was just the sort that spent his life trying to make up for all the times he was picked on in grade school. I had no patience for the type, but that didn't make him my traitor. If nothing else, I would have expected him to be a little more nervous. Who would betray a mob boss and then sit in a grubby bar with a Miller Lite in his hand?

It wasn't long before a woman joined him. She had short blonde hair, a skinny ass, and ridiculous heels – definitely not my type. She sauntered up to Steven and practically sat in his lap. The music was up a little, and I couldn't hear her at first. With practiced subtlety, I moved around the bar and sat with my back to both of them where I could hear pretty easily.

"So, no calls from work?" the blonde was asking.

"I told you, Maria, I did everything I needed to do earlier," Steven responded. "Part of what I like about working for Moretti – I get to set my own hours."

"He's a demanding boss, though," Maria said. "Maybe you'll get a call about him."

She kept asking questions, and the dumb-ass kept answering them for her. At one point, she said the words I needed to hear.

"So, how is Mario's mother?"

"I don't know," Stephen said. "Once he left Moretti's place, I didn't hear from him again. She went to the hospital in Gary – that's all I heard. Why do you care so much, anyway?"

Why, indeed?

She flirted and kissed on him for a while and then claimed she had errands to run and would meet up with him again later. As she left, I tossed some cash down on the table for my seltzer and followed her.

She wasn't all that bright.

"He hasn't heard a thing," she said into the phone as she walked away. "Tell Gavino no one is on to him – we're good to go."

It was all I needed to hear. I didn't even wait – I just moved up behind her while she was still distracted and on the phone. She hung up and started to rummage around in her purse for her keys. By the time she got the car door open, I was on her.

An elderly couple and a bum on the sidewalk both watched me as I grabbed her by the arm, covered her mouth with my other hand, and shoved her into her own car. I didn't care who saw me – eyewitnesses were unreliable at best – and the one person who was sure to remember me later wasn't going to live long enough to tell anyone about me.

I also just didn't care. It wasn't like I was going to go to prison for anything. If I was caught, I'd either be acquitted or dead. Prison wasn't going to enter into it.

Before she really grasped what was happening, I punched her once on the side of the face to stun her, then grabbed her keys and got the car going. By the time I pulled into traffic, I had my gun to her head.

"No words unless I ask you a question, and no movement – you understand?"

"Y…y…yes!"

"What's your name? And don't say Maria."

She didn't respond until I touched the business end of the Beretta against her temple.

"If I hit a pot hole, you're dead," I informed her. "You might want to answer my question so I can concentrate on my driving."

"Nina," she said quietly. "Nina Carson."

I knew who she was immediately. Killing James Carson is what had me sent to Arizona, and Nina was his sister. Greco was doing her cousin on the side.

"Take out your phone," I instructed.

With a shaking hand, she did as I said.

"Now call up Mister Hobbs and tell him you need to see him right away."

"But…but I just left him…"

"Tell him to meet you in the parking garage of the Chicago Sun Times."

"The garage?"

"You heard me."

She swallowed a couple of times, and I had to wonder what was going on in her head. She wasn't new to all this, that much was sure. It was entirely possible she knew exactly who I was, but not likely.

She made the call like her life depended on it, so maybe she did know who I was. She followed directions and told Steven right where to meet us but not why. She gave nothing away and sounded very convincing.

Proper little liar.

I pulled her car into a handicapped space in the parking garage next to a small, metal door. I kept my gun at her face, moved backwards out of the driver's side door, and then brought her through with me.

With her upper arm firmly in my grasp, I moved her past the piss-stained cement walls and to a small door. I twisted the knob, and it opened easily. Inside the room there were three chairs on the floor, a rusted metal toolbox in the corner, and a bare light bulb hanging from the ceiling.

I placed her in one of the chairs and grabbed both her wrists in one hand. From the toolbox I extracted plastic zip ties and secured her hands behind her.

"What's going on?" she asked. The panic in her voice was rising. I still didn't think she knew who I was, but she was getting the idea. "Please, I won't tell anyone–"

I gagged her with a rag from the toolbox, made a quick call to Rinaldo, and then waited at the door. Steven Hobbs arrived just a minute or two later, and I called out to him.

"Looking for a girl?" I asked. I beckoned with my hand. "She's in here."

The moron came right to the door, where I hauled him in and gave him a slight push towards Nina. He stumbled a little, turned, and looked at me quizzically as I closed the door behind us.

"What…what's going on?" Steven asked.

"Have a seat." I indicated the folding metal chair next to his girlfriend.

"Maria?" he said quietly.

"Try Nina," I corrected.

He just stared, confused. He was an idiot, like all men who did more thinking with their dicks than actually putting them to their natural use. I didn't even have to ask him about his past. I knew it as well as I knew my own.

Overweight in school, bullied on the playground, and always picked last on the team. He always thought he was much smarter than those who hazed him and thought that someday he'd have a great job and they'd have to grovel to him instead of laugh. Instead, he got a mediocre job, no date for the prom, and was now being used by a woman who probably hadn't even let him come in her.

I raised my gun and indicated the chair again. He sat and stared at me with wide eyes.

It was only a few minutes before I heard the sound of additional cars parking just outside the little office room. Footsteps followed, and then four short raps on the door. I took a step backwards to open it.

Rinaldo, Mario, and Terry Kramer were outside of the door.

They wasted no time in letting Hobbs know exactly why he was there.

"Mario, this man here decided it was a good idea to tell your family business to his piece of ass," Rinaldo said to his bodyguard. "What do you think of that?"

"I think he's an inconsiderate man," Mario said sternly.

I didn't really care for the games at this point. They were both going to have to die, and we all knew it. I never understood dragging it all out for the dramatic effect. Wasn't that the same sort of mentality that always screwed up the comic book villain's plans?

They went back and forth between berating him and administrating a little light torture until Steven was blubbering about how he didn't know anything about her. He went from defending her to accusing her in a short amount of time, and she struggled against her tied hands and gagged mouth as he told them everything she had said and done.

She used him to get information about Moretti's movements and gave that information back to Greco, who just waited for the proper time to use the information to eliminate the competition and take over his businesses. Fortunately for Rinaldo, I had been there to stop it from happening.

"She was nice to me!" Steven finally cried out as Kramer broke another knuckle.

Terry laughed.

"I believe Mario would like to take care of this man himself, Evan," Rinaldo said.

"Yes, sir," I replied.

"I could help–" Terry started to say, but Moretti interrupted him.

"Shut up, Terry," he said softly.

At least Terry had the good sense to listen.

Mario hauled Steven up by the back of his collar and hauled him out of the small office. Terry followed, leaving Rinaldo in the room with me and the girl tied to the chair.

"Mister Arden," Rinaldo said quietly. He waved a hand over at Nina. "Would you finish up please? Not here, though – this place is a bitch to clean."

"Yes, sir."

Nina's eyes were big as I hauled her up out of the chair. Comprehension was washing over her face, and if she hadn't known who I was before, she definitely knew me now. Whether by name or not, she knew who I was to Rinaldo and his organization.

Still in shock, she barely struggled as I hauled her out of the little garage office and back to her car. She did whimper a bit as I opened the trunk and shoved her inside, but I couldn't blame her for that. It was the last ride of her life after all.

I turned off the radio as I drove down to the water. It was late, and there wasn't much traffic as I crossed the West Grand Avenue Bridge and then drove down a side street. It was a short trip, and I didn't want to listen to half a song. I pulled into a little drive area with a big sign that said the area was under twenty-four hour surveillance.

Sometimes they just made it easy.

I barely had to aim since I had shot out this particular camera so many times. It shattered into pieces all over the asphalt as I got back into the car and headed to the parking lot just south of the bridge. I pulled up close to the building and parked in the shadows.

Nina struggled as I pulled her out of the trunk and onto her feet. She didn't come close to breaking away from my grip, and I wasn't sure where the hell she thought she was going to go, anyway. The building was inaccessible, and there was nothing here but gravel and the edge of the river. Even if she did make it the full five-hundred yards and over the fence without me catching her – which she wouldn't – what was she going to do? Hide in one of the nearby ocean containers?

My grip on her upper arm tightened, and I hauled her down to the edge of the water. There was a ledge between the building and the water where boats could come up and exchange supplies if any of that shit still happened today.

"Please…please don't," she begged. Her nails dug into my knuckles, which stung a bit.

I didn't answer her; I wasn't really listening. I'd heard it all before – the pleas, the promises – they meant nothing to me. I had a job to do, and I was going to do it. Nothing she said was going to make any difference in the outcome.

"Go on," I said. I gave her shoulder a little push ahead and got her walking while I followed closely behind. I wanted her under the bridge where it was darkest. If someone did happen to hear the shot, I didn't want to be visible from Chicago Avenue. She tripped over the asphalt once in her high heels, but I kept a hold of her so she wouldn't fall onto the concrete.

No reason to die with skinned knees.

"Why? Why?" she asked over and over again.

As if she didn't know.

We made it to the spot on the ledge in the combined shadow of two buildings and a roadway. I positioned her close to the edge, where there was less than a ten foot drop into the river. She looked over the edge and into the water, turned around, and dropped in front of me. She reached out to me with her hands, like she was trying to reach the hand of some god she saw in my eyes.

As if she'd find salvation there.

I looked down at the pricey heels on her feet, now covered in mud, and the designer dress strangling her twiggy figure. I pulled my Beretta out of the back of my jeans and fitted the end with a silencer. There wasn't any reason to make unnecessary noise.

"Please," she cried. "I'll do anything you want – I swear!"

Tears streamed down her cheeks as I raised the barrel of the weapon to her face. There wasn't any reason to drag it out – that would just be cruel.

I pulled the trigger, and her body slumped sideways. One shove from my foot sent her into the water. She'd be found, no doubt – probably before morning. It wasn't about making her disappear – it was about making sure Greco knew what had happened to her.

With the Beretta down the back of my pants again, I climbed into her car and drove it out to the airport to leave it in long-term parking, and then I took the L back into town.

I loved riding the trains and buses in Chicago. I was a people watcher, and it was always entertaining as hell to be on public transportation with anything from a drunk, crazy homeless guy to an equally crazy high-class, sorority bitch. If you were lucky, the two would run into each other and some kind of explosion would ensue.

No such luck this time, though. All the nuts must have taken the night off. Instead, I ended up leaning back in the seat and closing my eyes. I didn't drift off or anything – I still couldn't sleep – but my mind started wandering.

"What's your name?" she asks.

"Evan," I tell her.

"I'm Lia," she says with a smile. I'm not sure if it is due to her continued nervousness or if she really just wants to be polite. I watch her closely but don't respond. "Um...Lia Antonio."

Smooth, flawless skin and warm, brown eyes. When I thought about her, I always pictured how she looked when I woke up with my head resting on her stomach and her fingers running through my hair. It had gotten long while I was in Arizona. Well, long for me, anyway.

She smiles at me, and it feels like I've been turned inside out.

I closed my eyes and shook my head.

"Stop that shit," I muttered. "She was just some girl you fucked."

A pair of tourists with shopping bags glanced at me nervously, but I ignored them.

It was late when I arrived home, but if Odin was ticked off at me he didn't show it. I took him for an extra long walk around the park and played fetch with him in the living room for a bit before I had a bite to eat. He appreciated the extra attention when I sat down on the floor and rubbed his belly.

"I'm gonna have to ditch you for a while again," I informed him. He looked at me and snuffed through his nose. "Just a couple days, I think. No more than that."

His tail thumped against the carpet, and I rubbed his stomach once more before I got up and headed to the shower. The water was extra hot, and I loved the feeling of the moist heat. It relaxed me, and I hoped it meant I was going to get some decent sleep tonight.

My shower finished, I crawled into bed naked. Just as I was about to drop off, the phone rang.

Rinaldo.

"Sir?"

"You did good today, Evan," he said. "Real good."

"Thank you, sir. It just needed to be done."

"It's good to know there's someone around I can really trust. Damn good thing to know."

"Anything you need from me," I assured him, "just tell me. It'll get done."

"I know it will, son," Rinaldo said. "I know it will."

Son.

Leaning my head back, I closed my eyes and smiled slightly.

There was just no better feeling than pleasing the boss.

CHAPTER SIX

Brief Surrender

New Year's Eve.

Every year I was invited to Rinaldo Moretti's house to celebrate the coming of a new year, and every year I went. Each party was exactly like the previous year's with only the dates on people's paper hats changing. I clanged champagne glasses with Rinaldo at midnight, kissed Mrs. Moretti on the cheek, and put up with a bunch of assholes patting me on the back and telling me how promising the next year was going to be.

Whatever.

At exactly one in the morning, I felt I had paid my due respects and had the valet bring my car to me. He dropped the keys to the Mazda in my hand with a look of distaste, but I only took the convertible out in nice weather. Apparently a forty-thousand-dollar car wasn't up to his usual standards, so I didn't bother to tip the asshole.

The Audi convertible I had was actually acquired without cost to me since I kept it after killing its original owner. I never would have spent that much money on a car. I was a relatively frugal guy, and tended to keep my money liquid and close to me. At some point the winds could change, and having a good escape plan involved a decent amount of cash. Why waste it when the public transportation was so close to my apartment? I liked taking the bus most of the time, anyway – it was always good for people watching.

The ride home brought me within a couple of blocks of where I figured Bridgett would be. I had almost considered giving her up as some kind of New Year's resolution – I was starting to feel dependent on her. If I was in town on the weekend, I almost always had her over for a night.

Sometimes two.

It didn't exactly fit my miserly nature, but I needed the release and the sleep. More and more often, I was finding myself unable to think as clearly as I normally did, and it worried me more than I cared to admit. My sessions with Bridgett were more expensive than going to see Mark the Shrink, but they kept me going, and I had a lot to get done. Talking to him left me cold inside – Bridgett was warm.

I had seen Mark Duncan again the other day.

"How do you think your experiences changed you?"

"They didn't."

"Evan, no one comes out of something like that without some damage."

"Not a mark on me – they were really careful about that."

"There are other kinds of scars."

I blinked a few times to bring myself back to the present.

After a bit of internal debate regarding resolutions and finances, I finally came to a conclusion. I had no actual target to go after for the evening, and I decided New Year's Eve was really a crappy night to start resolutions after all.

The light changed to green, and I looked behind my shoulder before I quickly changed lanes and headed in the opposite direction from my apartment. There were nothing but drunks, cops, and me out on the road, so I drove with caution over to the red light district and the street corner by the drug store where Bridgett's pimp could usually be found.

Two minutes later, Bridgett was in the passenger seat, and I was driving us back to my apartment.

"Happy New Year," she said with a smile.

"Nice outfit," I commented back.

Bridgett looked down at her dress, if you could call it that. It showed the top of her nipples, with her tits outlined in red sequins. Happy New Year was scrawled in blue sequins across her bare belly.

"You like it?" she asked with another big smile.

"It's atrocious," I replied honestly, "and you look like you're freezing."

"I am," she admitted.

I cranked up the heat.

"You're all decked out," she said as she reached up and ran her fingers over the edge of the bowtie. "A tux? You been out partying?"

"I guess," I said. "I was at a party, anyway."

"You aren't much of a partier, are you?"

"Probably not in the way you mean."

Her fingers made their way down the lapels of the jacket and then to my thigh.

"You look nice," she said softly.

Her hand gripped my leg, and my cock seemed to recognize the touch. I was briefly temped to have her blow me or jerk me off there in the car, but it was New Year's Eve and I was bound to get pulled over with her lips around my dick.

"Save that thought, babe," I said. "I don't think you want us to get arrested."

Bridgett's hand moved up and brushed the edge of my dick before she pulled it away and ran it up her own thigh. Her skirt moved up a little, following the motion.

"Vixen," I murmured.

Bridgett giggled.

By the time we reached the elevator of my apartment, her hands were all over me. She reached around the cummerbund and into the tux pants, yanked out the button down shirt, and ran her hand down inside and over my ass.

"Eagar tonight?" I asked with a raise of my brows.

Her response was to crush her lips to mine. My hand grabbed the back of her head and held her there as my tongue explored her mouth. Her fingers dug into my ass, and my free hand moved up to cup one of her tits, which was still seriously cold from the night wind.

Then the elevator door opened.

Bridgett tensed and jumped back a bit, but there wasn't anyone there. I took her hand and led her out the door but only just into the hallway. I quickly undid the tux trousers and pulled them open.

"On your knees," I commanded.

"Here?" she asked as she glanced up and down the hallway. "What happened to not wanting to get arrested?"

"No one is going to arrest me here," I told her. "My boss owns this place. Now get on your knees and suck me off."

I took a step back and leaned against the wall. Pulling her closer to me, I put a hand on her shoulder and guided her down to the floor. She glanced down the hall once, then back up at me as she positioned herself right in front of my crotch.

"Did you think you could just tease me in the car and get away with it?" I asked with a slight smirk. I reached in, took my cock out of my tuxedo pants, and guided her head to the tip. "Suck."

Her warm mouth engulfed me, and I watched her eyes seduce me as her lips moved around my shaft. My fingers traced over the frigid skin of her cheek, and I found myself mildly annoyed that her pimp had them all out in the cold dressed like they were.

All hookers should work in Florida or something.

"You look good like that," I told her. My hand moved into her hair and set a slightly faster rhythm for her. "On your knees, out here in the open with your lips around my cock. You love pleasing me, don't you?"

She hummed around my dick, and I tilted my face towards the ceiling as I unloaded into her warm mouth. My eyes dropped back down, and she sucked and tongued until there was nothing left to clean off.

She'd definitely honed her skills in the blowjob department.

I reached down and helped her up with one hand and put my dick away with the other. Bridgett wiped her mouth, and we went into my apartment. I took Odin out for a quick piss and came back to Bridgett hanging out on my couch.

It looked very…familiar.

With a slight shake of my head, I went into the kitchen, pulled out a bottle of water, and offered one to Bridgett as well.

"So what party did you go to?" she asked.

"Just a basic New Year's party," I answered.

"That's all you have to say about it?"

"Pretty much." I took a long sip of my water, leaned back against the couch, and closed my eyes.

She didn't take the hint.

"You don't like holidays much, do you?"

"Not really."

"Why not?" she asked.

I sighed and opened my eyes enough to glare at her.

"I really just want to rehydrate a bit and then go to bed, okay? I didn't pay you to run your mouth."

Her eyes narrowed at me for a moment, but then she smiled what I assumed was supposed to be an apology and snuggled up to me. I put an arm around her shoulders, leaned back against the couch again, and just felt her fingers trace over my chest.

Of course, that didn't last long.

"You've been picking me up at least once a week for three months," Bridgett said, "but you never tell me anything about yourself."

"That's because you're my favorite hooker," I replied, "and not my shrink."

"You have a shrink?" Her head tilted up to look at me, and her hair tickled my chin as she moved.

My eyes flicked over to her for a moment as I studied her expression. She was surprised to hear me say it and waited for the confirmation. There was something else in her gaze as well, something that wanted to claim she knew it all along.

Her expression softened slightly before she spoke again.

"For what happened to you…over in the Middle East, right?"

Unexpected words.

I was taken off-guard and couldn't respond right away.

"What makes you say that?" I finally asked. I cleared my throat, turned my eyes from her, and sipped my water. I racked my brain trying to remember what I might have told her, but I didn't come up with much. She knew I was in the Marines, but I hadn't told her anything else.

"You talk in your sleep."

"What the fuck? I do not."

"Not often," she said, "but you have – a couple of times."

I watched her carefully, but she didn't appear to be lying about it.

"What did I say?"

"Oh no," she replied. "I'm not that easy."

I had to roll my eyes at her, which earned me a giggle. I set my bottle of water down on the end table and reached over to grab her by the waist and pull her into my lap. With one hand, I held her down against my cock while the other one circled both her wrists and held them behind her back. I brought her up against my chest and leaned forward until our noses were almost touching.

"Not easy?" I raised an eyebrow at her. "I think you need to remember who's paying for you tonight."

"You don't have to say shit like that you know."

"Say what?"

"Say that you pay for me."

"I do pay for you."

Bridgett sighed and looked away for a moment. Her lips mashed together, and her chest rose with a deep, frustrated breath.

"It's only fucking," I reminded her *again*. If she kept this up, I was going to have to replace her. Actually, I was already quite sure that was the right thing to do, but something was keeping me from just heading to another street corner for another convenient ass.

"It would only be fucking if you ever fucked me," Bridgett countered. "You don't fuck me. You just want to fool around and then fall asleep."

I raised an eyebrow at her but had to consider her words. I hadn't fucked her – not really. Blow jobs, titty fucking, hand jobs in the car – all of that, but I hadn't actually fucked her.

I pulled her down against my cock again and tilted my hips at the same time to push up against her core. She gasped a little, and her tongue reached out to wet her bottom lip.

"I want your ass," I told her. "You don't like it in the ass."

"Why do you say that?"

I rolled my eyes. The sheer amount of evidence I had collected on that subject would have taken a good ten minutes to divulge.

"Are you saying you *do* like it in the ass?" I asked, challenging her.

Her eyes stayed on mine for a moment.

"It would be okay with *you*," she finally said.

There were other words on the tip of her tongue – words about what other men had done to her – but she was smart enough not to say anything about them. When I was paying for her, I didn't want her talking about other johns she was fucking.

"I don't need this," I informed her. "You're here to help me relax and sleep, not to give me a line of bullshit. If I wanted that, I'd get a real girlfriend."

She tensed a little.

"Don't do that," she said quietly.

My fingers grabbed a hold of her chin, and I forced her to look at me.

"Do I need to find someone else?" I asked her.

"Why are you saying that?"

"Because you're trying to take this someplace it's not going," I said. "You are trying to make this shit something it's never going to be. I told you this was about fucking from the beginning, and you're still trying to make it something else."

"You don't fuck me," she said again.

"You want to get fucked?"

"At least it would be about fucking then!" she snapped back.

For a long moment we just stared at each other. Her fingers flexed and gripped my shoulders, and my hardened cock pressed tightly between her legs.

I felt challenged, and I wasn't sure if I liked the feeling or not.

"Get in there," I finally said coldly.

Her tongue darted out over her lips, and her eyes dropped from my gaze to my mouth and then back again. She glanced over at the bedroom door like she didn't already know what was behind it.

I grabbed her chin again and turned her towards me.

"You want me to fuck you in the ass or not?"

Her head nodded slightly.

"Then get in that bedroom, get your clothes off, and get on your hands and knees."

At first, she didn't move but just looked at me for another long moment. I raised an eyebrow at her, and she suddenly disengaged herself from my lap and rushed into the bedroom.

I smiled, gave her a minute, and then walked into the room myself.

Just as instructed, she was naked in the center of the bed on all fours, waiting for me. I went from semi-erect to raging hard-on in about four seconds as I approached the bed. I walked around it, taking in the sight on her spread out and waiting for me. Her thighs trembled a bit as I made my way around the bed to the nightstand. Her eyes followed me as I opened a drawer and took out a bottle and a condom. I could hear her breath quicken as I moved back behind her, reached out, and ran my hand over her backside.

"Nice," I said softly as I let my fingers trail down the back of her leg. "You ready for me?"

"Yes," she said with a breathless whisper.

Hesitating, I crawled onto the bed behind her, ran my hands up and down her legs, and then paused at the top. I took her ass in both hands, fondled and played with it, spreading the cheeks and feeling my heartbeat increase as my goal was revealed.

I let my hands travel up and down her back once before releasing her and ripping open the condom wrapper. As I placed the condom at the end of my dick, I realized I hadn't actually had the need to use one with Bridgett before. After three months, we still hadn't been quite that intimate. I pushed the thought from my mind as I rolled it up my shaft. With a small bottle of water-based lube in my hand, I crawled up behind her and surveyed the sight from close proximity.

The globes of her ass were as fabulous as they could be – a little bigger than average, round, and jiggly. I dropped the lube to the side and used both hands to run all over them, squeeze them, get to know them some more.

I hadn't done that with her before – really gotten to know her ass. I usually did with women, but it had been so obvious she had bad experiences with anal in the past that I didn't want to push it or tease myself. Now I took the time, felt her flesh intimately, and watched it move in the mesmerizing way only ass-flesh could.

Bridgett turned to look back at me, and I could see the apprehension in her face, even if she did say she wanted it. Part of me knew better. Part of me knew this was going to take us someplace I didn't want to go and she wouldn't want to go if she knew any better. She didn't though, and I was happy enough forcing the logical thoughts out of my head for a piece of ass.

It just looked so good, and I hadn't really fucked a girl since Lia.

I closed my eyes a moment and mentally rolled my eyes at myself for thinking about a girl from the past while I was about to fuck another one. I forced thoughts of Lia away and focused on the ass in front of me.

One hand dropped down over her thigh and grabbed the lube. I dispensed a good amount on two of my fingers as my other hand gripped her butt and parted her cheeks. Her little puckered hole winked back at me as I slid a lubricated fingertip over it.

Bridgett let out a sharp breath, and I paused for a moment before I started inserting my finger in her ass slowly, just to the first knuckle as I worked that much in her. It was obvious she had taken cock here before, and my finger entered her pretty easily, but I still wanted to go slow.

I liked going slow.

Once my finger was inside, I pulled it back, joined it with another, and worked that one in, too. Her body didn't resist. Whether or not she enjoyed it, she at least knew what to do.

I covered my condom-enclosed dick with more lube and positioned myself behind her. With cock in hand, I moved the tip to her hole and slowly inserted it.

"Fuck, yeah," I moaned.

Bridgett gasped and her arms shook just a little.

"Relax, baby," I said softly. My hand caressed her butt cheek and then moved up her back. "Just stay up on your knees. You don't have to hold yourself up with your arms. Lie down and spread your legs a bit more."

She nodded once, then moved her arms out to the side and turned her head so her cheek was against the mattress. Her eyes found mine, and they were still apprehensive.

"That's it, baby."

Slowly I entered her again, going just slightly deeper before backing out. Her ass was tight and warm, and my cock was throbbing to get all the way inside of it, but the slow burn was so worth the reward at the end. I'd keep my slow pace.

A little further, back out again, a little more.

My hands gripped both cheeks, spreading them to make way for my cock and squeezing them gently at the same time. The sight was beautiful as her body gave way to me, and my dick slipped further inside her bowels.

Half way.

"You feel so good," I said, "so tight on my cock."

I closed my eyes and pushed a little farther, back again, forward. I moved slowly in and out of her until I finally, finally, buried myself up to my balls in her ass.

I practically collapsed over the top of her for a moment while I got used to the felling of being in her. The muscles in her ass tensed, squeezing my cock and making me sigh out loud. Warm breath traveled over her back, and Bridgett shivered.

"You okay?" I asked.

"I'm okay," she replied. Her voice was breathless but her eyes less worried. The tension in her shoulders diminished as I kissed one of them before rising back up onto my knees.

With one arm wrapped around her waist and the other reaching up to palm one of her tits, I started moving. Slow, deep, gentle. My eyes closed as I placed my forehead on her back and just felt.

If I believed in a god, it would be the god of women's asses.

My hand moved to her belly, running my fingers over her skin. I could feel a couple of the ridiculous sequins that had been glued to her skin come off as my hand brushed over them. I traveled lower, felt the smooth skin between her legs, found her opening, and slid my finger inside.

Bridgett cried out, and her fingers gripped the sheet. They coiled around the fabric tight enough to make me pause briefly, assessing her and ultimately deciding her cries were of pleasure. My fingers moved inside of her, and my thumb brushed over her clit.

"Evan!"

With one hand on her breast and the fingers of the other sliding in and out of her, she began to push back against my cock.

"That's it, baby," I whispered. "Feel that."

Bridgett moaned into the mattress, and I decided the sound was a pretty good one. My thumb rubbed her clit in circles, then pressed as I thrust deeper, then rolled again in time with my hips. My fingers kept up with the same rhythm, and though the angle reaching around her was a little difficult, it was worth it to feel her pussy clenching around my fingers as my cock filled her ass.

My hand moved from her tit to her hip, and I used it as leverage to set a little faster pace. The grip her body had on my dick was fantastic, and every time I pulled back it felt like she was dragging me right back in.

Warm, tight hole and big, round ass cheeks bouncing around as I thrust into her…

Perfection.

"Do you know how easy it would be to fuck you in the ass from this position?"

My own echoed words floated around in my head, causing me to pause for a moment before refocusing my attention on the woman in front of me. She was rocking back and forth on her knees, trying to keep up with my movements. I leaned over her back and placed my mouth against her shoulder blade.

"Feels so good," I mumbled against her skin. "My cock in your ass…love how that feels."

She shuddered, and her hand reached back as if she was trying to touch me – touch *us* – but she couldn't quite reach. My hand moved over hers, laced our fingers together, and I started thrusting faster. My thumb and fingers kept pace, and when I pushed down against her I could feel her walls clenching around my fingers, my cock – everything.

I pressed against her with the pad of my thumb, and she cried out incoherently. Her legs trembled, and I reached around her waist to keep her from falling to the sheets. I stroked her with my fingers a couple more times as she panted beneath me, then raised myself up, grabbed her hips, and started to move again.

Not faster, but deeper and with more purpose. I didn't hold back but felt her body give way to mine, hugging my cock and giving me everything that was her.

I arched my back, thrust into her one final time, and let myself go. My cock shuddered and released into the condom as I held my hips tight up against her ass. My fingers gripped her backside as I pulled her against me just a bit more and then released her.

My hand went to the base of my shaft, gripped the edge of the condom, and then pulled back slowly. Bridgett gasped as my cock left her and dropped to her stomach as I backed away from her and got off the bed. I tossed the condom into the trash in the bathroom and then came back.

She was still on her stomach, and her eyes were closed. I climbed back into bed and wrapped my arms around her, holding her against my chest.

"You did good," I told her, though I wasn't sure why I felt the need to say it.

"It felt good," she whispered. "No one ever…used their fingers like that. I don't think I've ever come so hard in my life."

I snickered quietly through my nose and was about to ask her what she thought of the other times I had made her come when I suddenly stopped before the words started.

I'd never given her an orgasm before.

Blowjobs and coming on her face had been the norms with her – I hadn't even given it a second thought prior to ramming her ass.

Should I have?

With my shoulders tensed, my mind wandered to other hookers I'd had in the past – all single night hookups, and as I looked back on it, I hadn't tried to bring them to orgasm, either. I had paid for the sex, and in my mind that meant they weren't entitled to orgasm as well. Of course, it had always been a one-time thing before, and Bridgett was over here all the time.

It just didn't occur to me.

I wasn't even sure why it bothered me, but I couldn't get it out of my head. She was right about not fucking her before, of course, but she hadn't mentioned the orgasms, and I hadn't thought about it. Now I couldn't stop thinking about it, and I didn't understand that, either.

So I rolled her onto her back and fingered her until she was screaming my name.

And then I did it again.

I took her in the ass once more, going slowly and making sure she was moaning in pleasure repeatedly before I took my own. Then later I had her suck me off in the shower, then took her back to bed and brought her to orgasm with my tongue. By the time we actually slept, we were both exhausted.

As soon as we woke up, I made breakfast and we started all over again.

After nearly two days of spending every minute either fucking or sleeping, I had to admit I was ready to go to work.

My target awaited his destiny.

All right, *he* wasn't waiting for it, but *I* was ready. I had to be in Atlanta in the morning to start my new job as his security guard, and I planned on taking the earliest opportunity to end him and come back to my boss with the news.

I was packing light so I could get in and out quickly – just a backpack with two changes of clothes. I could have them laundered at the hotel. My plan was to be there only a day or two before I took him out, but I also had to plan for the worst. It was possible I was going to have to earn his trust before he let me that close.

I was hoping to earn his *lust* a little quicker.

Bridgett watched me pack.

"Where are you going?" she asked.

"Don't ask." I tossed a small toiletry bag into the front pocket of my backpack and zipped it up. A paperback novel I had been meaning to read went in on top of my clothes to occupy my head during the plane ride to the Atlanta airport.

"Why not?"

"Don't ask that, either."

"You suck as a conversationalist," she said with a laugh.

"It's a good thing you spend a lot of time with my cock in your mouth, then," I quipped.

Silence.

The lack of question-barrage was so nice, I didn't actually notice it right away. I threw a couple more things in the bag, zipped it up, hauled it up over my shoulder, and then started towards the bedroom door.

Bridgett followed slowly.

Odin sneezed, glared at me, and then ran behind one of the chairs in the living room. He knew when I was going on a longer-than-usual trip. I wasn't sure how, but he always knew. I coaxed him out from behind the chair, leashed him, and then looked back at Bridgett.

She wasn't actually crying, but her eyes were downcast and her shoulders slumped.

It hit me then why giving a whore an orgasm wasn't necessarily a great idea, especially not this one. She was having a hard enough time remembering what our relationship was, and I had just provided her with quite the holiday weekend.

"What?" I asked. I was being rather gruff, but I also had this feeling she was getting in far too deep for anyone's benefit.

If I had to really admit it – which I didn't, so I wouldn't – I probably liked her. I wasn't in love with her or anything ridiculous like that, and I wasn't about to take her on as my girlfriend instead of my whore, but there was something about her I found intriguing besides the warmth of her mouth on my cock.

She gave me something I needed in the form of comfort and sleep.

I didn't like the idea of needing her for anything. I didn't want to have to rely on anyone for anything. It just wasn't a good idea in this business to spread yourself too thin in the loyalty department. I had already been tested when I had to investigate Jonathan for an alibi, and he was as close to being a friend as anyone I knew.

The fact was, I had only one person who held my loyalty, and that was because he paid me for it.

Handsomely.

I walked over and placed my fingers around her upper arms. Her muscles tensed, and I could tell she wanted to back away from me, but she didn't.

"What's the problem?" I snapped.

Odin crouched down behind the edge of the couch and whined slightly. Bridgett glanced at him out of the corner of her eye.

"Nothing," she replied softly. "It's all good."

My hands slid up to her shoulders, and I crouched slightly to get a look into her eyes.

"You need to get something through your head, Bridgett," I said as I gripped her shoulders just a bit more. "I've said this before, and you don't have any clever ways of word-smithing it now. This is fucking – nothing more, nothing less. My cock goes in various places around your body for cash. You're a whore, and I'm a regular john. There is nothing *special* here."

She didn't look up, and her muscles remained tense. It occurred to me that she might have thought I was going to hit her. I wouldn't have – it wasn't my style. If I was going to kill her that would be a whole other story, but I didn't usually hit people I was going to kill. Not unless I really needed to do so.

"You got that?" I asked once more.

"I got it," she answered quietly.

"You need me to cut you off? Find someone else?"

She looked up at me, and her eyes glistened. Her throat bobbed as she swallowed twice before she shook her head. She looked away from me and down to the floor.

"Truth hurts, huh?" I said bluntly, and she flinched as a tear finally escaped from her dampened lashes.

Maybe it was cruel, but it had to be done. The last thing I needed was a hooker who thought she was more to me than she was, and the last thing *she* needed was for someone in a rival boss' business getting the idea she was important to me.

There was just no way I could give her what she wanted.

CHAPTER SEVEN
Easy Murder

Atlanta was always one of my favorite towns. It was decently warm, didn't have the constant wind of Chicago, and the people were as entertaining as they could possibly be. Everyone always seemed just thrilled to death to be where they were, even if where they were was begging on a street corner or drunk in an alley. Even the drunks on the street entertained me.

"You see that guy?"

"What guy?" I asked the fifty-something black dude who was drinking a foul smelling liquid out of a paper bag. He'd been doing so since I sat down by the steps of the Marquis One Tower near one of the funky statues that may or may not be lions.

"The one over there!" He reached his arm out to its full extent, added a pointing finger, and shook it around in the air like a flopping fish on the rocks.

I laughed.

"There are twenty guys over there!"

"C'mon!" he insisted, and I had to get up to follow him.

As we rounded the corner, we faced the valet parking area of the

Marriott Marquis. It was a beautiful area with a giant fountain underneath part of the hotel. The echo of the water as it moved over the cement structure was more deafening than the noise from the cars waiting to be valeted.

"That guy right there!" the drunk said as he waved his arms around a bit more. He reminded me of one of the characters from *Sponge Bob*, but I couldn't remember which one. "It's that guy! That one guy – from the movies!"

My ears perked up a bit. I was supposed to meet Jim in an hour at the Hyatt, not the Marriott, which was right across the street. I wondered if something was wrong, though I knew the two hotels were attached by a skywalk. Scanning the motor area, I didn't see any sign of either of them, so I looked back at my inebriated friend.

"It's Mel Gibson!" the drunk suddenly yelled out, and my shoulders dropped in relaxation.

I looked over where he was pointing, and though the guy did vaguely resemble Gibson, it definitely wasn't him. The drunken dude continued to squeal about *Braveheart*, but the show had lost its appeal. I gave up on the entertainment and hiked up the numerous back steps of the Hyatt, then followed the escalator to the lobby and bar area. There was a football game on, so I figured it was as good a place as any to be found when Jim showed up.

The bartender at the Hyatt was a good one, and I do like a good bartender even though I didn't drink often. He was a dark-skinned, bald guy who didn't weigh more than about a hundred and twelve pounds. He had a Caribbean accent of some sort, but I couldn't quite discern from where. He poured me two fingers of some decent scotch and let me just sit there and watch the game at one of the tall, round tables. I paid just enough attention to figure out who was playing, who was probably going to win, and to take note of at least one egregious foul I could bitch about later with Jim if he cared to talk football.

It was a team Jonathan favored, and I wondered if he was watching the same game back in Chicago. I hadn't seen him outside of work for a while, and I considered sending him a quick text suggesting we hang when I got back into town, but of course I couldn't. My regular phone was turned off so I couldn't be tracked back to the area.

Jim showed up just a few minutes late with one of the other security guys I had seen before, though only through my scope. He said his name was Damon, and he shook my hand like someone once told him a firm handshake would impress people. He made a lot of eye contact as well, also something he'd been taught and followed to a tee – not because he saw the value of it, but because someone he believed told him it was the right thing to do.

He probably thought he intimidated people, but I just found it comical. It wasn't like I was going to be told to go home at this point – Ashton was too paranoid to be down a security guy while waiting for all the background checks to be done. A thorough dig might have come up with the death certificate for Marshall Miller in a piss-ant town in Louisiana, but probably not. The rest of his record was clean.

Within an hour of his overly enthusiastic handshake, Damon was fitting me with a little earpiece and introducing me to Phillip Tanner, Ashton's public relations guy. He was the last stop before the man himself, and he spent a good forty-five seconds just looking me up and down.

"Umm…hmmm," he hummed under his breath. "I'm sure Mister Ashton will like this one."

I glanced at Jim, who just looked away from me. Their behavior confirmed my suspicions about Brad Ashton's preferences. I was also introduced to Alex something-or-another, whose main job seemed to be to stand right outside the door to the hotel room and glare at people.

"Marshall Miller," Phillip announced as he opened up the door to the hotel suite and allowed me and the other security guys through.

Ashton was on the far side of the room with a phone up to his ear, looking bored as he leaned back in the office chair by the desk, staring at his fingernails. His eyes moved over to the group entering the room, and he appraised me similarly to the way Phillip had outside. The look he gave me was decidedly less subtle than the one from his PR guy. There might have been some actual drool, which made me wonder if there wasn't some other plan that might be just as effective. The way he was looking at me made my stomach tighten up.

I wondered if Bridgett felt the same way when guys looked at her.

We all just stood there for a while, and I felt myself automatically enter the *at attention* mindset – mostly blank in the head but still listening closely. It was a pose I actually found very relaxing, though training camps used it to drive recruits crazy. I always felt it was a good opportunity to let go and reset, and it usually left me feeling recharged. I could stand still like that for hours, though the others around me began to fidget after only two or three minutes.

Once Brad Ashton finally hung up the phone, he stood and walked slowly over to the group. He barely looked at anyone else but looked me up and down more than once.

"This must be the new guy," he said with a smile.

"Marshall Miller," I said as I extended my palm for him to shake.

He took my hand with his manicured fingers and held it a little longer than he needed to for just a handshake.

"A pleasure," he said quietly. "Welcome to the team."

His attention went to his PR guy after that, and we discussed the boring details of the main event of the evening. Ashton would be escorted through the lobby downstairs via the service elevator, over to the ballroom where he'd participate in an interview and a panel discussion with a couple other actors and the director of his next flick. The details didn't interest me. Now that everyone else's attention was occupied, I could examine the inside of the hotel room.

It was a good-sized suite with a separate room leading to a king-sized bed and a nice view of the street below. In the main room there were two balconies and a wet bar. There was another door on the other side of the suite, which was closed with the bolt secured.

With the room's layout captured in my head, I was now able to watch the dynamics of the group.

Phillip mooned over Ashton, barely taking his eyes off the man like he was some sort of golden god. Jim nodded a lot, but his expression told me his mind was somewhere else. He glanced at me a couple of times, and it occurred to me that he might have taken a risk bringing me on without any additional credentials.

When the proper time came, we escorted Ashton down the elevator to his interview, then to a table way in the back of the hotel's restaurant for his dinner with some producer from Universal Studios. I was stationed between the lobby and the entrance to the restaurant to watch for anything that looked suspicious.

The next day was pretty much the same, only it was an autograph and photo opportunity thing, and I watched the ticket-takers make sure everyone had the right kind of tickets.

The whole standing-at-attention, mind-numbing activity came in handy again.

Damon and Jim were much closer to Brad Ashton physically than I ever was, and Ashton hadn't said a word to me since that first meeting. Apparently, I wasn't giving off the right kind of vibe. Normally that would be perfectly fine with me, but I needed Ashton to make a move, and he was only going to be in this city for a total of three days. I racked my mind for various ways of giving him the impression I might be interested and could only come up with things I might do to attract a woman, which didn't seem quite right.

What attracted me?

Tits and ass, that's what.

No help there.

I had about come to the conclusion that I was going to have to get a little more drastic. Every time Ashton went out anywhere, there were at least three of us with him, and usually four. When Brad Ashton retired to his room at night, it was never completely alone. Alex was always outside the door, and Phillip was often inside. I hadn't caught any additional company outside of the core group, and I didn't think there had been anyone else sneaking inside, but I wasn't positive.

I had to be sure, so I watched carefully.

Alex was as diligent as they came, and he took no breaks during his shift. No one went in or out of the door to Ashton's private room without Alex knowing about it. Ashton's room was connected to a common room as well, which was where we would all meet before heading to the elevator for an event of some kind. Though the room didn't have its own guard, there were almost always other people in it – usually other actors or people in the business, at least. It was where Jim slept on a roll-away bed when he wasn't on duty. Still, there was potential with a third adjoining room which wasn't being used by the group

There had to be another way to either get in or out. The two balconies in the common room were just a bit far off the ground to consider climbing up to them. There was no easy way to get up there from the street, and scaling up five stories using other balcony rails would have been beyond stupid.

I had to get Ashton to come out, but he never left the damn room without a plethora of escorts.

Jim and I walked a few paces behind Ashton as we moved from one area of the hotel to another, stopping every few feet for pictures and autographs. Alex was in front of him and Phillip just to one side. Every time a young woman approached him, Ashton smiled, flirted, and then usually looked a little nauseated once she was out of view again.

And he was supposed to be such a great actor.

We made our way slowly back to his room, where he moved straight to the wet bar in the common area and started rummaging around. Phillip tried to entice him with a large bottle of wine, but Ashton wasn't interested. Instead, he found one of those small bottles of vodka in the mini bar fridge. Phillip handed him a glass, which Ashton took roughly from the PR guy before pouring the vodka and tonic water carelessly into it. Some of the liquid spilled on the counter, but no one bothered to wipe it up.

"Looks like you are good for the night," Alex said to Jim.

Jim nodded, exchanged some notes with Damon, and then we all started to head out of the room. I glanced back at Brad once more and found his eyes on me.

"Why don't you hang around for a little while, Marshall?"

Jim's eyes met mine, and the little shine in them gave me a pretty good idea that Jim was well aware of Brad Ashton's preferences. I wondered if he'd ever been asked to hang around as well.

Brad held up his cocktail.

"I hate drinking alone," he said. He flashed me a toothy, actor-practiced smile. It was probably known to drop panties or something, but I wore boxers.

This was really, really hard to fake.

"Of course, sir," I replied.

Jim and the others were waved out of the room, and I couldn't believe how lucky I had gotten to be left alone with him. Of course, the main problem now was the number of people here in his organization who knew my face if not my name. I just needed to work on getting him away from his room now so I wasn't a completely obvious suspect.

"Please, have a seat."

I hesitated, and he pointed to the chair next to him.

"Please, I insist."

"I'm…ah…I'm still on the clock, Mister Ashton," I said.

"Hmm," he hummed. "You should call me Brad."

"Brad," I replied softly.

He stood and walked towards me, still sipping from his glass of vodka tonic. He came up very close, though not quite touching me. I went back to *at attention*, which seemed to make his grin wider.

"Am I making you nervous?" he asked as he took another step closer.

"Ah…um…a little," I admitted. At least I didn't have to fake that one.

Brad wasn't one to be dissuaded that easily, though. He tilted his head to one side as he looked me up and down again. His hand moved out as if he was going to touch me, but his fingers didn't quite make it. Instead, his hand hovered in the air right in front of me.

"You are a…a very *well-built* young man, Marshall," Brad said softly.

I smiled slightly and looked down, feigning embarrassment. I tried to will myself to blush, but I wasn't sure if I was pulling it off or not. This whole plan was actually ending up a lot harder than I thought it would be.

"You aren't used to men saying that to you, are you?"

"Um…no, sir." Again, at least I didn't have to make it up.

"Sir," he repeated, letting the sound draw out a bit. "You keep calling me that."

"Sorry, sir…um…sorry." I took an exaggerated breath and glanced back up at him. "I used to be in the military. Hard habit to break."

"Yes, Phillip mentioned that," he murmured as he took one more sip out of his glass before setting it down on the table.

Once his hands were free, he came right back up to me again.

"You are very attractive, too," he told me. "I bet you have heard that from *someone* before."

I swallowed and refused to make eye contact. When I felt his hand on my arm, I followed the motion with my eyes as his fingers traced my flesh down to the end of my sleeve where they met with the back of my bare hand.

"You are at least curious, right?" he said. "I'm not completely off base here, am I? I mean, if I am, say something."

I let my tongue dart over my lips.

"I…I'm not sure."

"Have you been with a man before?"

He was a straightforward little fucker at least. I had to give him credit for that.

"Not…um…not really," I said quietly. "I mean, there was one guy who…well, nothing really happened, you know?"

"I do know."

Glancing away, I shuffled my feet a bit.

"Thought about it since then?" he pressed.

I swallowed again as I nodded once. I had actually thought about sex with a man – thought about it, sure. Actually, really, truly considered it? That was a completely different question.

Brad Ashton wasn't really interested in any kind of reality, though, so my answer was exactly what he thought he wanted. His mouth curved into a smile as he focused on my lips. One of his hands moved up to my shoulder and then over my jaw while the other one latched onto a belt loop to pull me closer to him.

My heart began to beat faster, and I forced my face to only show my feigned nervousness over this whole situation and not my actual nervousness. What Brad Ashton wanted was blindingly obvious, but I'd never given anything up for a guy and didn't particularly care to now. I hadn't actually planned to let it get as far as that.

Ultimately, I had a job to do though, and this was going to be the best way to get it done.

His lips touched mine, and his hand moved to the back of my

neck to pull me a little closer to him. I responded reluctantly, both because it wasn't something I was interested in, but also in hopes of showing *Marshall's* hesitance.

"Not so sure," he whispered against my lips.

"Everyone…everyone keeps telling me I shouldn't," I said. "In the military…"

I let my voice trail off, figuring the rest of that sentence pretty much spoke for itself. Brad gave me an understanding smile and ran his index finger over the edge of my jaw, down my neck, and to my chest. He rested his palm there, presumably feeling the beat of my heart under his skin.

His lips brushed against mine again, softy and unhurriedly. My response was a little more encouraging, but only just. His hand gripped my shoulder a little more before running up the back of my neck and into my hair.

"Are you nervous, Marshall?" Brad pulled back and looked into my eyes.

I swallowed hard and nodded slightly.

"I don't want you to feel pressured," he told me. "You are in my employ, after all, but this has nothing to do with that. I'm afraid I chased off your predecessor when he believed it was all part of his job. It's not, I promise you. This is only if you are interested."

I let my tongue draw over my lips as I looked at his. My gaze flickered back and forth from his mouth to his eyes as the remainder of my plan began to form in my mind.

"I…I don't know," I stammered.

"Maybe just hang out for a little while?" he suggested. "Get to know each other?"

The finger in my belt loop pulled again, and the pressure I felt on my leg was pretty damn obvious. I mean, the guy was just huge.

No pressure. *Right.*

"I don't know," I replied again quietly. I took a hesitant step backwards, and he released me. "I…I just hadn't thought about it. I mean, you're *Brad Ashton* for Christ's sake. I've seen every one of your movies."

"All of them?" He raised an eyebrow, and I thought I managed to actually blush that time.

"Yeah," I replied quietly. "Even the…ah…the early stuff."

"You mean the porn?" he laughed.

"Yeah, that."

"Meaningless," he informed me with a wave of his hand. "If there is nothing else fame has taught me, it's taught me to go after what you want, when you want it. I want you – tonight. Who knows what will happen to us tomorrow?"

Who knows what might happen to you tonight?

I let my tongue lick at my lips, glanced from the floor up to Brad's eyes, and then over to the door. I wondered what Alex could hear from there and if Phillip would be returning any time soon.

"Stay here, Marshall," Brad said. His head tilted to one side, and he gave me one of those half smiles that seemed to make his female fans start dropping articles of clothing around his feet. "I mean…if you aren't busy or anything. I was going to order dinner in."

I glanced at the door as it opened and Phillip entered, answering my earlier question. His eyes widened just enough to show his annoyance and possibly a little jealousy. He didn't look at me or at Ashton as he moved around the room, and I figured this was probably a pretty common occurrence.

Staying right now wasn't a good idea. I couldn't kill Ashton in his own room – not with Phillip and Alex hanging about. Besides, the plan was forming, and I wasn't ready for this particular job just yet.

Need to get some condoms.

No, I wasn't going to let it get that far…was I? I just needed to do a little recon around the area and pick up some *other* supplies.

"I, ah…" I stammered a bit. "We were gonna go watch some

football. Um…Jim and I. He's probably already wondering where I am. Do you…um…you want to join us?"

"Me in a public bar?" Brad snorted. "No, that's all right."

He took in a long breath and blew it slowly out his nose.

"Go on," he said, "but think about it, okay?"

I nodded and headed out the door and down the hallway. Playing hard to get would make him a lot more likely to agree to go somewhere else with me later, and I needed him to be willing to leave. If he wasn't, well, I could always drag him out, but he looked like a screamer, and that would definitely cause some commotion.

Jim was hanging out around the corner as I left the suite, and he pushed the down button for the elevator as I appeared.

"You're dodging the bullet there," Jim snickered as we headed down the elevator.

I just shrugged at him.

After a couple light beers, I claimed to be tired and headed back up the elevator. Reaching into my back pocket, I quickly stepped into the skywalk heading to the other hotels in the area as I called Jonathan with the pre-paid phone.

"Hyatt Regency in Atlanta," I said when he answered. "I need room 555 in the International tower. Can you check it?"

"Sure thing, bro." I could hear clacking of the keyboard as Jonathan's magic fingers poked around until he announced he was inside the hotel's firewall or whatever. "It's open. What name you need it in?"

"Marshall Miller."

"Got it." More clacking. "Give me a few and I'll call ya back."

After shoving the phone back in my pocket, I headed down the stairs of the Marriott and out onto the street. It was getting late, and it shouldn't be too hard to come up with what I needed, even if my connections weren't very strong in this area. Even if they were, I wouldn't use them. It would just place Evan Arden in this area, and I wasn't going to chance that.

I found a juvenile delinquent near the Hard Rock Café and scored exactly what I needed.

"You don't look like the type that would need these," the teen said as he handed me a few pills and I handed him some cash.

"Depends on what you want," I answered quietly.

My phone vibrated in my pocket. I walked away from the kid and headed up the long stairway to the Hyatt entrance again as I answered.

"All set?"

"You should be good."

"You rock," I said. "Thanks a bunch."

I hung up and walked over to the hotel's front desk.

"Hey," I told the lady at the counter. "I lost my key – can you get me a new one?"

I handed her my ID with Marshall Miller's name on it, and she handed me a new key for room 555. I took the steps – it wasn't too far – and quickly opened the room. I checked around, and was pleased to find Jonathan had been right – there wasn't anyone already staying in the room. I didn't have any luggage to leave around, but hopefully Ashton wasn't going to notice that. I did mess up the bed and put a couple of the hotel glasses and the ice bucket on the desk to give the place a bit of a lived-in look.

I slipped out again, then walked down the hall to the elevators, turned, and headed back in the other direction. When I got to the end of the hall, Alex was there. He raised his eyebrows a bit when I asked if Mr. Ashton was still awake.

"I just need to…um…speak to him a minute," I explained.

Alex gave me what I supposed was a look of both disdain and annoyance before knocking lightly. Brad opened up and smiled as he turned to one side and let me in. As soon as the door closed, he was giving me a coy look and smile which were as sarcastic as looks could be.

I stared intently at him for about seven seconds, took a deep breath, and then rushed forward, grabbed him by the back of the head, and crashed my lips to his. His fingers gripped my biceps as he tilted his head backwards, giving me control as he opened his mouth to me.

With closed eyes, I might have been able to pretend he was Bridgett or some other chick, but the stubble on his upper lip made that impossible. Still, I had work to do, and not all work was the pleasant kind. I performed as I had to and kissed him with as much passion as I could find within myself.

I felt his hands move up my back, grip my shoulders, and then one of them moved back down to my ass. He pulled me against himself, and I could feel without a doubt that it wasn't a rabbit in his pocket. I pushed back a bit, breaking our kiss and breathing hard.

"Not here," I whispered. "I can't do this here. The other guard – the one outside – he saw me. The way he looked at me – I can't let him think something is going on. I have a military pension and shit…I don't want to lose that."

"I understand," Brad said softly. "Discretion – right?"

"Yeah," I answered. "It's important. I can't let anyone know…my family…"

"I know," he whispered softly. "Don't you worry, sweetheart, I understand."

"What do we do?" I asked.

"We should meet somewhere else."

"Another hotel?"

"Exactly."

"But…your fans…"

"I know how to be sneaky," he said with a smile. He lifted himself up on his toes and brought his lips to mine briefly.

"What about Alex?"

Brad rolled his eyes.

"He knows how to keep his mouth shut."

"About you, yes," I agreed. "What about me? Seriously, I can't just...you know...come out. My family..."

I let my voice trail off, and Ashton pursed his lips as he looked into my eyes.

"I have the room next door," I said quietly.

"What's that?"

"My room," I said as I nodded towards the door at the other end of the suite, "it's that one right there. We can't...I don't want to stay there, but you could get out that way."

A slow smile spread over his face.

"You are a sneaky thing," he commented.

I tried to make myself blush as I looked away. I wasn't sure if I pulled it off or not, but it was enough for him to grab my head and kiss me again.

"You are hot and adorable," he informed me. "Give me about an hour to convince Alex and Phillip you aren't coming back and that I'm going to bed. We'll have the whole night."

I nodded and smiled.

Too damn easy.

Shortly after eleven that night, Brad and I opened the adjoining suite doors, clomped down the back stairs of the International Tower, and out the side door. He wore a baseball cap pulled down over his face and some dark glasses, which looked ridiculous in the dark. You would likely notice that he was hiding something, but what he was hiding would have been anyone's guess.

We quickly booked a room at the Westin just down the street under Marshall's name again and hurried up the elevator. He was all over me as soon as the door to the room closed, and I had to just go with it for a few minutes to keep him off his guard.

His hand dropped down my chest, over my abs, and cupped my

crotch. I closed my eyes and thought of all the porn I could remember to get myself to react a little.

"You're still nervous," Brad commented.

"Yeah, I bit, I guess." *Either that or my dick really only worked for chicks.*

"Don't be," he said quietly. "We can go as slow as you want to."

"Okay," I replied. I cleared my throat. "Maybe some wine or something?"

"Good idea."

There was a small bottle in the tiny hotel room bar, which I opened and poured into two glasses. Checking over my shoulder, I quickly added Rohyphenol tablets to one of the glasses, stirred the drug until it dissolved into the liquid, and then handed it to Brad.

It didn't take long for the drug to take effect. Not that I needed any of that to rape him, as had become the drug's more common usage, but it did make him nicely stupid and easy to manipulate. Actually, he took to the stuff like I imagined a schoolgirl would.

In other words, he just dropped to the bed and started to giggle.

"I think maybe that wine hit you a little too hard," I informed him.

"Hard," he slurred. "I want to see you hard."

More giggling.

"Let's get a little fresh air first."

He agreed. He would have agreed to anything at that point, up to and including taking a leap off the balcony. If I had thought about it beforehand, and if his death should have looked like an accident, I might have gone that route. He was a message, though – like most of my work: Don't fuck with Rinaldo Moretti. It didn't matter who you were or how many people there were around you – you were going to get killed.

Ashton half fell against me, and I felt his mouth on my neck.

"So fuckin' sexy..."

"Yeah, I'm a dream," I replied. I sat him down on the bed as my phone began to buzz.

I glanced at the number, but other than being a Chicago area code, I wasn't sure who it was. Under most circumstances, I didn't answer when I didn't know the number – it was more often someone wanting me to buy something than anything else – but this time I did.

"So where you hanging out tonight?"

"Terry Kramer?" My eyes narrowed as I looked at the phone again. I had a number in there for Terry, but this one wasn't it. "What do you want?"

"Just wonderin' what you were up ta," he said. "I heard you might have left town."

"Who told you that?"

"No one in particula'," he said.

I could just about see his ridiculous, nonsensical grin in my head.

"Well, your information sucks," I told him.

"So, you wanna go have a drink somewhere?"

"Busy," I replied.

"Oh yeah? Doin' what?"

"I gotta date," I said right before I hung up. I looked down at Ashton, who had flopped over to his side on the bed and closed his eyes. He muttered something as I hoisted him back onto his feet again, but I couldn't understand a word of it.

I carried my "drunk" friend out the back of the Westin and down the street to a quiet, deserted alley. I found exactly what I needed about halfway down the dank passage, and I helped Brad sit down on the curb by the sewer cover. It was heavy, but I managed to loop my fingers into it and haul it up.

"Whatcha doin', hottie?" he mumbled.

"I'm going to kill you, sweetheart," I answered.

With one hand firmly around his waist, I turned his body so his head was right at the top of the storm sewer entrance.

"Whoa," he said with another giggle. "That makes me dizzy."

"It won't last long," I promised.

I made sure my grip was firm enough to keep him from falling before I was done with him, reached down my leg to the small gun holstered beside my boot, and put it to his head.

"Rinaldo says don't worry about paying him back this time," I told him.

Brad's eyes widened in recognition, but I fired before he could start to struggle.

With his head in the manhole, the spatter all went down and I stayed mostly clean. There was a little blood on my boot, but it would come off easily enough. All I had to do was release my grip for his body to fall into the sewer and out of sight. I stood, replaced the lid, and walked back down the street. A cab took me to the bus station.

I leaned back in the seat and let out a long sigh which turned into a big smile.

I felt like the end of an *A-Team* episode when everything worked out, and the heroes all got to go home and live happily ever after while the bad guys were put in jail. Except, of course, *I* was the bad guy.

Whatever.

It still felt awesome to have had everything come together so nicely. Ashton was dead, Rinaldo would be happy, and I didn't have to actually take my clothes off to get it done.

There was just no way I could have gone through with that.

CHAPTER EIGHT
Wretched Patient

I was fucking sick.

My head was absolutely pounding, and my knees ached from all the kneeling in front of the toilet I had been doing. Though I still hated vomiting with a passion, I was almost too exhausted to give a shit if my insides did start coming up.

I almost never so much as caught a cold, but whatever I had this time was nasty and unshakable. I had no idea where I might have picked it up, but I had spent the last day and a half puking up anything and everything I put in my mouth. Other than calling a dog-walking service to take Odin out on a regular basis, I had barely moved since yesterday morning.

To top it all off, every time I closed my eyes, I was hit with hideous dreams of blood, dust, and bodies all around me. Even when I could drag myself out of the bathroom, I couldn't get any actual sleep. When I got to the point where I was feeling too weak to even get myself a glass of water, which I would undoubtedly throw back up, I reached for my phone.

Pride didn't even enter into it – I knew when I was defeated.

"What's up, brotha?" Jonathan said when he answered. "Haven't seen ya in a while."

"Hey dude," I replied, "I need a favor."

I started coughing as soon as I got the words out. My head started pounding in my temples again, and the pain was enough to make me squeeze my eyes shut.

"You sound like shit."

"I feel like shit," I agreed when I could speak again. "Can you go pick something up for me?"

"Sure," Jon said.

"Awesome." I swallowed a couple of times as my stomach lurched and the hammer inside my head began to nail up drywall on the inside of my skull. "You know that pimp dude that hangs out by Mario's old place? Marvin or something, I think his name is?"

"Melvin," Jonathan corrected. "I know the guy."

"He's got a hooker named Bridgett," I said. "Pick her up and bring her here, will ya? I'll Paypal ya later."

"You got your own hooker?" Jon laughed.

"Just pick her up," I moaned.

"Will do," he replied. "Be there shortly."

It didn't take him long at all. At least, I didn't think so. It was also possible I passed out and lost track of time between the phone call and their arrival. Either way, it seemed only a short time later someone was knocking at the door. I dragged myself off the floor of the bathroom to answer it.

They were both there – Bridgett in her usual tiny skirt and fishnets, and Jonathan with an unlit cigarette sticking out between his lips. Odin peeked out at both of them from the edge of the couch.

"You are a mess," Bridgett said as soon as the door opened.

"Shut up and get in bed," I mumbled.

Jonathan laughed and chewed on the end of his cigarette.

"She's right, bro, you *are* a mess."

"Fuck you."

"Yeah, you're welcome, asshole." Jonathan laughed and then apologized. "Sorry, bro – that was just mean. You do look like shit, though – I can't lie about that."

"S'okay," I muttered. My stomach lurched. "Thanks for pickin' her up."

"No problem, bro," he said. "I'm gettin' outa here – you ain't paying me to catch this shit."

With Jonathan gone, Bridgett put her hands on her hips and looked me up and down. Her eyes narrowed as she took a step forward and placed her palm against the side of my face. As soon as she did, her look softened again.

Her hand felt cold on my skin.

"You are burning up," she said quietly. Her hand trailed down the side of my face and then came to rest on my bare chest. "How long have you been like this?"

I shrugged and ignored her question. Any additional actions would have put me in a coma.

"I just need sleep," I told her. "I swear I haven't slept in days, so get in bed, okay?"

"When was the last time you drank anything?"

"I'm not that kind of sick!" I snapped. My head began to spin a bit, and standing became quite a chore.

"You are that kind of dehydrated!" she retorted.

She probably had a pretty good point there.

Moaning, I turned and dropped down on the couch because I just couldn't manage to get myself back to the bedroom. At least there wasn't anything in my stomach to puke up. Bridgett started going through my refrigerator looking for something to force me to drink. I heard her thumping around, and the noise took the shape of the aching in my head. I leaned sideways until my head hit the arm of the couch and then I closed my eyes.

"Do you have any Gatorade?" Bridgett asked.

"I have no idea," I groaned back.

She came around the couch holding a bottle of water with a straw sticking out of it. I had no idea where she even came up with a straw, but I let her hold my head up a bit as I took a drink. She disappeared for a minute and then came back out to shove a couple of pills down my throat and make me take another drink.

"It won't stay down," I mumbled.

"Maybe," she said, "but it's better than nothing. How long have you really been like this?"

Completely relentless in her questioning, she kept harping on it until I finally told her.

"Since yesterday morning."

"Could be worse," she mumbled.

Her hands grasped onto my bicep, and she helped me off the couch and into the bedroom. Once we got there, I flopped down on the bed and went completely immobile. I was actually pretty sure if I did move, it would be my last action. The water and pills in my stomach felt like they were being dragged behind one of those circus shows with the chick on the horse chasing dogs or something. Maybe it was dogs riding elephants – I wasn't sure. I just knew it was all threatening to come back up again.

"Do you have a thermometer?" Bridgett called out from the bathroom.

I couldn't answer her, so I just moaned in response. I only wanted her here to help me sleep, not to play nursemaid. I might have told her that if I could have formed a coherent sentence without my head exploding.

"This is the cleanest medicine cabinet I have ever seen," she was saying from the bathroom located just off the far side of the bedroom. "It would be more useful if there was something in it beside a razor and an extra toothbrush."

"It's for you," I mumbled. "In case you forgot yours."

She poked her head out of the bathroom and looked over at me. I returned the gaze, but I couldn't really focus on her. She shook her head and placed her hands on her hips again.

"What am I going to do with you?" she asked rhetorically.

"Please lay down." Yes, I had resorted to begging.

With an overdramatic sigh, Bridgett climbed into bed with me. My arms immediately wrapped around her, and I placed my head against her shoulder. Even though I was currently going through an episode of feeling cold instead of hot, it feel good to have her cooler skin against my face.

Her hand trailed from my temple down my jaw line. I didn't open my eyes, but I could both hear and feel her long sigh as she wrapped an arm around my head. My body seemed to melt into her, and I thought for a brief moment that nothing else could feel this welcoming. A warm, heavy feeling came over me, and I wondered if this was how it felt to be on heroin.

Then I was asleep.

There were times when I knew she was waking me up to get me to take a drink or medicine or whatever. I was pretty sure at one point I heard her take Odin out as well, but I couldn't be sure. There were also dreams – lots and lots of dreams. Some were benign, but most were far from it. They weren't awful, though, and when I woke up, Bridgett would be there. Usually she was sitting up in the bed with my head on her stomach or against her shoulder. Sometimes she was reading one of my books, and other times she would be reaching down to scratch Odin's head with one hand while she ran her fingers over my hair with the other. One time she was asleep beside me when I woke up.

My head had been pounding and was especially achy on one side right near my cheek. Reflexively, I reached up and found a hand there. I pulled it down against my chest as I opened my eyes and looked into Bridgett's sleeping face.

She was curled up next to me with her head pressed into the pillow slightly above where I lay. Her face was relaxed in deep sleep, and her breathing slow and regular. I reached out and touched her cheek, and the touch made her flinch from whatever dream was going on in her head. I moved my arm up around her middle and pulled her against me, which seemed to settle her down.

I swallowed a couple of times, which made me wince from the pain in my dry throat. I had to pee, and my head spun around as I tried to get myself out of the bed. I stumbled towards the bathroom and ended up having to actually sit down on the seat with my boxers around my ankles because I couldn't stand long enough to take a piss.

When I stumbled out of the bathroom, Bridgett was there to take me back to bed, give me some nasty tasting liquid medicine, and then tuck herself around me as I fell back to sleep. The dreams came back, but they were foggy and muted.

Sand. Constant, relentless sand.

I know there is no way I will ever enjoy a vacation at the beach again.

It's in my nose and throat, making me cough all the time. As if that isn't bad enough, the meager food I am offered contains the shit as well.

I still eat it. I'm far beyond being stubborn about taking anything from them. My assumption is that they will kill me eventually – when they decide once and for all that I won't tell them anything and that the U.S. government wasn't going to give into any demands to get me back.

Trying to move, my shoulder cramps up painfully. I can't move enough to get it out of the position it has been in for weeks, and I think it's possible it's been dislocated. The ache is so familiar; now I barely notice it.

A sound.

Footsteps in the sand off to my right. I turn my blindfolded head towards the distraction, and open my mouth as foul-tasting water is poured into it.

Disoriented, sweaty, and confused, I woke with my head on a soft stomach and feminine scent all around me. My head was pounding, but there was some comfort in the small hand running over the top of my head. I recognized the scene immediately.

"Lia," I mumbled as I tucked my head against her.

Her body went a little tense, and her hand stopped moving. I realized how pissed off at me she must be and tightened my grip on her.

"I'm sorry I left like that. I didn't want to." I tried to turn and look at her, but the throbbing inside my temples forced my eyes closed and sent me back to unconsciousness.

"What the fuck?"

I hear the sound of a woman's laugh all around me.

"I've always wanted to try this. You were in the military – it's just like the quarter test on the bed after you've made it up.

"What, on my ass?"

"Exactly!"

The giggles are back, and they join my own laughter as Lia flings a quarter at my ass over and over again. Every time she misses, it clangs on the floor.

"I can't find it!" she calls out.

I roll over to help her look, but the wooden floor of the cabin has turned to sand. As my hand reaches into the dry grains, I feel the round, metal object but can't quite reach it with my fingers. I push to the side of the bed but lose my balance and fall. Sand fills my mouth…

When I woke, I really had no idea how long I had been out – only that Bridgett was still there with me. I recognized her scent immediately and found it comforting. I didn't even bother to open my eyes. My fingers twitched slightly against her side, and I pushed my nose into the skin of her neck.

Her soft voice curled into my ears. The sound was far away, muted and windy-sounding. After a minute or so, the words took form and began to make sense.

"I can't really do that…I would have to wake him up…"

My eyes opened a crack to see her with one of those cheap flip-phones held to her ear. Her expression was worried, and her fingers tensed minutely against the device as she spoke softly into it.

"You'll have to take my word for it," she continued. There was tightness around the edge of her mouth. "I don't know if…no, Mel, he's just sleeping…he's been using me pretty hard."

She shifted a little, and her hand came up to the back of my head. Her fingers moved through my hair.

"No, I can't. I really don't think he wants people knowing where he lives…"

I ran a hand up the side of her body as I stretched and yawned. For the first time in a long time, my head was not pounding so hard that I couldn't hear anything in my ears outside of my own heartbeat.

"Is that your pimp?" I mumbled against her skin.

Bridgett's head turned to look at me, her eyes widened, and she nodded once. Her teeth bit into her lower lip as she watched me. I held out my hand, palm up, but she just continued to look at me and not move.

"Give me the phone," I eventually said. I could still hear the pimp's muffled voice coming from the phone in her hand.

"Okay, Mel," she said quietly, "he's awake, and he says he wants to talk to you."

She moved the phone away from her head and out towards me as her teeth continued to try to pierce her lip. With an exaggerated sigh, I took it from her and held it close, but not too close, to my mouth.

"What's the asshole's name?" I asked loud enough for him to hear through the speaker.

"Um…" Bridgett cleared her throat. "Mel…um…Melvin."

I placed the phone against the side of my face. The device felt hot, like she had been talking to him for a long time.

"Melvin, this is Evan Arden," I said smoothly and emotionlessly. My throat was still dry, and I hoped I wouldn't actually break into a coughing fit, which definitely wouldn't help with the reputation. "Is there some kind of problem?"

"Uh-uh-um…" he stammered.

"Excuse me?" I said in the same deadpan voice. I swallowed a couple of times to coat my throat in moisture.

"I was just checking up on my bitch," the pimp said with a little more confidence. "She's been gone for some time, and–"

"Melvin," I interrupted, "did one of my guys pick her up and say he was bringing her to me?"

"Uh…yes. Yes he did."

"Do you think if I kept your property for an extended period of time, or returned it damaged, that I would refuse to compensate you for that loss?"

There was a long pause before he answered. I had the feeling he was choosing his words pretty carefully at this point.

"Um…you…ah, no, I never thought you'd do that," he said. "You've always been a good customer."

"Do you think I'm somehow not good for the money all of a sudden?"

"No! No, man – not at all!"

"Do you think that I want to be disturbed right at this time?" I asked.

"Uh…no…"

"Do you think calling your whore and harassing her when she's with me is in your best interest?"

"No," he replied softly. "No, sir."

"Then why are you calling and interfering with the business of my dick?"

"Sorry, um…"

"Don't call again," I said. "I'll bring your bitch back when I feel like it."

The phone closed with a click, and I tossed it on the floor before I wrapped my arm back around Bridgett and nestled against her soft body. That warm, comfortable feeling was all around me, and I didn't want it getting chased away by being pissed off at her troll of a pimp.

She said nothing as I dozed a little but couldn't seem to actually get back to sleep. My hip hurt, and I had the feeling I had been lying like that for way too long. I grumbled as I rolled to my back and stared at the ceiling.

"Do you want to try to drink something?" Bridgett asked.

"Not really."

"You should."

"Just thinking about it makes my stomach churn," I told her.

Again, she was relentless and eventually convinced me to drink from a bottle of water. After a few minutes, she was convinced it wasn't coming back up and made me drink some more. With the partially empty bottle sitting on the nightstand, she sat close to me on the edge of the bed as her fingers traced the side of my face.

"You don't feel as warm," she commented. "Will you let me take your temperature?"

I shook my head.

"Come on," she coaxed, "we've done this before."

"We have?" The next thing I knew, there was a thermometer in my mouth. I didn't even recall owning one, but it was suddenly under my tongue and going *beep* a minute later.

"Normal," Bridgett announced as she beamed at me like I had just won a fucking triathlon. "That's good! Do you feel better?"

"I feel like I've been run over by a tank," I replied honestly. I closed my eyes and tried to bury my head against the side of her body. I was tempted to go back to sleep, but the ache in my hip wasn't going to let me.

As I lay there and contemplated the idea that I just might survive this shit after all, Bridgett's fingers moved up my back and into my hair again. They traveled down my cheek and over my jaw. There was several days' worth of growth on my face, which I absolutely fucking hated.

"I should get a shower and shave," I announced, but the actual idea of standing up to get to the bathroom was less appealing than the idea of having my body magically groom itself without having to move.

Someone should invent that.

Bridgett's fingers ran the opposite way up my cheek, which made sounds like sandpaper over a two-by-four, and I grumbled again.

"I think it's kind of hot." Bridgett giggled.

"I hate having a scratchy face," I replied. "No stubble in the Marines. It's worse than needing a haircut."

"You really seem to have liked being in the military," Bridgett said.

"Yeah, I guess," I replied with a slight shrug.

"So why did you leave?"

I should have ignored her or told her to just shut up, just like I did with anyone who asked me about that shit. Maybe it was because I still wasn't in my right mind or something, but for some reason I opened up my mouth. I went against all my good sense and actually answered her question honestly.

"I was…discharged," I told her. I closed my eyes and look a long breath through my nose. It was already more than most people knew, and I still had a strange impulse to tell her more.

"You didn't want to leave," she finally said softly.

I wasn't sure if it was a question or a statement.

"Not really," I said. "I had been in the desert a long time. They just…"

My chest rose and fell with another deep breath as my fingers tensed against her hip. Visions from my dreams came back into my head, causing the back of my neck to sweat.

"They just decided after what I had been through that I was no longer fit to serve."

"I'm fine, sir."

"No, son – I don't think you are."

"I'm a Marine," I remind him. "I'm perfectly fine."

A hand on my shoulder that is supposed to be comforting isn't.

"No one expects you to just walk away from that unscathed, Evan. Consider it early retirement for a job well done."

Fingers over my cheek again brought me back to the present. Another long, drawn-out pause ensued until Bridgett finally asked in a whisper I could barely hear, like she thought I might kill her for uttering the words.

"What did you go through?"

I felt her body still beside me. She didn't quite go tense, but I could tell she was just *waiting*. She didn't know what she was waiting for, but she knew there was more, and she was going to try to out-patience me, and I let her. I never should have – I never should have let her get as close as she did. I never should have said anything at all to her.

It could only end in tears.

Or blood.

"I was a POW," I finally told her. "I was captured and held for a year and a half somewhere in the Middle East – Iraq, Afghanistan, or possibly both. I couldn't really tell, and the people who did it weren't exactly forthcoming with a lot of information. Once I was found and brought back to the States, the Colonel didn't think I was fit for the military anymore."

"You were…captured?"

I could barely hear her words, but I knew what she was saying – I'd heard similar reactions many times. It was part of the reason why

I didn't talk about it. It was everyone's initial reaction – the disbelief that seemed to turn itself to some sort of plea to be told it was all a sick joke.

Like anyone would joke about that shit.

"The rest of my unit was killed a mile from our camp," I told her. "Since I was the only officer, they figured I must have information, so I was taken prisoner and tortured for eighteen months."

"Oh my God," she whispered under her breath.

"Don't do that," I growled. I turned my eyes on her and glared. "It was years ago. I don't want that shit from you, got it? That's just why I left – they said after all of that, the doctors didn't think I was fit for combat any more, and I didn't want some fucking desk job, so I was discharged."

My head was pounding again, and my chest ached with the labor of breathing. Aside from that, I still felt absolutely grimy, and talk of what had happened to me just made me think of sweat, sand, and dust.

"I need a shower," I muttered as I tried to push myself back out of bed.

As soon as my feet hit the floor, I got dizzy and stumbled. I didn't quite fall, but I had to put the palm of my hand on the mattress to keep the floor from coming right up to my face.

Bridgett practically had to walk me all the way to the bathroom. Once I was there, the dizziness left just long enough for me to take a piss in private. I turned on the shower but immediately starting cussing the damn thing out when I couldn't get the temperature right.

"How about I help you?"

Bridgett opened the door and moved up beside me. She reached around, adjusted the water, stripped, and then got in with me.

"I need to shave first," I told her as she reached for the bottle of shampoo.

She looked up to my face.

"I'm not sure I could do that for you."

"I can do it." I wasn't sure, but it was going to drive me crazy if I didn't. She got the razor for me and helped me lather up my face, and then I used the little round mirror in the shower to make sure I didn't miss anywhere.

I felt a thousand times better.

"We're going to have to make this quick,' Bridgett said when I was done. "You look like you're going to pass out. Just lean against the tiles."

I was too weak to argue with her.

The tiles were cold on my back, but the water and Bridgett's hands were warm. She started with a small handful of shampoo, and I had to lean forward a bit so she could reach around my head and wash my hair. Her fingers massaged my scalp, and I didn't want to think about how good it felt.

She moved down my neck to my shoulders, filling her hands with liquid body-wash and coating my skin in lather. She washed my chest, my stomach, and down my legs. My eyes closed as she ran her hands all over me, and my cock remembered the way she had touched me in the past.

With my eyes opened just a slit, I watched her mouth move close to the head of my cock as she washed my feet and legs. As my body reacted to her on her knees in front of me, Bridgett glanced up at me – her look questioning.

I shook my head.

"I'd just fall over," I informed her, and she nodded.

Her hands still ran over me, cleaned me from top to bottom, and I made a mental note to bring her back in here when I was healthy again. Images of her sucking my cock or with her back up against the tiles floated around in my dizzy head until she pulled me into the water, rinsed and dried me, and then hauled me back to bed, naked.

By the time she got herself dried off, I was already asleep.

The next morning I was markedly better. I even took Odin out for a quick trip to the grassy area of Lake Shore East Park. It ended up being all I was up for, but I figured it was still progress. The air was warm for the end of February, and after I brought Odin back up to the apartment, I went out on the balcony and looked over at the lake.

"You have such a beautiful view up here," Bridgett said as she came up behind me. She wrapped her arms around my waist and placed her head against my shoulder. "Is that Millennium Park over there?"

She pointed off to the south.

"Yep," I replied.

"It's on my list of places to visit," she said quietly.

"Visit?"

"Yeah, when I first moved here I had this big long list of places I wanted to see – the Art Institute, the Shedd Aquarium – all those places. I haven't been to many yet."

"What about The Bean?"

Bridgett snickered.

"Never *been* there," she said with the emphasis on the pun, which I ignored.

"What do you mean you've never been to The Bean?"

Bridgett shrugged.

"I only moved here a few months ago," she said. "I haven't exactly had a lot of time to check out the city. It was always part of the plan, but then again – there are a lot of things I had planned that didn't happen. Ultimately, I have to make a living, and that pretty much takes up all my time. I never got around to doing any sightseeing."

"So what places in the city have you gone to?" I asked.

"A friend took me up to the Observatory when I first arrived," she said. "I've been out to Navy Pier and went to the area where all the museums are but never actually saw the exhibits. I was just applying for jobs."

"Why didn't you go work at one of those places?"

"I didn't get hired," she shrugged.

I looked over to her and carefully observed her posture as she looked out over the balcony rail, obviously not actually looking at anything outside of her own mind. I watched her hidden memories move around in her head as her tears formed in the corners of her eyes but wouldn't fall from her lashes.

She'd come here – from where? – looking for something new, something better. So many people did. She was actually far luckier than a lot of those who ended up homeless and strung out on the street. Not that she was in the best of places, of course, but I had seen far worse. She had a good head on her shoulders, and had found a practical way she could get by. It was far from the ideal, but there were far worse options.

Part of me wanted to keep asking questions – to pry into her background, her history, and get to know her better. The rest of me knew that was a really, really bad idea.

This was just fucking.

"You should see The Bean," I finally said as I turned to go back inside.

There was just no way she could live in Chicago without seeing The Bean.

CHAPTER NINE
Evening Interlude

"There's something in the back for you."

I wouldn't have admitted it to anyone, but I was really looking forward to tonight. Reservations were made, certain people expecting us, and I even suited up, which I didn't do often. I was decked out in a pinstripe suit, white button-down, dark purple tie, and dress shoes. I wasn't wearing any socks – a habit I picked up from my Italian co-workers. I had planned for tonight far more than I had for anything that didn't involve my Barrett and a hole in someone's head.

Bridgett glanced at me over the hood of the car with suspicion in her eyes. She'd been giving me the same look since I picked her up, and she asked why I was all dressed up. She leaned back a bit and looked at the package on the back seat of the car before she looked up at me again.

"Get it," I said with a nod, "but don't open it until we get upstairs."

She pulled the box out from behind the seat and followed me up to my apartment.

"I didn't have you pegged as the gift-giving type," Bridgett said as she sat down on the couch with the box in her hands.

"Just open it," I said as I rolled my eyes.

Bridgett's eyes opened wide as she stared into the box with the Armani name on the lid. The sleek dress inside of it was deep purple, matched my tie exactly, and had a black, wool shawl to go with it so she would stay warm. There was also a pair of black heels with straps that would go around her ankles. They weren't too high, so she could still walk comfortably, but they were sexy as hell.

"Put it all on," I told her. "We're going out to dinner."

"Are you serious?"

"Of course I am."

She looked back to the box and slowly pulled out the dress.

"It looks like the right size," she commented.

"It *is* the right size," I said.

She looked up at me for a moment but didn't say anything else. Her eyes went back to the dress and then the shawl below it.

"This, too?" Bridgett asked as she held it up.

"Of course," I said. "That fucking rodent in Pennsylvania might have thought spring was coming, but he's an idiot. It's cold out there, and I don't want you to freeze your ass off. I have plans for it later."

I raised my eyebrows at her, and she shook her head at me. Moving up behind her, I wrapped my arms around her waist.

"I'm taking you for a night on the town – dinner, drinks, shopping – everything. You go get yourself ready."

I smacked her ass with the palm of my hand, and she shrieked as she ran to change in the bedroom. I leaned against the kitchen counter and sipped from a bottle of flavored water, which didn't taste too bad. Jonathan had been going on about them lately, so I had finally given them a shot. They were all full of vitamins instead of sugar, so they had to be better for you than a soda.

Bridgett came out of the bedroom looking like she belonged on the television as a fucking fashion show celebrity. I had to admit that I had done a great job picking out the dress – it fit her perfectly – but the rest was all her. Round ass, long legs, face cleaned off of whore paint and just lightly made-up. She was all looks.

"Beautiful."

She blushed.

For dinner, we went to the restaurant on the other side of the little park behind my apartment building. It was a nice steak place, cozy and quiet enough that Bridgett didn't seem to be overwhelmed or anything. Once we were done with our meal, I wrapped the shawl back around her shoulders and walked her out the front and over to Millennium Park.

She started laughing immediately.

"It *is* a giant bean!" she squealed.

I couldn't help but smile. I also couldn't explain why I loved the sculpture. Sure, there were a lot of people who considered it more comical than artistic, but I thought it was absolutely brilliant.

And shiny.

I took a picture of our reflections in the polished silver with my phone before we walked back towards my building. I held her hand and helped her down the long staircase on the east side of the park, then across the sidewalk and into the parking garage.

"We're not going upstairs?" Bridgett asked.

"Not yet," I said. "We're going to the Magnificent Mile."

I led her over to my parking areas but steered her away from the car she was used to being in.

"This is your car?" Bridgett's eyes widened as she examined the exterior of the Audi R8.

"Shut up and get in," I replied with a smile.

It wasn't quite warm enough to put the top down, but it was still a nicer ride than the Mazda for the kinds of places we were going. I drove in silence across the Michigan Avenue Bridge and up north towards all the best shops. Bridgett just stared out the window at the people going by, most of whom were looking over at us. Once I got to the general center of the area, I pulled off in front of a hotel and let the valet take the car.

"Checking in, sir?"

"No, just shopping," I replied as I handed him some cash.

"Very good, sir."

I took Bridgett's hand again as she stepped out of the car and then escorted her across the street and up the sidewalk to one of the shops. I held out my hand to allow her to enter first.

"Evan, what are you doing?"

"Taking you shopping on the Magnificent Mile," I informed her. "Once we've hit the highlights, we'll have drinks at one of my favorite bars. It's got a great view of Michigan Avenue."

"You can't be serious," she said quietly. "You aren't going to *buy* anything here. The dress I can understand for the place we had dinner, but …"

Her voice trailed off, and I just gave her a half smile as I grabbed her waist and shoved her through the revolving doors and into Tiffany and Co's.

The thing I found most noticeable about the store was just how sparkly everything was. It was like walking into a place full of tiny little disco balls – there were rainbows everywhere. I thought that chick who wrote about the sparkly vampires must have gotten the idea by standing in the Tiffany's store and staring at the diamonds.

I had a feeling Bridgett wasn't going to just pick something out for herself, so I already had something in mind. I led her to the back where all the charms were kept.

"Mister Arden?" A tall, lean blonde walked around the counter and held out her hand.

"Hello," I replied. I reached out and shook the salesperson's hand. She smiled at Bridgett before leading us around to the back counter. She brought over a velvet box and opened it up as I watched Bridgett's expression go from curiosity, to surprise, to bemusement.

"That's a gold bean, isn't it?" she asked.

"It is," I said with a smile. "Rose gold with earrings to match."

The salesperson held Bridgett's hand and slipped the gold chain around her wrist. The bracelet included a rose gold bean as well as a traditional Tiffany's padlock charm.

"Beautiful," the salesperson said as she affixed the charm around Bridgett's wrist. It jingled as she moved, and when she turned her wrist slightly, the charms sparkled in the store's lights.

"Evan…" Bridgett's voice evaporated again, and her eyes started to brim over with tears.

"Stop that," I said quietly. I took my finger and placed it under her chin. "You deserve a night on the town after putting up with me for all that time when I was sick, and I'm going to make sure your night is perfect. This is just a little memento of the evening."

"It's hardly a little thing," she argued. "This is…"

She glanced over at the salesperson, but she was now ringing up the bill and a bit out of earshot. Bridgett lowered her voice anyway.

"This is more than you would pay for me for a whole week," she said.

"So?"

I ignored her remaining protests, took her by the hand, and led her back out onto the street. We stopped at a few more stores but mostly just window-shopped. I pointed out the window of the Armani place where I had acquired Bridgett's dress – she hadn't known Armani catered to women as well – but we didn't go inside. I wasn't in need of a new suit just yet and probably wouldn't need one until Moretti's daughter got hitched or something. Then I'd come get one.

Ice cream at Ghirardelli's Chocolate and a quick carriage ride down a few blocks to my favorite drinking establishment came next.

The 676 Restaurant and Bar was just a block down from the famous Tiffany's jewelry store and in the same building as the Omni Hotel. I helped Bridgett dodge the drunks and other pedestrians as we made our way into the building. The downstairs was your usual hotel stuff – front desk, concierge, bellhops – but upstairs there was a small restaurant and bar that mostly catered to the hotel's guests.

I wasn't sure what was better – the food, the drinks, or the banter between the staff.

"This place is…nice," Bridgett said softly.

"Good service, too," I informed her. "They have the best martinis in the city. You like martinis, right?"

"Sure, I guess."

Her hesitation caused me to stop in front of the elevator and take her by the elbow.

"It's okay?" I asked. I had no idea why I was feeling suddenly hesitant. I hadn't been to 676 for a while, but I was there enough in the past to be considered as much of a regular as anyone was. I'd never actually taken a girl up there with me, though. I'd taken a couple away – or at least as far as their hotel rooms upstairs – but never brought one in with me.

"Whatever you like," Bridgett responded.

I scowled at her lack of answer, which seemed to make her smile. Her hand reached up and touched the side of my face.

"It's fine," she said.

I leaned over and placed my lips against hers.

"You'll love it," I swore to her.

I took her up the elevator to the fourth floor and held her hand as we walked into the bar area. I recognized almost everyone there immediately and was glad to see familiar faces. Michele was tending bar, and Patrick was managing. They were an interesting duo – and just watching the two of them interact was worth the price of the drinks.

The drinks were damn good, too.

"What do you want?" Bridgett said. "A beer or something?"

"No," I said, "definitely not. Do you like raspberries?"

"I guess so."

"Hey, Michele!"

The bartender smiled and waltzed over to me. Her dangling silver hoop earrings danced around on her shoulders as she moved, and her mahogany hair swung back and forth in a high ponytail. She had on basic black from head to toe, like pretty much every bartender there, and her smile earned her a lot of big tips.

"Hey there, Evan," she said with that award-winning smile. "What can I get for you?"

"Give me one of those raspberry martinis you make," I said, "and Lagavulin, neat."

"Who's this?" she asked with a sly grin as she started to make the drinks.

"Michele, this is Bridgett," I said. They both smiled at each other. "Bridgett, this is Michele with one 'L.'"

"Don't forget it!" Michele laughed and nodded her head, which caused her ponytail to bounce around. She reached up on a high shelf to retrieve my scotch and then moved farther down the bar to gather the ingredients for the martini quickly and efficiently.

"You really are going all out here, aren't you?" Bridgett commented as Michele set our drinks in front of us.

"I figured after last week, you kinda deserved it," I said with a shrug. "A night on the town is the least I can do to make up for a night with me sick as a dog."

"Four nights," she reminded me.

"Right."

I sipped my scotch and watched her take in the surroundings. It was a nice place – posh, in the heart of the Magnificent Mile, and with a good view of Michigan Avenue. Michele exhibited her usual rockin' service and seemed to be going the extra mile to be nice to Bridgett, even if she did keep glancing at me sideways. The way she raised her eyebrows, I wondered if she suspected Bridgett's occupation. Not that it mattered to me – I didn't give a shit what she thought of my date.

Patrick stopped by and placed his hand on my shoulder.

"Good to see you again, Evan!" he said with a big Doogie Howser smile. "Haven't seen you in ages!"

"Been busy," I replied. My eyes bore into his. "I've been working a lot lately."

Patrick removed his hand, cleared his throat, and gave me another managerial smile.

"Make sure you treat this guy well, Michele!"

She gave him a "thumbs up" as she went back to mixing drinks for a couple farther down the bar.

I tried not to watch Michele too much. She was hot – no doubt about it – but she was also married. Not that I gave a shit; I didn't. I did actually have some scruples, just not in that particular area. However, she had turned me down every time I came on to her over the past year since I first found the place, so I had given up. Still, I liked watching her work, but I had to make sure I wasn't paying too much attention to her shakin' and stirrin'.

I ordered a PB&J waffle, and Bridgett just stared at me like I was nuts.

"I'll give you a bite," I promised her. "You won't regret it."

"I already do," she stated.

Michele brought out another round of drinks and rolled her eyes at me once she got a good look at Bridgett, which confirmed my suspicions. I wasn't sure how she knew, but I could tell by her expression that she understood the situation. I gave her the evil eye back – the last thing I needed was someone who served me drinks judging me for the quality of my date.

Thankfully, Bridgett didn't seem to notice, not that I cared what Michele or anyone else thought about me or my date. However, this was supposed to be a nice night for Bridgett, and I didn't want something stupid to ruin it. So far, everything had been perfect.

"These drinks really are fantastic!" Bridgett said as she sipped the fruity martini.

"All of the drinks here are great," I told her. "They have awesome food, too."

We ordered a couple more drinks, and as crowds rolled in, the manager tried to help out at the bar. He scratched his head, stared at the rows of bottles on the shelf, and looked lost.

It was kind of like cabaret.

"You put cranberries in it, right?" he asked.

"It's a raspberry martini," Michele replied, "so you put raspberries in it."

"Got it." Patrick looked around the bar, then under it. "Umm…where are they?"

"You need a glass," Michele informed him. She pulled four beers and placed them neatly on a tray before walking off.

"Do you know what vodka Michele was using?" Patrick asked me as he held up two bottles.

"The good shit," I replied, which made Bridgett giggle.

He put both bottles back and grabbed a tall bottle of Grey Goose.

"You have no idea what you're doing," Michele mumbled as she came back and took the shaker from him.

The drinks were made, and the banter continued.

"Did you need a glass, George?"

"You have to pour it in the mouth!"

"This shirt keeps coming un-tucked – I look like a total loser."

"You are a total loser."

"You can't talk to me like that!"

"So, where can I go to find a hooker?"

Maybe the patron thought he was being quiet or subtle, but he wasn't. The concierge chuckled and rubbed the spot between his eyes, which made his glasses bounce up and down on his face. I glanced over at Bridgett, who had obviously heard the guy's question. She wrapped her fingers around the edge of her new drink and stared at the floating fruit.

I reached over and placed the end of my finger under her chin to turn her towards me. For a long moment, we just looked at each other, and then I leaned in to press my lips against hers. My tongue tasted the raspberry drink as it reached into her mouth.

I tilted my head and kissed her again.

And again.

Her fingers gripped my arm through my suit jacket as she pressed harder against me. When we parted, her eyes were glassy and her chest rose and fell with her breaths. I couldn't help but smile a bit at her expression, which seemed to cause her to blush.

She was a fucking sexy sight.

One of the other patrons noticed her, too, but one glare from me and he kept his eyes to himself.

"You are beautiful tonight," I whispered.

Before she could respond, the manager walked behind me, grumbling.

"I hate it when people wave their hand at me," Patrick mumbled under his breath. "What does she want me to do, jump over and serve her a drink?"

I glanced at the overweight woman with her hair up in a bun. She was waving frantically from one of the window-side tables. Patrick managed to put his smile back on before facing her, and Bridgett snickered.

"He's an interesting one," she said quietly.

"You haven't seen the half of it," I told her. I leaned in a little closer and pushed her hair off her shoulder. "I was in here once when Michele was on vacation – the guy couldn't figure out how to make a rum and Coke."

Michele brought out my PB&J waffle.

"Are you really going to eat that?" Bridgett asked as she looked down at the plate.

"Most definitely," I told her. "This shit is the best soul food in the world, right, Michele?"

"Better than chicken and biscuits," she agreed. "Actually, that's the only thing that could make them any better – put a piece of chicken in the middle and cover it all with gravy."

"We should totally try that!" Patrick said. "I'm gonna see if they'll make that in the kitchen."

Patrick disappeared, and Michele laughed. Bridgett shook her head and rolled her eyes at me. I took my fork and cut off a little piece of the waffle, which was oozing jelly. Picking it up with my fingers, I turned towards Bridgett and held it up to her mouth.

"You want to try this," I informed her.

"I really don't think I do!" she cringed and mashed her lips together.

With one finger, I traced up the side of her neck.

"You would regret it for the rest of your life if you didn't try it."

"I'm okay with that."

"Come on," I urged. "If you can swallow guys' cocks all night, you can definitely try this."

She glared at me, and I realized what I said was pretty douchebaggish but ended up rolling my eyes back at her.

"Just try it."

With her eyes still slightly narrowed, she opened her mouth and took the little piece inside. As soon as she sunk her teeth into the homemade waffle oozing peanut butter and strawberry jelly, I knew she was hooked, and she had totally forgotten what I had said.

"This is incredible!" she exclaimed.

"It's awesome, right? Food of the fucking gods."

"I have never eaten anything quite like this," Bridgett said. "It's amazing."

We shared the remainder with me feeding her chunks of it alternated with my own bites. When it was gone, Bridgett excused herself to wash the sticky jelly off her face where I kept missing her mouth.

"What the hell, Evan?" Michele with one "L" stepped up in front of me from the other side of the bar.

She was giving me one of those looks that, despite my other observation skills, I had never understood. It was a look I'd only seen from women, and though it seemed to coincide with something whatever guy she was with did, I never understood what it was actually supposed to *mean.* It always ended up with the husband or boyfriend in trouble, though. Often, he ended up alone.

"What?" I asked.

Michele leaned over the bar on her elbows and looked up at me.

"That's a hooker," she stated.

"So?"

"So, what the hell?"

"I always fuck hookers."

She rolled her eyes.

"Do you always dress them up like they spend half their lives at Saks for a night on the town?"

I glared at her.

"What difference does that make?" I leaned back on the stool and folded my arms across my chest. "If I'm paying for her, what the fuck difference does it make what I do with her?"

"You are such a man." She tossed her hands up and started walking away.

"Well, yeah!" I called back. "You want to check out my dick?"

She looked quickly over to Patrick, her manager, to make sure he wasn't looking in her direction, flipped me off, and then moved to the far end of the bar to serve someone else. Bridgett came back, and I never did get the chance to ask Michele what she was going on about.

Bridgett and I still spent a couple hours at 676 just talking and hanging out. At some point we moved over to the more comfortable chairs near the windows overlooking Michigan Avenue. I put my arm around Bridgett's shoulders, and we watched the traffic go by. When the fascination with the view seemed to have waned, I took her by the hand and led her back downstairs to the valet.

Bridgett was quiet as we drove back to my place and continued her silence as we parked the car, went up to the apartment, and then took Odin out for a walk around the park. Though technically closed in the later hours of the night, we made our way over to the dog run where I could let Odin off his leash so he could run around a bit.

I leaned against the fence at one side of the park and tried to ignore the beeping sounds from the parking garage behind me. Ever since the day the damn garage went in, the electronic warning signal when the parking garage door went up had been driving me nuts. When the balcony door was open, I could hear it from the living room.

I glared at the large metal door as the wind from the lake picked up and blew some trash down the street. Bridgett shivered and pulled the shawl tighter around her shoulders. Reaching out, I took her by the waist and pulled her back against my chest. My lips found her neck as I began to remember the feeling of her tight ass gripping my shaft. My hand moved from her hip to her stomach and then farther up to palm her tit.

Odin raced from one shrub to the other, watering and fertilizing as he went.

"Did you have a good time?" I whispered into her ear.

Bridgett nodded quickly.

My tongue flicked out over her skin.

"You look so good tonight," I told her. "I thought I might have to kill one of the guys at the bar for staring at you."

She stiffened and took a step away from me. Her hands pushed at my arms until I let go of her, and she moved out of my reach.

"What are you doing, Evan?" Bridgett turned and glared up at me with tears streaming down her face. "What the fuck is this, huh? What happened to all that 'it's just fucking' garbage? Is that what this is?"

She ripped the bracelet from her wrist and shook it at me.

"You going to fuck me with this?"

I took a half step back as my insides began to feel as if they were slipping down into my feet, leaving the top half of me cold.

"I just…I thought since you…" I stopped and shook my head to clear it. "You took care of me when I was sick – I wanted to thank you."

"Thank me?" she scoffed. "Why did you even have that guy come and get me, huh? What made you think I'd come and take care of you, Evan?"

Another half step backwards and I hit my back on the fence. The tension that immediately flowed through my body was familiar and frightening. Bridgett was too close to me to get around her effectively, and I couldn't turn and jump the fence without hitting her in the process.

I looked up towards the skyline to try to free my head of the enclosed feeling, but it was a cloudy night and I couldn't see any open space. There were high rise buildings all around us.

The closed-up feeling increased, and then the fucking parking garage door began to beep again.

"What the hell is wrong with you?" I growled at her. "You said you had a good time!"

"I did have a good time!" she yelled back at me. "Don't you see? That's the problem!"

My mouth probably dropped open as I tried to figure out what the hell she was talking about. Though normally pretty apt when it came to reading people's body language, the combination of the claustrophobia and Bridgett's sudden change in behavior completely took me aback.

Not a feeling I liked.

Not at all.

"Damn, you bitches make no sense!" I snapped at her.

Odin was suddenly at my side, snuffling at my hand. I grabbed it away from him and pointed a finger at Bridgett.

"I told you what this was," I snarled at her, "and you know full well what I am. I give you money, and you let me use your body for whatever the fuck I want. That's what this is, and that's how this works."

"You are so full of shit," she snapped back. "Who sends for their favorite whore when they have a tummy ache?"

Irrespective of the point made, I refused to back down. In fact, knowing she had such a good point made me have to take it that much further.

"And what kind of whore falls for her hit man john? Didn't it occur to you that the only way this ends is you with a bullet in your brain?"

I stood there glowering at her as Odin whined by my side, and Bridgett stared at me for a long moment. Without another word, she turned and ran out of the park and up the stairs towards Columbia Drive. About half way up, she stopped, cursed loud enough for me to hear from where I was, reached down, and took off her shoes. A moment later, she was completely out of my sight, and I was left alone with the dog.

My heart was still pounding in my chest.

"What the fuck?" I muttered.

I took Odin back up to the apartment, ditched the tie, and then went back outside.

There was no way I was going to admit to myself or anyone else that I was looking for her. I wasn't. I was only going for a nice walk in the evening.

Well, nearly midnight.

I walked between the buildings and past various sculptures on which the good people of Chicago spent a lot of money just so I could have the privilege of walking past them in the middle of the night. They were mostly modern art – swirly shapes and strange, metal animals. Modern art didn't really make any sense to me, though some of it definitely caught my eye.

No Bridgett.

Not that I was looking for her.

A homeless guy wandered out from between the metal animals and tried to talk to me. He didn't have any teeth, and I couldn't figure out if the napkin-wrapped beer bottle he was holding out was an offering or a request. I finally shoved past him and made my way back out to Michigan Avenue and the nearest bar.

Unfortunately, that was Sweetwater and the place was a zoo. Without Jon's mad skills and phone apps, I was going to have to wait forever for a table, which just wasn't going to happen. My least favorite dude was tending bar, and though the drink he made was fine, I wasn't comfortable just standing around staring at the television screens showing games I didn't give a shit about. I stood by the bar for all of five minutes before I gave up on my vodka, threw ten bucks on the counter, and walked out.

My mind was still spinning, and I didn't know what to do with myself. I felt completely lost and out of control, and I was fighting the urge to pull out a gun and start shooting.

Without any better ideas in my head, I wandered back to The Bean and stared at the skyline reflected in the shiny surface. The chilled wind from the lake picked up and blew my clothing around as the tourists took pictures of themselves.

I wanted to pretend I didn't know what I had done wrong, but I couldn't quite manage it. I'd wanted her to have a good time. I'd wanted her to feel like it was more than it was. I just didn't want her to notice it felt like more than it was because that would screw it all up.

There was just no way this was happening.

CHAPTER TEN
Abrupt Change

"You're on edge today."

"Not sleeping."

My hands were jittery due to the lack of sleep, and there was absolutely nothing that pissed me off more than something that could affect my aim. Caffeine made it even worse. I was also ticked off at the dirt on my jeans, which I got courtesy of my shrink's car. As I walked past it, I managed to bump the fender, which was covered in mud – just like the rest of the Land Rover. I'd seen the vehicle before but never all muddy and figured the driver usually got their car washed during their lunch hour; my appointment had been moved up from the afternoon when I usually saw Mark.

I considered putting a bullet in the tires until I looked at the license plate that read "ID V EGO" and realized it had to be Mark's. There was also a toolbox on the passenger seat containing a bunch of those Habitat for Humanity fliers.

"I thought you had been doing better on that front."

I glanced up at him and scowled at his choice of words. His expression told me he hadn't realized what type of metaphor he had used.

"I was," I stated bluntly, "and now I'm not."

"What changed?"

My eyes dropped back to the area rug and its swirly, uninteresting patterns. My eyes followed a blue swirl around a green one. Did I really want to go into this with him? Did I want to tell him how apparently my pathetic, empty self had developed the need to share his bed with a hooker – not for the sex but for the sleep?

Did I want to tell him she left me?

How does a whore get the option anyway?

A shiver went through my body, my stomach clenched, and I tasted bile in the back of my throat.

"What's her name?"

"She's no one," I replied.

"Yet you have someone in mind when I ask the question," Mark said. "That pretty much makes her a *someone*."

I glared at him again.

"It's not what you think," I said.

"What do I think?"

"She's not a girlfriend or anything. She just…slept with me."

He paused and tapped his pen against his wrist before jotting something down.

"A prostitute?"

"Yeah." I clenched my hands into fists a couple of times to try to get rid of the shaking. I couldn't have been much worse off if I had been going through the DTs. "She'd stay overnight with me, and it helped to have someone else there. The dreams weren't as bad."

Saying it out loud made it sound even more pathetic.

"And she's no longer in the picture?"

"She's not."

"What happened to her?"

I ran my hand over the top of my head, mildly annoyed with myself for needing a haircut. I took in a long breath and figured it couldn't really make it any worse to tell him.

"I took her out, showed her a great time, fed her waffles, and then at the end of the night, when everything seemed to be going great, she took off."

"Why did she leave?"

"I have no idea."

"Seems like you missed some details in there somewhere."

"I don't miss details," I snapped.

"Apparently, you do."

The tension in my body had to be noticeable to Mark as I glared at him. I could almost see the crosshair on his forehead and figured I'd try a more mental shot than a physical one.

"You do a shit load of charity work," I told him. "You aren't married now but you were once, or at least engaged. No kids. You drive a Land Rover, and you like off-roading on the weekends. You probably tried to get into the military, but because of your foot, you didn't qualify for active service, and you used it as an excuse to go to school. Your dad probably hated the idea of you becoming a shrink, which is why you don't speak anymore."

Trying to keep my breaths calm, I stared at him as he opened and closed his mouth a few times. Eventually, he cringed a bit and found his tongue.

"Evan, have you been…spying on me?"

"No," I snapped. "You told me all of it, just not with your mouth. Don't ever think I miss the details."

It took him several minutes, but he eventually gathered his wits about himself again and continued on.

"I meant you might be missing some of the...*nuances* of female behavior."

"She was having a good time," I said. "I know how to tell when a chick is happy."

"And then...what?" Mark asked. "You are obviously observant, so tell me what you saw."

My tongue ran over my lips as I conjured up images of Bridgett running across the park and away from me. Playing the whole scene in reverse, I brought myself back to the dog park and her back pressed to my chest.

"I told her...I told her none of this shit was serious," I paraphrased. "She already knew that."

"She wanted more."

My eyes moved from the rug to his face, and I stared at him for a long moment before shaking my head and returning my gaze to the swirly patterns.

"There isn't anything else."

"You don't think you have anything to offer a woman?"

"I don't think anything I have to offer a woman is in her best interest. Seriously, you've got a better idea of how...of what I've...of what happened. How could I ever try to explain that to a date?"

"Lots of people deal with PTSD every day, Evan," he reminded me. "You don't do too badly for yourself. I know working under the table isn't ideal, but at least you're not a criminal, right?"

I tried not to actually laugh.

"Tell me one thing," Mark said as the session ended and I got up to leave, "how did you know about my father?"

"Your jackets don't fit right."

"What?"

I took a long, deep breath.

"You're fine in jeans and polos, but whenever I see you wearing a button down shirt, dress pants, or a jacket, they're wrinkled and they don't fit right. Rich kids get taught that shit. You're a blue-collar guy."

"You still haven't said anything about my father."

I rolled my eyes.

"No blue-collar guy goes into a white-collar profession without pissing off his dad."

Mark laughed, and I took the opportunity to get the hell out before he asked me anything else. Besides, I had a little side trip I wanted to take, and I needed to do something first.

I grabbed my phone out of my back pocket.

"Hey, Nick," I said when he answered.

"Hey there!" Nick replied.

"Am I interrupting anything?" I asked.

"Nah," he replied. "I'm just hanging out, shootin' the shit with some buddies. What's up with you?"

"Just wondering…" I paused, suddenly unsure how to even ask.

"You still there?"

"Yeah." I cleared my throat. "I was just wondering…what's the best way to apologize to a chick?"

"Oh, that's easy," Nick replied. "You gotta go down on her."

"Don't I have to get her to speak to me first?"

"It helps!" Nick laughed.

"So, how do I get her to talk to me again?"

"Just do something nice for her," Nick replied. "It doesn't even matter what, 'cause guys never do anything nice for chicks, so anything works. That's why the flower business is so good."

"So, buy her fucking flowers? That's it?"

"Yeah," he said. "Or one of those fancy vibrators."

Yeah – not gonna happen.

"I dunno." I leaned back and stared up at the cloudy sky. "Flowers seem kind of…cliché."

"There's a reason for that," Nick said. "They work."

I couldn't argue with him, so I stopped at a florist shop and wondered what kind of flowers said whatever it was I wanted to say. There were too many varieties – too many colors to choose from to actually come up with something that looked right. They all looked right. They all looked wrong, too. I couldn't think of any words to put on the card, either. Maybe the basics were best.

Roses are red,

Violets are blue.

I'm just a fucked up hit man,

And nothing rhymes with that.

It was entirely possible that poetry was not my strong point.

Whatever I did, I'm sorry.

Sorry.

SORRY.

The ridiculously simplistic note I left on top of the skewed sheets covering the worn out, twin-sized bed in Arizona fluttered down and landed at the forefront of my mind, mocking me. If there was anything I knew, I knew that I wasn't any good at this kind of shit.

I left the flower shop, ripped four daffodils out of the window box on someone's deck, and drove myself over to Bridgett's corner. Traffic was heavy since it was still the tail end of rush hour, but I was patient as I crawled along with the other travelers. I still wasn't sure what I should say, so I let different scenarios clamber around in my head while I waited for people and cars to get the fuck out of the way.

Once I reached the right corner, I saw Melvin, the pimp, leaning over the car in front of mine. My eyes scanned the area, but there wasn't any sign of Bridgett.

"Hey, baby. How about some sweet stuff?"

I recognized Candy as she swayed around from the back of my car and up to my window. She leaned over enough to put her tits in my face and asked what all she could do for me. She didn't seem to know where Bridgett was, though.

"Haven't seen her since the day before yesterday," the girl said. "She's got a regular john, so that's not so unusual."

Yeah, maybe – except I *was* the regular john.

"Where's she stay when she's not here?"

I had to give the whore fifty dollars to talk, which she slipped inside her shirt while watching Melvin out of the corner of her eye. I figured out what building Bridgett lived in by Candy's description, and it only took a minute to drive there.

There was only street parking, so I drove around the block twice before I found a spot. The sky was pretty much dark by the time I pushed open the door, found her apartment number on the mailbox, and went down a handful of stairs to the lower level units. I looked down at the daffodils in my hand and wondered just how ridiculous I was – apologizing to the chick I paid to fuck me – but I needed to sleep before I went completely over the edge.

I knocked.

I had to physically force myself to not tap my toe on the ground, stare at my watch, or start whistling. There was no way I was going to pull off any kind of casual encounter anyway – it was obvious what I was here to do. The daffodils kind of gave it away.

I knocked again.

There was that distinct feeling moving slowly up the sides of my spine that I had rarely felt outside of combat. It was a completely irrational knowing that came from nothing other than gut instinct, but it had served me many times in the past.

It was a gut instinct I trusted.

My mind and the memories within took over for a moment, and I felt the dry, stale heat of the desert air around me. It had been mid-summer in the desert, and the heat was absolutely unbearable. I had walked around the corner of a small building to reach just a bit of shade to relax a moment and take a piss when it all started.

One hand had touched the wall of the building as I leaned against it, while the other loosened my fatigues and pulled out my dick. There had been a noise from the other side of the building that I couldn't identify – something that didn't sound quite right. The hair on the back of my neck stood up.

There was something very, very wrong. I was sure of it.

"Bridgett?" I called as I brought myself out of the memory and banged harder against the door. "Bridgett – open the fucking door!"

Still no answer.

I didn't think – I just leaned back and kicked the handle. I had to kick twice before the shitty lock splintered the weak wooden doorjamb and the apartment was open to me.

I took everything in.

It was a small place – one room efficiency with a small cubby bathroom off to the side. There was a little half window with a view of a brick wall. It wouldn't have let any light in at any time of day and was probably too small for the fire marshal to allow without some kind of bribe involved. The stove looked like it might have worked well in the seventies, and the fridge was one of those half-sized ones you find in college dorm rooms.

Despite the size, the room was neat and orderly. Everything seemed to have its place, including a small shelf with books and an aloe plant, a box for mail, and a small candle. No pictures – none at all. There wasn't much in the way of furniture – just a card table with four plastic chairs, the book shelf, and a futon along one wall. It wasn't pulled out into a bed, though there was a body lying across it.

I knew she wasn't dead – there was no tell-tale smell of death, and the slight rise and fall of her shoulder made it obvious. Her back was to me, but I didn't need to see her face to know she was unconscious. The lack of reaction to having her door kicked in was evidence enough that she wasn't just asleep. Hesitating only slightly, I moved across the room and knelt next to the futon.

With my hand on her shoulder, I pulled her body towards me. The black and blue bruises that covered her face and shoulders were maybe a day and a half old, not much more than that. There was a cut over her lip, and her chin was streaked with blood.

As I pulled her closer to me, her arm fell away, and I could see the bruising on the rest of her naked body. Clear hand prints in purple circled her wrists, and the circular bruises on her thighs were clearly fist marks. The scent of stale semen on her was unmistakable.

"Bridgett?" I said and felt her jerk in my arms. My hand touched the side of her face where she wasn't bruised. "Open your eyes."

They fluttered at my order, and the lids parted. Her expression quickly moved from fear, to shock, and then to sadness. Sobs began to shake her body as her forehead pressed against my shoulder.

"Evan," she croaked. Her voice didn't sound right – it was rough and scratchy. I tilted my head to get a better look at her neck and saw the finger-shaped bruises there as well.

"Can you hold on to me?"

Her fingers gripped my shoulder as I wrapped the sheet back around her and lifted her up into my arms. I held her against my chest as I walked out the door, crushing the dropped daffodils as I left. I got a few looks from the bums on the street as I carried her off and lay her down in the passenger seat of my car, but no one said anything or tried to stop me. I was carrying a beat up girl, naked and wrapped in a sheet, and no one cared.

Nice fucking neighborhood.

Back at my apartment, I was a little more concerned. Since I was in the parking garage, it was easy enough to get to the elevator without anyone laying eyes on me or what I was carrying, but being in the elevator had me on edge until we got to my floor. Luckily, there was no one else around. The elevator doors opened, and I glanced quickly down the hall before carrying her to my apartment.

I dropped the sheet in the hallway, figuring I'd come back in a bit and throw it out. It stank of sweat, beer, and semen.

"I'm going to get you cleaned up, okay?" I said as I carried her through the bedroom door and into the master bathroom. "Can you stand on your own?"

I took off my jacket but couldn't seem to get my shirt unbuttoned while I kept Bridgett from falling, so I ended up taking her into the shower with my clothes still on. She kept her arms wrapped around my neck as I filled my palms with liquid soap and ran them over her skin.

When I washed between her legs, she flinched and started crying again. I ended up holding her for a minute, not having any idea what I was supposed to do. Eventually, she steadied enough for me to finish.

Once she was rinsed, I stood her on the bathmat and tried to dry her off, but it wasn't easy with one hand holding her up.

"I can do it," she said with a scratchy voice.

I steadied her as she ran the towel around and then rubbed at her hair.

"Do you…um…do you have a hairbrush?"

I laughed and ran my hand over my closely cropped hair.

"I guess you wouldn't, huh?" She smiled a little, but it seemed to hurt her busted lip.

She sat on a towel at the edge of my bed, wrapped up in my robe as she ran her fingers through the strands of brown hair. Her hair was a lot darker when it was wet, and I tried to force thoughts of another woman from my head for a while, but it didn't really work.

It never did.

I peeled off my wet clothes and hung them over the shower door. Once I was dry, I pulled on some clean ones and grabbed my phone.

"I could use a little help at my place," I said into the phone.

"You get shot?" the voice on the other end asked immediately.

Franklyn Johnson might have been a doctor once, and he might not have been. No one ever called him Doc or anything like that – just Franklyn. Still, he knew how to take a bullet out of a leg, stitch people up, and do a lot of other emergency room kinds of procedures. He did stuff like that when Rinaldo's people were hurt, and a hospital visit would end up causing questions.

He wasn't expecting a beat up hooker at my place.

"She's been through the wringer," Franklyn said when he left the bedroom. He reached up behind his head and scratched at the overgrown, graying mop there, which reminded me of Christopher Lloyd's character from Taxi. "I sedated her and gave her a morning after pill, but there isn't much else I can do."

"Anything more serious?"

"What, aside from the multiple rapes? What else do you think she needs?"

His eyes shot daggers.

"I found her, asshole," I growled, and his look towards me softened a bit.

"Nothing permanent," he finally said. "Well, not on the outside. I doubt she'll ever be the same on the inside. No broken bones, no internal bleeding. Dehydrated a bit – make sure you get some more water in her when she wakes up."

He left, and I went back inside to see how she was doing. She was asleep, and Odin was right there beside the bed, watching her.

"Are you finally going to make yourself useful as a guard dog?" I asked him.

He sneezed and then peered up at me through curly white hair.

"She'll be okay," I informed him, though I wasn't sure why I felt the need to do so. Odin dropped down on the floor next to the bed, and I moved around to the other side to get in.

As soon as I lay down, the exhaustion hit me. My mind didn't race from one horrific image to another but focused on the sweet scent of the woman beside me. I reached out and carefully wrapped my arms around her, making sure I didn't cause additional pain.

With Bridgett nestled against me, I finally got some sleep.

It was hours after I woke up when Bridgett finally came down from the sedative, but she fell back asleep almost immediately afterwards. I made her drink some water before she dozed off again and then just watched her for a while. When she woke up the second time, she seemed a little better, even with her black eye and bruised cheek.

"Do you know who it was?" I asked.

She didn't answer.

"Was he a regular john? Someone you'd seen before? Can you describe him? Or…um…*them*?"

Again, she said nothing.

I watched her carefully as the edge of her eye constricted a little, and her lips pressed together tighter. She knew who it was – she definitely knew. Why wouldn't she tell me?

There was really only one possible answer.

"It was him, wasn't it?" I asked. "That pimp of yours."

"It doesn't matter," she said quietly.

I brushed a bit of hair off her forehead and was pissed off at her reflexive flinch from my touch.

"It was him, wasn't it?" I pressed. "Who else?"

"I don't know," she said quietly. "I never saw them before."

I shoved myself off the bed, found a pair of jeans, and hauled them up over my hips.

"Evan, what are you doing?"

I didn't answer. I grabbed a T-shirt out of the drawer and pulled it on over my head. My boots went on my feet without socks, and I didn't even bother with my watch or anything like that. This was going to be a short trip.

"Evan!" Bridgett called out.

I glanced back to see her sitting up in the bed, her bruised face making her nearly unrecognizable from the girl I was used to seeing there. Before she could say anything else, I walked out of the bedroom and out the door.

I could hear her calling my name and telling me to stop, but I ignored her.

The pimp was easy enough to find – right there on the street corner with his bitches all around him. He reached into a car window, pulled out some cash, and then shoved one of the girls in the backseat. There were at least three guys in the car, and they drove off with a screech of tires.

My fingers tightened around the steering wheel, and my teeth ground together. There wasn't any actual parking on the street, and I wasn't about to go find a garage, so I pulled right up over the curb and onto the sidewalk. I got out of the car, leaving it running, and headed right for him.

"Mister Arden!"

Ignoring his words, I walked up to him quickly, grabbed him by the collection of gold chains around his neck, and shoved him backwards into the alley. Two of the girls started screaming, and a blonde one grabbed my arm. I flung my fist backwards, and she hit the sidewalk with a grunt and her heels in the air.

Melvin the pimp clawed at my hand, drawing blood. It didn't even register in my head that I was bleeding – I was far too focused on getting him off the street where we could have a little private moment. The most convenient place was the alley right next to his usual hangout, so that was where I dragged him.

I stepped around a foul-smelling puddle next to a dumpster and shoved Melvin up against the brick wall on the other side. He gasped and grabbed at his throat.

"Mister Arden," he croaked.

"Do you think being polite is going to help you right now?" I asked calmly.

Moving forward, I pushed my forearm across his neck, pinning him to the bricks and partially cutting off his air supply.

Again he clawed at my skin, but I just leaned forward and stared him in the eye until he stopped struggling.

"You scratched my car," I said quietly as I stared into his widened eyes. "Maybe it was a rental car, but you still scratched it. Now when I drive it, it just won't quite be the same."

I used my free hand to punch him in the face.

"I-I-I..." he stammered. "I didn't touch your car!"

I shook my head slowly at the asshole's ignorance and then punched him in the gut twice. He struggled to breathe as I shoved him up against the wall again. His skull knocked against it, and his eyes rolled for a moment before he could focus again.

"Okay! Okay! You mean that bitch...that girl of mine you like – Bridgett."

"Aren't you clever?" I replied coldly.

"I thought you were done with her!" he exclaimed. "You hadn't been around...she's been acting up and not bringing in her worth, ya know?"

"I have no idea," I said, "but I know little boys who don't take care of their toys end up losing them."

"I'm sorry, man," he said. "I didn't know...I didn't know you still wanted her..."

I stopped listening to his blather. My hand reached behind to pull my piece from the back of my jeans, but it wasn't there.

I'd left so quickly, I hadn't even taken a gun.

Mario was pretty good at beating people to death when it needed to be done. There were several ways – collapsing the trachea could do it, and you could always punch someone in the head enough to cause brain damage. I could have strangled him as well, but that took a lot longer than it looked like in the movies.

If someone were to ask, I'd probably admit to being a lazy killer.

"You have a piece on you?" I asked.

He blathered nonsensically until I punched him in the face again, busting his nose and spraying my shirt with his blood.

"I said, do you have a gun on you?"

"Y-y-yes!" he cried. "It's on my right ankle!"

"Raise your leg up," I instructed.

He obeyed, and I kept a good grip across his neck and chest with one arm while reaching for his pistol with the other. I pulled it out and put it in his face.

"You don't take care of your things," I told him bluntly. "I don't think you deserve to have them."

"It was just business!" he cried out. "They paid good money!"

"Oh yeah?" I asked. "How much?"

"A grand for an hour!" he told me. "You pay that for the whole night! You can have her right now – all night! No cost!"

I hummed and tilted my head to one side, lowering the gun a bit.

"Yeah, all right," I agreed. "I think I will take her tonight, no cost to me. Tomorrow, too."

"Anything you want!" he promised with a quick nod of his head. Sweat poured from his temples and down his neck.

"I think she's gonna keep the money from that last trick, too."

His brow creased, and for a moment he looked like he was going to argue. He thought better of it, though, and agreed with me.

"Whatever you want, Mister Arden," he said. "She can have it."

I nodded.

"Whatever I want, huh?"

"Anything!" he confirmed.

I nodded again.

"Okay." I raised the gun, kicked back the safety, and blew his brains into the bricks.

Several feminine screams came from behind me, but they were lost in my own personal disgust at the blood and tissue that sprayed back at me. I hated close range shots like this – as if that actor dude hadn't been bad enough. At least I had the manhole cover as a shield then. I hadn't thought enough about this one to avoid the mess, and I hated the mess. I needed to kill someone from a distance again. All this up close and personal shit didn't settle well with me.

I tore off the bottom of his shirt as I let him fall to the ground and used a bit of it to wipe off my face. It was better than nothing, but only barely. I threw the torn cloth to the side, skipped back around the puddle, and headed out of the alley past the hysterical whores.

One of them grabbed at me like she was going to be able to do something to stop what had already happened. I looked her in the eye, and she stepped back away quickly. Running around to the other side of the car, I jumped into the driver's seat and sped off without another word.

Bridgett was still lying on her side in my bed when I returned. Our eyes met, and I knew she had been crying. I didn't understand that, though. I didn't understand why she would cry for that shithead of a pimp.

I glanced down at my blood-covered hands and shirt.

"I'm going to take a shower," I said quietly.

Her eyes watched me, but she said nothing. I took off my bloody clothing and dropped it on the bathroom floor before stepping into the shower. I hoped it would clear my head a little, but it didn't work. I was just as tense as I had been before, and my head was full of…of…what was this?

Confusion?

My stomach was uneasy, and not from the blood that washed down the drain. There was a bizarre feeling of near-guilt, but that wasn't quite right either. I didn't regret killing that asshole. I never regretted anything, so I didn't know what this feeling was.

I guess that made it confusion.

Since Bridgett still had my robe, I walked over to the dresser naked, pulled on a clean pair of boxers, and then climbed into bed beside her. She didn't move to look at me when I wrapped my arms around her and pulled her against my chest, but she didn't resist, either. I lay my head just above hers on the pillow, inhaled the scent of her hair, and pressed my lips to her temple.

"You killed him," Bridgett whispered, "didn't you?"

My fingers trailed up her arm, over her shoulder, and to her lips. I didn't press down because of the cut there, but still made the point.

"Shh," I replied.

She turned then, and her red-rimmed, black-and-blue eyes turned to mine.

"Why?"

"Why what?"

"Why did you kill him?"

I raised an eyebrow at her. I wasn't going to answer a question when I had already refused to admit there was anything she could ask about anyway.

"What am I going to do?" Bridgett's voice cracked as her hand moved to cover her mouth. "I can't be on the street with no protection!"

"Carry a gun," I suggested.

"I've never even fired one!" she exclaimed.

"Then find another pimp," I said. It occurred to me that I could teach her to shoot, but making this about more than the sex had already caused an issue once. I didn't want to do that again. "That isn't the only street corner in the city, you know. You probably don't even have to go anywhere – some other dude will come up and take over the girls there."

"What about the other girls?"

"I don't really give a shit about the other girls," I said.

She glared at me.

"What if the new guy is one of the ones from across town?" she asked quietly. "The ones over by the warehouses."

I narrowed my eyes.

"You don't work for the fucking competition," I snarled.

"What competition?" she asked with feigned innocence. "You don't seem to actually have a job."

A couple hundred potential rebuttals went through my brain, but I knew when I was being baited. I also knew when a situation was likely to escalate quickly, and silence was the best way to combat it. We watched each other for a full two minutes before she sighed and put her head down on my shoulder.

"What am I going to do?" she asked again. "Even that apartment is in Melvin's name."

"I got some money for you," I said. I hadn't actually taken any cash from Melvin, but she didn't have to know that. I had twenty or thirty grand lying around in the back of my closet. "You already earned it."

"I'm not taking your money," she said.

I took her chin in my hand.

"First off, you will take the fucking money because it's yours, not mine. It's the money from those fucking bastards who hurt you. Secondly, if I decide to give you fucking money, you're going to fucking take it."

"Fucking am I?"

I tried to scowl, but she grinned at me.

"You can earn that money, too," I said. "As soon as you're up for it. You don't even have to have any other clients."

She gave me a strange look, like she wondered what the hell I was suggesting. I wondered myself until I heard it come out of my mouth.

"Just stay here," I said.

So much for keeping it only about the sex.

Immediately, the atmosphere between us changed, electrified, and heated the air. Bridgett's tongue darted over her cut lip as she processed what I had said.

"You want me to…what?" she asked. "Stay here and be your personal whore?"

I paused, thought about it, and decided that yes – that was exactly what I was suggesting. It made sense, in a way. She was here often enough before, and she wouldn't have to worry about bills and food – just fucking me. That way, it was still just about the sex.

More than anything, I'd sleep better if she was here every night, and I couldn't help but see that as a positive thing.

I looked in her eyes.

"Stay here," I said again. "No bills, no pimp, no worries."

"You're asking me to move in with you."

I hadn't quite thought of it like that.

"I'm saying, instead of me picking you up on some other street corner, you just stay here, and I can fuck you whenever."

"You can't be serious."

I watched her look at me and saw the last thing I wanted to see – the desperate need for it to be true. She wanted it. She wanted to stay here – to live with me – not because it was convenient, but just because she wanted to.

"It doesn't *change* anything," I told her. "This is still what it is."

"You don't even try for anything else," she said quietly.

She was right, of course. I didn't.

I wouldn't, and I won't – ever.

My fingers moved a strand of her hair away from the bruise around her eye.

"I don't have anything else to give you, Bridgett," I told her. "This is all there is."

There was just no way to make it something it wasn't.

CHAPTER ELEVEN
Painful Betrayal

"You better git yer ass over there," Jonathan informed me. "I didn't get the deets, but Mario was on edge and Rinaldo wasn't sayin' a damn thing. I read through his email but didn't see nothin' there."

"You hacked the boss's email?" I rolled my eyes at the phone as I slid into the back seat of the bus. "Are you crazy?"

"What? It ain't hard – the password's always 'Luisa' with a number after her name. He just increments it every month."

"Why does he do that?"

"I told him it was safer to change it every month instead of leavin' it the same."

Another eye roll before I hung up the phone. I could have sworn he did that kind of shit just to prove he could get away with it. I remembered that I hadn't given him the Save Ferris T-shirt yet and made a mental note to toss it in my car when I got home.

It was the first really hot day of spring, and the jacket I wore to conceal my Beretta was too warm for the afternoon sun. I rolled the sleeves up, but I was still sweaty and uncomfortable. I wished I had driven myself for once, but I jumped off the bus and walked the three blocks to Moretti's office.

Mario was there and Terry was just leaving. Rinaldo was standing behind his desk, waiting for me. He motioned for me to come in the office, and Mario stood just to one side of Rinaldo's desk chair. He gave me a nod, which I returned as I stood at-ease in front of them both.

Moretti didn't waste any time.

"You want to tell me why you decided to take out a pimp on my payroll?" Rinaldo asked simply.

"No, sir," I replied. I wasn't surprised by the question – I kind of assumed it was why Jonathan had told me to high-tail it over here. The only real surprise was that it had taken a week for him to call me out on it. I'd made two other kills for him during that time and had been glad to get back to sniping.

"You know his whole stable is all over the place now – a bunch of trained birds scattered to the winds and looking for a cage to nest in. It's not my favorite line of business, but now some of his property – property I had a vested interest in – is lost."

I looked up at him carefully but couldn't see any actual anger in his face or posture. He wasn't thrilled, but he wasn't all that pissed off, either. I hadn't expected him to be, but I had still prepared myself for the conversation.

"My apologies," I replied. "You want me to pay for it?"

Rinaldo laughed, and the tension in the atmosphere died down.

"No," he said, "I had another task in mind. Something more along the lines you're most comfortable with achieving. I've received some troubling information that a woman has been giving information about my business to Greco's men. No one seems sure exactly who she is, and I'll need you to find that out and take care it doesn't happen again."

"Yes, sir," I replied.

Rinaldo handed me the picture, and I tried not to show any reaction in my face as my mind starting jumping around and doing flips in the air.

"You sure this is the target?" I asked. I tapped the edge of the picture with my forefinger. "This girl?"

"You think my sources are unreliable?"

"No, sir," I replied. "I'm just…not sure what they'd want with her."

Rinaldo stared at me through narrowed eyes.

"Evan, do you have something to tell me? You know this bitch?"

I was going to have to play this very carefully.

I kept my expression completely lifeless, shrugged one shoulder one time, and then looked to Rinaldo's face as I tossed Bridgett's picture back onto the desk.

"I've been fucking her," I said simply. "So finding her isn't an issue."

Rinaldo's eyes narrowed and his eyebrows tried to meet each other in the middle of his head.

"Explain," he said quietly.

"She's a hooker."

"A hooker?" he repeated.

"Yes, sir."

His face darkened, and his jaw tightened. He took a step over to his desk chair and sat down heavily.

"She belonged to that pimp you killed, hmm?"

"Yes, sir."

Rinaldo leaned forward over the desk and pulled at his cuffs to straighten them.

"You better tell me everything," he said quietly.

I didn't like the tone of his voice, not in the slightest. It sounded way too much like the tone he used right before he exiled me to Arizona, and I did not want that happening again. The very thought of him being pissed off – *disappointed* in me – made my skin crawl.

"There isn't much to tell you, sir," I informed him. "I'm one of her regular clients. I pick her up on the street; she comes to my apartment. I fuck her, and she leaves. That's it."

"Until something happens and you kill her pimp."

"He crossed a line," I replied steadily.

"Beat her up, huh?"

I nodded my head once.

"Is this the same girl I hear you took out on the town?"

Fuck.

"Yes, sir," I admitted.

"Sounds like she's more than just a hooker you fuck."

"No, sir," I replied. "That is all she is."

He eyed me meaningfully for a moment, and I couldn't help but see it for what it was – fatherly concern for me. I liked that he did that, even if it was annoying at the same time. I had the feeling it was the way fathers were supposed to behave, and it made me feel strangely warm inside. I'd seen him do the same thing with his daughter on occasion.

And with Nick, for that matter.

"We'll see," he finally said. "Regardless, there's been talk that this girl is feeding information to one of Greco's boys about heroin shipments coming in from up north and about the Russian connection who came up dead the other day. Information you are privy to hearing."

My eyes met his, and I knew immediately what he was thinking.

"No," I said definitively. "No, sir. I do not discuss business while I'm fucking whores. Absolutely not."

Our eyes remained locked together as he seemed to be deciding something – most likely my fate. His chest rose as he took in a sharp breath and then huffed it out through his nose.

"All right, Arden," he said.

I hated that he was back to calling me by my last name. I glanced towards the door to make sure my face didn't show how I felt about it.

"You find out what's going on here," Rinaldo said, and he tapped his finger against the surface of his desk. "If what I've been told is correct…"

His voice trailed off, and I leveled my gaze at him.

"I will take care of it," I said.

I tried to keep my voice completely steady – completely normal. I didn't though. The very last syllable dropped as my throat went dry. It was enough for him to notice.

"Getting close to a girl," Rinaldo said, "can be a good thing. If you were someone else – someone less *complicated* – the worst that can happen is you don't work out. You're a complicated man, Arden, and you are in a complicated position. Bitches make it even more complicated."

"I'm aware, sir."

"*You're aware*," he mocked. "Will that change anything when someone finds out you give a shit? What better to hold over your head than a warm cunt, huh? You take better care not to show your affection for her. You've done a shit job on that front with that pup of yours."

His dark eyes darkened further as we stared at each other.

"You know Greco will use what he can to get at me," Rinaldo reminded me. "You are a good way to get at me. One of the reasons that makes you ideally suited for your job is because you have no attachments that could be used against you to get to me. You were always careful not to show your affection for the dog in public. You aren't as careful anymore."

"I'll remember that," I said to him, "but that still won't happen."

At least my voice stayed steady this time because if I thought about it deep inside, I wouldn't give Odin up. Not a fucking chance. I'd blow them all away first.

"You like this girl," he said.

"She's a whore," I replied.

"And my wife used to dance on a pole in one of my clubs," he retorted. "Married twenty-five years now with Luisa in our lives. You think that doesn't concern me sometimes?"

"I know it does, sir."

He paused significantly, and I didn't move.

"Divided thoughts," Rinaldo said softly. "That will never do for you."

I continued to look him squarely in the eye.

"I only have one loyalty," I informed him and then nodded my head towards him.

He returned the nod but gave me a long, increasingly sad look.

"No good can come of what you're doing, son," he said. "One of you will get hurt."

I looked up at my boss and shrugged one shoulder again. The word "son" flowed over my skin and warmed me as I answered him.

"It won't be me."

Finding Bridgett was supposed to be fairly straightforward because she was still supposed to be in my apartment where she was when I left. Like a typical woman, she wasn't going to be that easy, even if she was a whore.

Aside from Odin, the apartment was empty when I got back – no note or anything. She had been there for several days, and though she had gone out before, she usually told me first. I tried her cell, but she didn't pick up. I took a deep breath, jumped in the Mazda, and cruised around looking for her but to no avail.

When I returned, she was still gone.

She wasn't back the next day, either. I tried to tell myself that it didn't matter because there was a lot more I needed to figure out before I talked to her again. If there was even the slightest possibility that someone was framing her, I had to know who it was and quickly.

Who even knew about her?

I spent the next several days wandering around town, trying to catalog all the possibilities in my head. As sleep deprivation mounted, my thinking was a little less clear. The main problem was a lot of people knew about her. Just like Moretti had said, I wasn't being as careful as I usually was.

I blamed it on the lack of decent shuteye.

I had taken her to all the best spots around the Magnificent Mile on a freaking date, and anyone could have seen us together. Those at the 676 Restaurant and Bar certainly knew about her, as well as the people at the restaurant where we had dinner, and the saleslady at Tiffany's. Rinaldo knew I had been seeing someone prior to showing me the picture; he just didn't have a name to put with the face.

"Seeing someone?"

I shook my head to clear it.

Jonathan had picked her up and brought her to my apartment when I was sick. Just like it had been when Greco moved on Rinaldo, I had to consider him. Terry was always a suspect for anything, as far as I was concerned, because he was a douche.

For the next several days, I continued to drive around trying to find her. She didn't appear to have returned to her apartment. None of the other streetwalkers were admitting to seeing her, and she didn't come back to my place. She seemed to have disappeared completely.

I had to consider that it was all true, and the very thought sent me to the shooting range. The idea was so distasteful, I pushed it out of my tired mind, missed the bull's-eye twice, and left in a pissier mood than when I had arrived.

I just couldn't keep myself occupied anymore.

With no better direction, I continued to consider who knew of my relationship – however that was to be defined – with Bridgett.

Pete, the security guy in the apartment lobby – he saw her come up here to the apartment all the time. He'd been having trouble a few months ago with his wife, but I never followed up on the details. Maybe he knew something. Maybe he did something.

Why did I continue to assume she was being framed?

Because that made the most sense. If someone had seen me with her, then they might think they could use her to get to me. What easier way would they have than to plant the idea in someone's head that she's divulging information to Greco?

I also couldn't fathom the alternative.

Bridgett wouldn't betray me; I was sure of that. She wanted to live with me and set up house, for Christ's sakes. She wouldn't tell other people about my business. I never told her about shit I was doing, so there wasn't even anything for her to tell.

I wiped my forehead with the back of my hand. I was getting a headache from the lack of sleep. I hadn't had two hours of sleep in a row for a week, maybe more. I was starting to lose track of time a little.

I pulled out the phone logs Eddie Boy had dropped by – all paper copies instead of electronic. I couldn't take a risk of the information being intercepted electronically. I was combing through Jonathan's a bit more, and anytime I used my computer, he seemed to know about it. I didn't find anything interesting or unusual at all, except that he'd been calling his dad a lot.

Focusing was becoming more difficult, and I knew it was making it harder for me to figure out what the hell was going on with Bridgett and Greco, assuming there was a connection at all. That knowledge didn't offer me any answers, though, nor did it help me sleep.

Sleep.

"You talk in your sleep."

"What the fuck? I do not."

"Not often, but you have – a couple of times."

"What if I said something when I was sleeping?"

No.

No way.

"If I talked about Iraq, I could have said anything."

Odin snuffed at my shoe, and I realized I had been talking out loud. I reached down to rub the top of his head while my brain started forming a less-than-pleasant picture.

My eyes moved across the rooms in the apartment until they came to rest on my laptop, which I hadn't even had time to use for surfing since all of this started. I walked over to it carefully, like I was afraid of what might happen when I opened it. As the screen refreshed, the user ID and password screen popped up with the user ID already saved.

I entered my password incorrectly.

Incorrect password! You have reached the maximum attempts, and your account is now locked. Please contact your system administrator for assistance.

There were supposed to be *three* attempts. Always three attempts with three warnings before the system would lock you out on the fourth try. Someone had already tried, received the message, and then stopped. Unless Odin had some opposable thumbs hidden in his shaggy fur, there was only one other person who had been in my apartment.

"Motherfucker."

A few phone calls and a bus ride later, I was in front of Moretti.

"You found something."

"Not exactly," I admitted, "but there is a…a possibility."

He looked at me and waited for me to go on. I didn't miss Mario slightly shift in his footing, placing his weight at an easier distribution if he needed to draw his gun. I didn't think it was going to be necessary, but it depended on how Moretti took my news.

Full disclosure.

"It was more than fucking with that whore," I told him bluntly. His expression didn't show any surprise, but I also knew it wasn't what he was thinking. "She also…well, sir, she slept with me."

Mario snickered, and I glared at him. He raised both eyebrows back at me.

"Isn't that the same thing?" he asked.

"I mean, she'd stay at my apartment overnight," I clarified. "She slept in my bed with me, lots of times."

Moretti leaned back and folded his arms over his chest.

"What did you tell her?" Rinaldo asked coldly.

"Nothing," I swore. "Nothing *intentionally*."

Mario shifted again.

"I just remembered something she said a while ago – something she said about me."

"And what might that be?"

I took a deep breath.

"She said I talked in my sleep."

Mario laughed out loud, and I considered just shooting the bastard, but that wasn't going to help me out here.

"I haven't confirmed anything," I told him, "but I admit there's a…a possibility she heard something. I just need to know who told you she was squealing because that could help me figure all of this out."

Rinaldo nodded his head.

"You aren't going to like it," he said.

It was all I needed to hear.

"Terry Kramer."

Rinaldo's lips tuned up in a sardonic smile.

"You believed him," I said, trying not to sound accusatory.

"He had good information," Rinaldo corrected. "He knew things he shouldn't know about."

"I've caught him following me."

"Then you do have some detective work ahead of you," my boss agreed. "I want whoever passed sensitive information from my organization to Greco's dead. As long as that is your end goal, whose head you bring me isn't of consequence."

"I'll take care of it," I promised.

Moretti leaned forward on the desk and gazed at me. I tried to be patient, but all I really wanted to do was figure out what the hell was going on and kill whoever was trying to turn the small amount of comfort I had found upside down.

"You know what you need, Evan?" Rinaldo questioned.

I shook my head.

"A good woman, that's what. A woman who is actually capable of getting through that thick head of yours."

I half smiled and blew a sharp breath out of my nose. I blinked away thoughts of the flowing dark hair of the woman in the cabin.

"You got any suggestions, boss?"

He looked me in the face, and his expression changed as his smile faltered. His face became a mask of worry as he motioned for me to sit in the chair opposite his desk and told Mario to wait outside.

I sat down somewhat hesitantly. As soon as I sat, the heavy feeling of near unconsciousness shoved inside my brain and made me feel like I was going to fall over. I was pretty sure if I closed my eyes even for a second, I'd fall over onto the floor. The problem was I'd be awake ten minutes later – sweating and maybe even screaming.

I had to get some sleep.

"I'll tell you something, Evan," Rinaldo said as he leaned back in his chair and folded his hands together. "There is something I was considering."

"Considering, sir?"

"My daughter, Luisa."

My muscles wanted to stiffen significantly, but I forced myself to remain still and calm. Something wasn't right – he wasn't smiling or anything like he might have been if he was going to suggest I date her, but he didn't seem angry at all like he might have thought I touched her without permission. I couldn't read him – not at all.

I definitely needed some sleep. I was totally off my game.

"Your daughter, sir?"

"You know her."

It was a statement, not a question, but I nodded anyway.

"You are only three years apart in age," he remarked. "She is a beautiful girl."

Again, I nodded as I watched him closely, but he wasn't giving me any signs to indicate where this conversation was going. My hands went clammy, and I could feel my heart pounding in my wrists.

"I considered you for her," he finally said. He leaned forward and rested his elbows on the desk as his hands folded beneath his chin. "I considered you for a long time."

Considered – past tense. Considered only – not offering. I had done something wrong, but I had no idea what he was getting at. Was it because of my fuckup last year? I thought all had been forgiven at this point. Did finding Ashton's body somehow cause concerns? Every indication in the news said the authorities were stumped.

Because I killed the fucking pimp?

It wasn't that I wanted Luisa. She was beautiful and obviously from a very powerful family, and that came with a whole lot of perks I found interesting, no doubt. However, I didn't want her any more than I wanted any other woman in my life.

Well, except maybe one.

I couldn't think of anything to say, so I just kept the eye contact and waited. I had to be pretty damn patient, too.

"In many ways, you are the perfect choice," he said quietly when he finally decided I had sweated it out enough. "I have no son – so this is all hers."

Rinaldo waved his hand around the room, but of course he didn't mean the office or the building – he meant all of the businesses. I raised a brow but wasn't stupid enough to ask about Nick at that point. Biology aside, he wasn't going to let the illegitimate child that far inside. He was lenient enough with the guy as it was.

"Luisa is a strong woman like her mother, and she could take care of it, but having a man such as yourself looking after her would be a substantial bonus. It would keep those who might believe her to be an easier target at bay. There are also some who might feel a woman is not to be taken seriously, and I would trust you to take care of anyone who insulted her."

"Thank you, sir."

He went quiet for a moment.

"I trust you with my life, Evan," he said. "My life – the life of my daughter, the running of any of my businesses – I would trust you to be loyal to this family as much as I would anyone who shared our blood. Yes, in many ways you would be the perfect choice for her."

His lips tightened, and his eyes narrowed. I felt my muscles tense a bit because I knew the answer was coming. His focus on me was acute and palpable.

"You would never love her, though," he said, "would you?"

I blinked a couple of times.

"What, sir?"

"You would never love my daughter," he said again. "Even this hooker you killed for, you don't have any real feelings for her at all, do you?"

"I…I don't understand."

"If you had gone back to your apartment, found a letter from her saying she was moving out of the city, and you never saw her again, would you care?"

I didn't even know how to answer.

"I didn't think so," Rinaldo said. "That's why you will never touch my daughter. I hope you'll always be there to protect her if I am unable to do so myself."

"Of course," I responded immediately.

"That you understand," he commented. "Killing to keep her safe – you know just what to do with those instructions. But matters of the heart? You're lacking there, son."

My chest tightened up, and I didn't know what I was supposed to say. Cold sweat had formed on the back of my neck and trickled between my shoulder blades. The rest of my body tensed completely before I could stop it. I tasted sand in the back of my throat, but when I tried to swallow past the sensation, I couldn't.

"You don't even really understand what I mean, do you?" he asked. "You don't let anyone in that head long enough for you to understand them or to let them understand you."

"I have a shrink," I heard myself say.

"I know," Rinaldo replied. "I know everything, Evan. You don't think I'd let your past not be of my utmost concern?"

"I…I never thought about it." I hadn't, either, and now the sleepy feeling waned as it was replaced by feelings of stupidity.

"You endured more than most men ever will," Rinaldo said quietly. "You've had it worse than anyone you ever killed. They died quick and easy. You've been dying since they brought you home from that war."

I forced myself to swallow hard and found I was having a hard time looking at his face.

"You are going to crack someday, aren't you, Lieutenant?"

My eyes flashed to Rinaldo's, and I couldn't stop my hands from clenching into fists. The anger boiling inside of me had nowhere to go, and I was dangerously close to letting it loose on the one man whom I didn't want to hurt.

Had Mario been in the room, he would have noticed. He would have seen how close I was, and he probably would have shot me. Rinaldo only nodded slowly and sat back again.

"If there comes a time I need to put you down, I will," he said. "If there comes a time you *want* me to put you down, you let me know. You can go now, son."

I stood up, trying not to let my knees wobble as I did. I turned and walked as quickly as I could out of the room, trying not to comprehend what Rinaldo Moretti had just said to me.

I couldn't think.

I could barely breathe.

Even though spring was in full force, the temperature had fallen and the wind was bone-chilling. I dropped down on the bench inside the dog run and unhooked Odin's leash from his collar, so he could run around and sniff at the other neighborhood dogs. I needed to think – my head was just too jumbled up with all the recent information inside of it, but every time I tried to figure out what was happening to me, my head ached and reminded me how long it had been since I'd slept.

Well, kind of reminded me. I'd really lost track of how long it had been. I couldn't focus anymore – that's what I knew. I jumped at fucking everything, too, just like I had in the hospital after I had been brought back from the Middle East. It had been years since I felt that kind of paranoia, and I wasn't even sure how to begin to cope with it.

Where did things start going wrong?

Without warning, Lia's face came back into my head, and for once I just let it happen.

I closed my eyes and leaned back against the bench as the whole time she was with me raced through my brain. I remembered seeing her out there on the dry, dusty road walking aimlessly towards my cabin, and I remembered thinking I might just have to shoot her.

I didn't do it – I made her dinner instead. Once night fell, she crawled into the little twin bed and I ended up inside of her minutes later – *really* inside of her. I didn't push for a blowjob or anal – we just had straight sex. No condom, no barriers, no pretenses. I came in her over and over again, and I couldn't get enough.

Even though I had told her I'd be there when she got back, I knew it wasn't something I could ever have. I didn't get the kind of promises she could offer. I didn't deserve them. According to Rinaldo, I didn't even understand that sort of shit.

I did, though. I knew exactly what I was missing.

Why did I keep thinking about her? I didn't want to think about her. I'd been spending all my time since I left the cabin in Arizona doing things to stop myself from thinking about her, and it still wasn't working. Whether I was sweating at the gym, researching the next target, or firing at the shooting range, she was always in my head.

Silk-soft hair running down her back, easy smile that made my heart beat faster for no reason at all, and that shy, quick blush that had my cock ready to go again at a moment's notice.

From right behind me, the obnoxious sound of the parking garage door warning system went off and brought me out of the memory. I scowled over my shoulder at the car that moved out of the garage and around the loop North Field Boulevard made as it circled the park. The garage door went back down again.

What was I going to do about Bridgett? Did she really hear things I said in my sleep and tell Greco's men about them? Who did she even know in his organization? I couldn't quite fathom how she could have hidden such things from me, but then again, I was usually completely exhausted by the time I went to pick her up.

I remembered how quickly she talked about going to work over by the warehouses and considered maybe she had been working for them the whole time. Maybe her connection had always been there. Maybe *she* contacted Terry.

I wasn't sure. They had both completely disappeared.

That didn't make sense, though. What would she have been doing on Melvin's corner, then? Not waiting for me – I had never even picked up a girl at that location before. I had always gone further south and used one of the hotels you could pay for by the hour.

She was chosen because I was in a hurry, wanted to fuck her at my apartment, and because she had the roundest ass of the group. There was no way that was a plant. Someone had to have gotten to her after they realized I was fucking her regularly.

I was back to the list of those who knew about her and frustrated that I had been so stupid as to take her out in public where we could have been seen by anyone. It made the list insane.

Top possibilities, then.

Melvin.

Jonathan.

Terry.

Mario.

One of the other hookers – Candy, maybe. What did I know about her?

Michele with one "L" at the bar.

There were too many and very little else to go on. Maybe I needed to figure out just which one of Greco's boys was getting the information and see if that led me in the right direction. Something had to show itself, but it wasn't going to happen out here in the park. The parking garage door was going to drive me over the edge before I came to any reasonable conclusions. I grabbed Odin and headed back upstairs, knowing there was one name that came up more than anyone else's.

Only name that really made any sense.

Terry Kramer. His phone logs were far more interesting than Jonathan's with several to a prepaid phone that seemed to find itself in the vicinity of my apartment pretty frequently, especially at night when a certain hooker should have been asleep in my bed. I dug back to earlier in the year and found two calls to Bridgett's number from the last surviving payphone in Chicago, as far as I knew, which happened to be near Terry's place.

There was no doubt that Terry would look for an excuse to get me run out of Moretti's organization – I was his superior in skill and position, and he knew it. As long as I was around and the favorite, he couldn't move up from where he was – nothing more than a two-bit thug.

Was Terry stupid enough to be working for the competition or just trying to get me out of the way?

My hands were jittery, and I was starting to feel really nauseated. I lay myself down to try to get some sleep, but it didn't come easily. When it finally arrived, it brought forth some of the worst of the nightmares, and I woke sweating with a scream in my throat.

I took the dog out for a midnight walk to clear my head. It wasn't particularly successful, but it was probably better than nothing. My cell phone began to ring just as Odin and I returned to the apartment.

I didn't recognize the number, but I answered it.

"Evan?"

I froze just inside the doorway, paused for a moment and then reached down to unhook Odin's leash. I wanted to yell and scream, but I knew I had to at least appear calm.

"Bridgett. You've been a little out of touch." My voice was cold.

"I need to see you," she said quietly. "I need to talk to you."

"Where are you?"

"Would you meet me somewhere?"

She didn't want to come here or have me pick her up. She wanted to meet somewhere – somewhere else, somewhere not alone.

Could she be any more suspicious?

"Where?"

"What about that place you took me on Michigan Avenue? The bar with the martinis and the waffles?"

"676," I said. "I'll be there in ten minutes."

I knew what she was doing – trying to get me to meet her in a public place because she had something to say she knew I wasn't going to like hearing and she was afraid of my reaction. The fact that she had stooped to such a level didn't give me any kind of calming feeling. I was as tense as I could be.

"What did she fucking do?"

I took the Audi, drove up to the valet in front of the Omni, gave the guy a fifty to just hold my car there for a minute, and headed into the lobby. When I turned the corner to head upstairs, I saw Bridgett right by the elevator, waiting for it to arrive and carry her upstairs.

Not going to happen.

I walked over swiftly, took her by the elbow, and began to lead her back to the front of the building. As I had hoped, she was taken off guard enough that she didn't have time to scream or consider what was happening until I had her outside the building.

"Evan–" she started, but I shushed her.

"Not a fucking word," I growled. "Don't you say anything; don't you do anything. Just get in the fucking car."

I escorted her around to where the valet was holding open the door, seated her with a smile, and then quickly climbed into my side. I drove off before anyone had a chance to even consider what had just happened.

"Evan," Bridgett whispered from the other side of the car.

I glanced sideways at her, my jaw tight.

"Tell me," I snapped. "Tell me everything. Tell me how you know Greco, and tell me what your relationship with him is. Tell me what the fuck you think you are doing!"

The precious little grasp I had over my emotions was waning, and there didn't seem to be anything I could do to stop it.

"I don't know what you're talking about!" she cried.

As I looked ahead into traffic, I could still see her press herself against the car door like she might jump out and make a run for it. It wouldn't work, though. I wouldn't let that happen.

"I came back; you were gone." I turned around the block and started heading down Grand, over the bridge, and towards the boss's office. "You want to start by explaining that?"

"I-I-I went outside," she said. "I just wanted to get some air, but he was there. He said I had to go with him, and we went to an office building – he had a room there in the basement."

"What office?"

"Just a small one," she said quietly. "It was brick and didn't have any windows at all."

Could he really have been hiding out in the basement of the boss's main office building? Had he been there, right under my feet the whole time I was looking for him? Was it even who I suspected?

"Who?" I demanded. "What's his name?"

She didn't answer.

"Who did you go with?" I snarled through clenched teeth. I already knew the answer. The little fucker had been trolling around my apartment, and he had sucked Bridgett into whatever his sick little game was to take my position in Moretti's organization.

"Take my position in his *life*."

"What?" Bridgett whispered.

"Tell me his name!"

"His name is Terry! I didn't know him. He just found me!"

"And you told him what?"

"I didn't want to tell him anything," she said. "I stopped talking to him a long time ago."

The cold feeling I always associate with what it must feel like to drown coated me from my head to my feet. My knuckles went white as my hands gripped the steering wheel, and I made a quick turn towards the boss's office building.

"A long time ago?" I repeated.

"Yes," she whispered back. "He used to…to ask me about you all the time."

"What did you tell him?" I asked in a low voice.

"Nothing," she replied.

I didn't believe a word of it.

We were nearing Moretti's primary office building, and the parking lot behind it was devoid of any cars this late at night. I pulled up to the side of the building near the door and then thought better of it.

"What are you doing?"

Ignoring Bridgett's question, I maneuvered the car back behind the row of dumpsters on the far side of the lot instead. I got the car mostly out of sight before turning it off.

"You have to *explain*," I informed her. "It doesn't make any fucking sense, and you have to *explain* it!"

"Please, Evan, you're scaring me!"

I looked over to my passenger and smiled.

"Maybe you ought to be scared," I suggested. "Get out."

"How did you know this was the place?" she asked.

"Just get out of the car."

Moving swiftly around the Audi, I made it to the other side before she was completely out the door. I took her elbow again and led her across the lot and down the back stairs to the basement. There weren't many rooms down there, and Bridgett showed me which one she had been staying in.

I'd been in it before once or twice, though it didn't serve any specific purpose. There was a time I recalled some goods being stored there very briefly before they were moved over to the docks by the river for shipment, but that was it.

Now there was a twin sized bed in the room, a small table, and a suitcase with women's clothes in it. The whole scene reminded me of Arizona, which made my already pissed-off self angrier.

There was no one there.

"Damnit." I turned back to Bridgett.

"How do you know him?" I interrogated.

"Who?"

My hand reached back into my jeans and wrapped around the handle of my Beretta. I pulled my arm back around and pushed it against her shoulder as her face twisted into terror.

"Do *not*," I said, "play any fucking games with me. Tell me how you know Terry Kramer before I put a hole in your head."

"I didn't know what he wanted!" she said. "He kept following me and telling me he needed to talk to me. He said I couldn't tell you about it, or we'd both end up dead. He said if I just told him what you told me, then…then…"

"Then *what*?" I snarled. "Did he pay you?"

"No!"

"Did you fuck him?" The very idea that Terry, the motherfucking piss-ant wannabe, had his cock in her made me livid.

She didn't answer, which was answer enough. I leaned forward and slammed my hand against the wall right next to her head.

"Tell me why you did it!" I screamed. "What did you tell him, and why did you do it?"

"He said…he said he'd kill you if I didn't cooperate!" she finally cried.

"You…you thought he was a threat to me?" What had been a cold snarl escalated into a scream. "That little fuck was somehow a danger to me? *Me*?"

"He…he….he said–" Her words were too choked to be understandable. "I-I-I thought–"

"I don't give a fuck what he said!" I screamed back in her face. "There is nothing – nothing – he could have said that would ever, ever make you…make you…"

I couldn't even say the words.

Like some kind of primordial ooze making its way out of the ocean, Terry chose that moment to walk into the dimly lit room. There was no consideration to my actions. No thought behind them – just movement and quick, practiced muscle memory.

My arm rose.

My gun aimed at his face.

I pulled the trigger.

Bridgett stifled her scream as Terry's face exploded in blood and his body hit the floor.

"You see how big a fucking threat he is?" I growled as I turned back to her.

My head was spinning. The pit of my stomach felt heavy, and the back of my throat tasted sour. I felt like I was trapped in some never-ending fog, and I couldn't see in which direction I should go. There was no end or beginning in sight and no answers in any direction.

"You never really said anything to me." Bridgett's voice was barely audible. "I didn't think…I didn't think what I said to him was a big deal, and he always seemed happy enough with what I had to leave you alone…leave *us* alone."

The drowning feeling came over me again, and my eyes burned as I pointed the business end of the Beretta towards Bridgett.

"You fucking betrayed me," I said.

"No, no!" she cried as she shook her head violently. "Evan – no! I didn't; I swear! I never meant it like that!"

"But that's what it was," I said. "You were right there in my bed listening to shit I said when I was asleep. Then you took what you thought he'd find interesting, and you told him about it."

"I didn't think any of it was important," she whispered through her tears. "I thought if he kept hearing all this stuff that didn't matter, he'd leave me alone – leave *us* alone!"

"Us?" I laughed, but there was nothing friendly or amusing about the sound. I tilted my arm up and tapped the side of my head with the barrel of the weapon. "You were delusional from the beginning, weren't you? Was this your way of getting closer, huh? Be a part of the business, but on the wrong side?"

"No…Evan, I swear!"

"Yeah, your promises aren't holding any weight at the moment." My head throbbed along with my heart, and nausea crept up from my stomach to the back of my throat. "What kind of stuff did I say?"

"Nothing important," she said quietly, her eyes refusing to meet with mine.

"*Sure*." I flavored the word with enough sarcasm to drown a horse. "That's why he kept coming back for more. That's why you're shacked up with him now."

I could tell by the way her eyes widened that she knew exactly what I meant. I nodded, knowing that my deductive skills were still in full effect – just like they always were. My chest tightened, and the nasty taste in the back of my mouth worsened. My temples throbbed, and for a moment I couldn't see anything around me.

"Evan, please…" Her voice trailed off.

My feet stumbled slightly; I regained my balance, and faced her fully.

"Please *what*?" I yelled. My arm rose up, and the Beretta in my hand found its barrel pointed in her direction again. "What exactly do you want? More information?"

"No! I don't want anything, please – just let me go!"

"Let me go! Please, just let me go!"

"Not until you tell us what we want to know!"

"There weren't any more units! Ours was the only one!"

"We found two others near you, so I know you lie."

A blow to my head rattles in my skull.

"I wasn't privy to…to any…information…"

"You're an officer!"

I grunt as a sack full of hard, lumpy objects makes contact with my stomach again. It moves around to my kidneys with another blow, and then the lower half of my chest, knocking the wind from me and causing me to vomit onto the sand…

"Let you go," I said, my voice dropping to a near whisper. "Yeah, that's what I'm going to do."

The noise in the small room was deafening.

I dropped to my knees, and the cold cement floor sent a shockwave through my body as she slumped to the floor against the wall. I looked to her face and the neat hole in the center of her forehead, willing the impossible.

"Fuck…no…"

My mouth and throat felt as though they were filled with sand, and I coughed to try to rid myself of it. I could feel it – taste it – but when I touched my fingers to my tongue, there was nothing there. I couldn't swallow, and for a moment I couldn't breathe, either.

"What the fuck did you do?"

I coughed again, and the coughing turned into choking. Choking sobs that were completely uncontrollable filled the air as my Beretta dropped to the floor with a clang. I scrambled for it quickly, cradling it against my body.

"Why did you do it?" I screamed at the slumped figure in front of me. "Why did you listen to him? *Why*?"

There was no answer.

There would never be an answer.

Like so many other questions, I'd never know the real answer.

My fingers reached out and touched hers, as if somehow that would make any difference. It didn't, and though they were still warm, I knew they would be cold soon enough.

"I told you it was going to end this way," I whispered. "Why didn't you listen to me?"

Too many whys.

I dropped back on my ass, wrapped my arms around my knees, and began to rock back and forth. I didn't understand what was happening inside me, and I didn't like it. My thoughts couldn't seem to stay in one place, and instead, they bounced around from one memory to another.

The first time I saw her on the street corner.

The feel of her fingers across my chest in the shower.

The scent of her skin.

Holding her against me as we slept.

Would I ever sleep again?

There was just no way I was going to survive this.

CHAPTER TWELVE
Lost Sanity

My feet felt oddly disconnected as I plodded up the stairs of the CTA 146 bus heading north. It was pretty much completely full, and I had to stand there holding the bar for a couple of stops before there was a seat available. At the next stop, a bunch more people got on again, and I could barely see anything except asses. A little girl nearly fell in front of me as she tripped over people's feet, and her father leaned down to pick her up and hold her to his chest. After a couple more stops, they also found seats right at the back.

She was an African-American girl of about four years old, and her head was covered with a hat that looked like it had been cut from one of those fuzzy bathroom rugs in bright pink. There were two long pieces of fuzzy fabric that I figured were supposed to form a scarf, but instead of wrapping around her neck, they just hung down on her shoulders. At the end of them were felt pieces made to look like an animal's face. It was obviously warm and looked both ridiculous and adorably cute all at the same time.

What the fuck did I do?

More people crowded on, and the driver yelled at everyone to step toward the back of the bus to make more room. A couple in Muslim garb slipped past some of the other people standing in the middle of the aisle and moved near the back door to my right. She wore a black dress, and her head was covered in bright blue fabric. He was in a button-down white shirt with a high collar, and his beard was dark and full.

I wasn't so far gone as to believe that the pair were Al Qaida sympathizers or insurgents just because of the way they were dressed or what holy book they happened to read on which day and in which building. Usually my reaction was no more than a slight flinch if they got too close, and then I would be silently berating myself for a couple minutes about being stupid.

This time was a little different.

I reached up and rubbed my hand over my face to rid myself of the sweat forming on my forehead. My eyes looked back towards the other end of the bus, but the hairs on the back of my neck continued to stand up and tickle at the inside of my head. My bladder felt the need to empty itself, and when I closed my eyes it all came back.

Middle of the afternoon, just east of base but right along the border. Insurgents had been taking potshots at the base, and we'd already had one suicide bomber blown to bits near the motor pool.

Send in the snipers.

We're tasked with taking out the guys hiding in the hills, but the day's been a wash. No people, no shooting.

"Where are you going, LT?"

"Thirty seconds, Private," I respond. "Nature calls."

He laughs nervously, and I move around the end of the pale beige building. I flip my rifle over to my back and release my dick from my fatigues. Something doesn't feel right, but I shake off the feeling, and I sigh as a steady stream wets the sand in front of me.

Shots.

Screams.

The perimeter alarm begins to blare.

Trying to get my rifle back around my shoulder while simultaneously getting my dick into my pants. I stumble backwards, right myself, and then aim my weapon as I move around the building.

Bodies everywhere.

Ortega, Matthews, Davis, Ryans – all on the ground, none moving.

Pain in the back of my head, and the sand rushes up to connect with my face.

My eyes flew open, and I had to blink several times to get myself back into the present. The bus was even more crowded than before, and the Muslim couple had moved closer to me. My chest tightened as I tried to take a calming breath and failed.

"She's dead."

The guy across from me looked up and narrowed his eyes a little, but I ignored him.

The bus stopped again, and though I hoped the couple might get off at this stop, they didn't. Instead, a guy in a camouflage-colored coat stepped on, and I felt myself tense. It wasn't desert camo, at least, but for some reason it still set my heart beating faster. I looked away quickly and crossed my arms in front of myself. As I closed my eyes and gripped my biceps with my fingers, I could feel Bridgett's phantom fingers run down the side of my face, cooling my heated skin when I was sick.

"Stop it."

But it didn't stop.

The rumbling of the seat below me felt like the aftershocks of bombs going off around me. The sound of the bus against the street as it took off again was transformed to tank movements on grimy sand. The bus lurched to a stop, and I felt myself bump into the woman next to me on the bench seat. Again, my muscles tensed, and the butt end of my weapon dug into my back. I considered pulling it out of my waistband.

Of course, everyone would have been able to see it then – not such a great move.

Was it?

I closed my eyes again, and various visions of high school shootings and gunmen from rooftops invaded my head. Despite the carnage of the scenes played for everyone's viewing in the media, my mind found peace with the idea. There was always the same ending to the instigator of that kind of violence.

End being the focus.

"Tired."

Tired of playing this role, tired of just moving through the city like I was some kind of god or demon here to bring Rinaldo Moretti's version of justice to those who crossed my path. None of it even mattered to me – all I got out of it was a wad of cash and a twisted idea of loyalty to someone who told me I did a good job and occasionally called me "son."

When I opened my eyes, the Muslim woman was looking at me. My already tense body coiled, and my hand slipped down to the end of the seat – closer to my weapon. I had seven rounds loaded and two more clips on me. My mind counted how many people I could take out with what I had. I could easily build a barrier of bodies around myself.

How would that look to the woman who was eyeing me? Would she try to come at me? Would she throw herself in front of her husband or he in front of her?

It wouldn't make any difference. They would both die. So would the guy wearing that stupid camo coat and the plethora of oblivious teens with their earbuds shoved into their ears and their electronic devices shoved in their faces. They had no idea what was going on around them, and it was about time for someone to wake them all up.

I couldn't save those in my unit – couldn't protect them. There was nothing I could do now – no one to save, no one to protect. The deaths would be meaningless and senseless – every last one of them.

All deaths were.

My fingers reached behind my back and touched the warm handle of my Beretta. It felt good. I maneuvered the weapon around to my front, though still underneath my jacket.

My mind continued to swim around me, but there wasn't any war going on inside. Even when I tried to come up with shit I might regret not knowing or not doing, I couldn't come up with much. I wished I had a pizza for lunch instead of the damn hotdog I'd grabbed from a cart. I wished I'd seen that new GI Joe movie that was supposed to come out soon – the previews looked good, and I had always liked GI Joe.

My head moved up slowly, and I opened my eyes.

There really wasn't any reason to delay.

"It's decided."

This was how it was going to end.

I looked around from right to left, starting with the Muslim couple. My eyes traversed the teens, the camo-coated guy, a woman with a Macy's shopping bag, and the guy holding his little girl.

The little girl's eyes left her father and focused on me. Our gazes locked on each other, and the fuzz of the pink hat blew around in the wind from the bus doors as they opened and closed at the next stop. My heart beat louder in my chest, and I could feel the blood flowing rapidly through my veins. I didn't know how long she and I just looked at each other. I only knew that she would be collateral damage in my half-assed plan.

The doors of the bus opened, and the fuzzy hat blew around in the cool breeze again. I shoved off the seat, pushed my gun into the front waistband of my pants, and got the fuck off the bus.

I was far past my own stop – up north on Michigan Avenue near the John Hancock Observatory. I crossed the street but didn't bother to get on another bus – it seemed risky. My feet carried me past the Water Works and the Columbia sportswear store. I went by Tiffany's and Co and tried not to think of my date with Bridgett.

The smell of tomato sauce and cheese dragged me into a nearby pizzeria, where I ordered a cheese stuffed pizza with extra sauce, ate half of it, and then leaned back and wondered if my stomach was going to explode.

I walked back home and dropped down to the floor as Odin came up to me and whined. He sniffed at my hands, and I swear he knew what I had done.

"I shouldn't have done it. I don't even know why I did it."

My throat tightened, choking off my words.

"I could have taken a piss on the other side of the building where I might have seen them coming up. If I had, I could have taken them out from there – lots of cover."

Dizziness tried to knock me further to the ground, but I fought my way back to my feet. Maybe I was dehydrated – my throat was certainly dry. After guzzling a bottle of water, I decided to take Odin outside. He wagged his tail at me, and I felt like a total schmuck for not even thinking about what would happen to him if I was gone. I rubbed his shaggy head and attached the leash to his collar.

The weather was about the perfect temperature for his coat, and he seemed pretty thrilled when I didn't steer us towards the park but headed out down Wacker and towards Navy Pier. It was a good distance, but Odin loved to walk out by the lake.

He moved towards a group of seagulls, and I ran with him so he could chase them. My feet pounded the ground, and my head filled with memories.

Heavy artillery fire and an explosion. I can barely lift my head at this point, but I want to know what's going on outside. Something big. Something noisy.

I can only hope whatever it is will finally end me.

There is shouting, the sound of feet running, and the added sound of a helicopter way too close to the ground.

More explosions, more shouting – this time in English, but I assume that is nothing more than a dream – another hallucination.

I can't even pretend I still have hope.

Tired from the run, we walked back to the apartment. I fed Odin and sat down at my computer to check email.

Maybe if I just kept myself occupied with the mundane, I could manage to pull out of this.

"You killed her. She fucking trusted you – depended on you."

"Shut up."

Email never changed.

Some attorney in the UK was sure I was the long lost relative of some Irish land baron and would like to send me a lot of money.

The Art Institute had free admission to Chicago residents to the Picasso exhibit on Monday.

The place where I just had dinner wants me to save ten bucks on my next visit.

Nothing interesting, so I closed it and sat on the couch for a while, flipping through channels. It didn't work, of course. I even tried some pay-per-view-porn, but it did nothing for me. My head was pounding too much.

"Better off with a hooker; they're just not better off with you."

"Shut up."

I had to do something to clear my head, so I grabbed Odin's leash and led him back outside and over to the dog run.

The sun was beginning to fade behind the buildings, but there was still plenty of daylight and lots of people around. The kids on the playground were loud, but all seemed to be having fun. The damn parking garage door sang out to all around that a car was about to exit, and I tensed at the blaring noise. Shaking my head to clear it, I sat numbly on the bench and let Odin do his thing.

My head was still throbbing, and I rubbed my fingers over my temples. When I brought them back down again, I saw a spatter of blood on my thumb.

"Is it hers? His?"

I rubbed at it and then laughed at myself.

"Out, out, damn spot!"

"Bleep! Bleep! Bleep!"

My arms tightened around my body, and I doubled over a bit. I hadn't realized it before, but the sound was just a little too close to the perimeter alarm that blared in the middle of the night, signifying that someone had breached the exterior of our base. It was usually a false alarm, but it still woke everyone up.

"Too tired. Need sleep."

Odin ran up and slobbered on my leg.

"Disgusting," I told him, but I rubbed his head anyway. With our connection reaffirmed, he ran over to a yippie terrier and chased it around a tree with funky orange bark.

The damn garage door behind me went up again, accompanied by the detestable and continuous warning sounds. My back and shoulders tensed, and my heart rate increased.

My mind continued to flash back and forth – the Iraqi desert, Bridgett's body on the floor of my boss's office building, Lia's moans as I slid inside of her, and the taste of sand.

It was too much…just too much.

"Bleep! Bleep! Bleep!"

"Motherfucker!" I growled low as the sound from behind me made my teeth clench. My right index finger gripped back against my palm, letting me know what my body wanted.

The woman who apparently owned the yippie terrier glanced over at me dubiously. My eyes met hers, and I held her gaze until she looked away. She quickly moved herself and her dog to the other side of the small park.

"Like that's gonna help you."

Thirty seconds after it stopped, the blaring, beeping sound began again.

I capitulated to the growing need inside of me.

Whistling for Odin, I snapped his leash back on his collar and marched across the park to my apartment building. Odin whined at me and actually pulled back a bit at his leash, which he never did. I glanced back at him, and he nearly cowered.

I didn't have time for that, though. I had other things to do, so I hauled him to the building against his will.

"Come on, come on, come on," I muttered as the elevator took forever to get to my floor. I pressed the button several dozen times, but it didn't seem to help. As soon as the doors opened, I hauled Odin down the hallway and into my apartment. I released his leash, filled his water dish, and then turned to something far more desirable.

In my bedroom closet, way in the back, were my desert fatigues. I hadn't worn them since my forced retirement, but they still fit pretty well. I pulled the dog tags that sat at the bottom of the ceramic dish on my dresser over my head, and then I turned back to the closet.

Odin whined from the doorway.

I pulled my Barrett rifle out of its duffle bag, assembled it, and opened up my balcony door. I knelt down on the ground and opened up the bipod to stabilize the weapon and then lay down behind it. With my feet sticking out through the balcony rails on one side, I took careful aim across the park through the scope. I placed the cross hairs right at the light next to the door and waited.

It was only a minute or two before the light started to blink, the door started to open, and the *bleep bleep bleep* warning signal screeched across the area.

"You are going to crack someday, aren't you, Lieutenant?"

"Sure am."

I fired.

The light exploded, but the noise continued. In a smooth arch, I moved my aim and fired at a box to the left of the door, which sent shrapnel around the sidewalk but still didn't end the noise. There was another small electric box up near the corner of the garage door, and my third shot destroyed it and left the park in blessed electronic silence.

The people noise, however, increased significantly.

There was screaming from around the park, people rushing out of the Mexican restaurant at the end of the strip mall, and barking dogs from the dog run. There was a row of windows in the red brick building that housed the offending garage, and I blew them out one by one. The glass fell to the sidewalk and shattered further as spent cases began to cover my balcony.

The parents of children on the playground wrapped their arms around their offspring and ducked under slides and swings. Owners tried to leash their dogs and get out of the open.

I switched to a new magazine and then kept firing.

My ears were ringing, and I could hear Odin barking from the room behind me, but I shut out everything I could. The remaining windows in the building shattered as I fired repeatedly. It was just me, the trigger, and the recoil of the weapon against my shoulder.

I wanted more, though.

The crosshairs found one of the restaurant patrons, and I focused right above her eye.

"You don't even know her."

I shook my head, closed my eyes tightly, and tried to catch my breath.

"And you're fucking talking to yourself!" I spat back. I looked down the scope again, but the woman had disappeared inside. Refocusing, the crosshairs found the woman with the terrier. She had scooped up the small dog and was running across the park with a couple other screamers. I was pretty sure I could take them both out in one shot.

"Why? What's the fucking purpose?"

"Shut up!"

My hands started to shake, and sweat poured from my forehead into my eyes. I hadn't put on a bandana to keep it away, and my accuracy was going to suffer. The shaking was totally fucking me up when it came to placing the crosshair over my target, and when I fired, I missed completely.

Sirens.

"Waited too fucking long."

I let go for a moment, wiped sweat and whatever out of my eyes, shook my hands, and took a deep breath.

"You can do this shit. You're good at this shit."

As I glanced away from the scope and down the side of the building, I could see multiple people in flak jackets and helmets beginning to evacuate the park and surround my apartment building. I could have gone over and down the side of the building at that point, but figured it was probably too late, so I went back to firing.

Seven cars lost tires, but nothing was as satisfying as the parking garage door. I switched to my last magazine and shifted my aim to the right. The SWAT team hadn't surrounded that area yet, and there were lots of bystanders around. If I killed one of them, they were probably going to locate their own sniper to take me out. I could hear a helicopter in the distance and figured that's where he'd be. It was either that or open up fire on the SWAT guys, but the helmets made it more difficult.

I blew out the windows of the residential building on the right side of the park and then focused on someone standing half way down the stairs leading to North Columbia Drive. The crosshairs found where an ear was hidden underneath dark, silken hair.

Beautiful hair.

She turned, and the fading sun glittered off the necklace around her throat. It was a simple, silver chain with a large, round pendant of some sort. No wait, not a pendant – it was a…a…

"A quarter."

My finger stopped moving. My breath stopped. Hell, my heart might have stopped beating at that point.

"No fucking way."

Odin barked, yelped, and then went silent.

The noise from the screaming people below was overshadowed by the noise from behind me. Their words meant little, even though I knew they were likely screaming at me to let go of the weapon and stop trying to blow up the fucking neighborhood.

Whatever.

I couldn't take my eyes from the shining quarter necklace and the familiar face above it.

"Lia."

"Release the weapon now!"

It had to be a hallucination.

There was no way – no way she could possibly be here.

Absolutely impossible.

"Release your weapon now, or I will be forced to fire!"

Fatigue covered me. I couldn't fight it anymore. My hands moved to the ground below the gun, and I pushed back away from it even as I kept my eye on the scope. I had already dropped my hand from the trigger, but nothing was making any sense to me in the slow motion events to follow.

I didn't want to be there, and I didn't want to be doing what I was doing. I never wanted any of it to come to this. Rinaldo wouldn't like it – this wasn't something he would approve of at all, and I couldn't take it back now.

The figure in the crosshairs turned, held her hand up to shade her eyes, and looked up towards me. The same eyes, the same swishing motion of her hair as she turned, and the same curve of her bottom lip as her teeth sank into it.

Then she was gone.

My hands were wrenched behind me, and I was abruptly facedown on the balcony floor, my cheek scraping on the concrete. Immediately, I could hear the muffled, distant-memory sound of gunfire and explosions. I could taste the sand and feel it in my lungs.

"Please…no – please don't kill me! I have a wife! Her name's Marie, and my daughters, Evelyn and Jennie…"

A muffled click, and when I turn towards the sound, someone grabs my head and pushes it down again.

"Kill me! I don't even have a fucking family! Just kill me!"

I didn't move, didn't resist. I barely felt their hands on me.

"Kill me," I whispered. "Kill me, please…just kill me."

More voices joined the conglomerate around me. There was a new set of hands holding one of my shoulders down. Radios crackled, and the sound of a helicopter overhead made me try to lift my head to see what kind. Police? Traffic? Military? Was there a sniper inside, as I suspected, ready to end me?

The gunfire in my head continued, occasionally causing me to flinch. Whenever I did that, the two people holding my body to the ground leaned harder against me, though I wasn't resisting. My head dropped back to the ground, and I could see out over the edge of the balcony towards the park, which was now devoid of people. There was no one there at all now – not a woman, a man, or even a dog.

"Odin?"

I tried to get my head up enough to look into the apartment, but I was shoved back down.

"Odin!"

I heard nothing in response.

My chest started to seize up, and I couldn't breathe. He had been barking, something he almost never did, but was now silent. Where was he? What did they do to him? Did he go after them in order to protect me?

"No…no…"

Odin…God, no…Odin…

I squeezed my eyes shut. Someone was holding the back of my neck, and I could taste sand in my mouth. I could feel the wire wrapped around my wrists as it cut into my skin, and I could hear desert winds blowing around me.

"Not real."

Forcing air into my lungs, I traded not breathing for hyperventilating. I glanced over my shoulder and saw four men around me, holding me to the ground as cuffs were placed around my wrists. Another man near the sliding glass door held a shotgun at my head.

"Where's my…where's my dog? Odin!"

No one replied. No one said a word.

The dizziness in my head threatened to end my consciousness as they hauled me to my feet. I stumbled as I stared towards the stairs where the figure with the quarter-themed necklace had been, but there was no one there now except a man with a rifle and a SWAT uniform.

"He's got dog tags."

The chain around my neck is tightened, cutting off most of my airflow. When he shakes it, I feel the skin from the base of my throat scraped clean as my tags jingle in his grasp.

"You think this means something to me? To us? You are nothing! They are nothing! You have been here how many months? Do you even know? There is no rescue for you - they care nothing for you! One of your own men told us where you were!"

The private had betrayed me.

"Doesn't mean anything."

"Lieutenant?"

My head turned towards the sound – a reflexive action. I didn't know the man standing in front of me with the round face, blue uniform, and flak jacket. I'd never seen him before.

"Where's Odin?" I asked.

"I'm going to read you your rights," the man said.

The familiar words flowed from his mouth, and I was reminded of a thousand movies and television shows where similar words were spoken.

"Do you understand these rights?"

"There was a girl down there," I told him. "Did you see her? She had a quarter around her neck."

"He's gone, sir."

"Let's just get him in."

I was pushed through the opening and back into the apartment, through the bedroom, and into the living room. My breath caught in my chest as I saw the pile of white fur near the couch, but before I could react to the sight, Odin's muzzled head came up and his tail began to thump against the floor. An officer had a leash around his neck and kept him from coming closer to me.

I gasped out a breath and nearly fell in relief as I was escorted across the room, through the open door, and into the hallway. The elevators were blocked open down at the end of the hall, and there was an officer arguing with a woman near the stairway.

Not a woman – *the* woman.

Lia stood with her hands on her hips and her hair pulled up into one of those ridiculous, lumpy buns at the top of her head. Strands fell all around her neck and moved with her as she turned to look towards me.

Her mouth opened, and she tried to take a step forward. The officer blocked her path, so we just continued to look at each other.

I remembered everything I thought about while driving back to the cabin after dropping her off at the bus stop. This was exactly why I didn't want to bring her into my life, but here she was anyway – watching me get dragged to jail. She was damn lucky I didn't shoot her.

My stomach tightened at the thought.

The officers on either side of my body urged me forward towards the elevators. It was the closest to her I would get.

"Evan?" My name was a plea on her tongue.

I could only stare at her in return.

"What…what happened?" she asked, as if I would have an answer that made any sense.

I didn't. I probably never would.

I turned away from her as they started to shove me into the elevator. There certainly wasn't going to be any kind of understandable reason for anything I did. I couldn't even understand it myself, so how would anyone else? They'd be better off talking to the dog.

"Lia!" I turned back to Lia and caught her eyes with mine. "Take Odin – please. Please take him with you – make sure he's okay. Please? Will you? Please?"

"I will," she said quietly.

"Let her?" I begged the guy holding my left arm. "Let her take my dog, okay?"

He said nothing.

"What are you going to do with him?" I demanded as I was shoved towards the elevator. "Let her take him! Please!"

"It's all good, Lieutenant," the round-faced officer said as he came up in front of me. "The dog's fine, and after a little processing, we'll make sure he ends up in the young lady's care. All right?"

I nodded.

My eyes met Lia's again, and I saw a single tear escape her lashes and roll down her cheek. The need to wipe away the tear was overwhelming, but I couldn't move.

"Sorry," I whispered.

Her teeth dug into her bottom lip, and more tears flowed as she whispered my name again.

"I'll take care of Odin," she told me. "I'll…I'll figure it out. You just need…you need…"

Her voice trailed off, and I had to give her a half smile for the effort. I didn't need anything other than what Moretti had said he would do – I needed to be put down.

They were supposed to take me out. Why did I stop firing? If I hadn't stopped, they would have ended me. Glancing back at Lia again gave me the answer – I couldn't continue knowing she was in the area.

There was nothing else to be done, and no way were my usual tactics going to be able to keep me from thinking about her constantly now. I had seen her again, no longer just a memory, and I could feel myself drawn to her presence. Even as the police officers blocked us from actually coming into physical contact with one another, it felt as though we were touching.

I didn't need to touch her – I could feel her from across the hall.

I had felt her all along; from the time she boarded the bus to see her mother until the moment our eyes met in the hallway. I might have found some ways to push her to the back of my mind, but I knew she was always there. It was like she was inside of me, and there was no way she was going away, no matter where I ended up.

I would be the death of her, quite possibly in a very literal sense.

There was no way I could let that happen. I couldn't allow her to become a part of my fucked up life without her ending up just like Bridgett – either with my bullet or someone else's. I wasn't going to allow that, because…because…

Because Rinaldo Moretti was wrong about me.

I knew exactly what he had meant – I felt it.

Looking at her one final time, I soaked in everything about her that I could. My mind captured her long, dark hair, eyes glistening with tears, the shining quarter hanging around her neck, and committed it all to permanent memory. I knew this would be the end of it, and that was what was best for her. I knew it with all my warm, beating heart. The only thing left was to find a new way to get her out of my head.

Prison seemed as good a distraction as anything.

So I let them haul me out.

Cuffs around my wrists.

And remained otherwise occupied.

EPILOGUE

Lia

This was fucking crazy.

What had I walked into?

The hallway was bright, clean, and expensively decorated. It wasn't quite posh but certainly counted as upscale. The scene filling the corridor didn't fit in the slightest.

Several SWAT team members lined the walls, some of them with guns drawn and pointed at the man their comrades brought out of the apartment at the far end. They tensed as he emerged, and their fingers twitched against the triggers but not enough to fire.

My gaze was drawn to their target.

The face I looked at was the same one that had obsessed me for months, but the clear blue eyes were red and swollen, and the tight, military haircut outgrown and unkempt. The desert-style fatigues I had never seen before, but at least the look fit what I was expecting. The rest of the scene and the look on Evan Arden's face were completely bizarre.

For months I had been searching for this man based on nothing more than a name and military affiliation, but all records of him seemed to completely disappear after he returned from the Middle East. My search had led me to the terrifying video of him on his knees while the man next to him was executed and pictures of him being brought back to the United States after he was found in an undisclosed location during a raid on a suspected Al Qaida base.

Though faded, the bruises in the photos were still quite visible. His arm had been in a sling due to a dislocated shoulder, but he had been reported to be otherwise unharmed.

But his eyes…

They had been haunted and haunting. The somewhat hesitant but bright and alive glimmer I had witnessed in Arizona was nowhere to be found. I hadn't been able to reconcile the pictures of the man brought back from war with the cool and confident one who locked eyes with me in his tiny bed and told me to touch him. Now that I had found him, I was watching him with the exact same look in his eyes, being taken away in handcuffs by a half dozen men.

He had been shooting at people.

Still, it wasn't the look of a callous murderer, but more like a lost puppy – desperate, hungry, and terrified – biting at the ominous hand reaching underneath the couch to pull him out. There were tears streaming down his face, though he seemed oblivious to their presence.

All of the fantasies that had cavorted around in my head while I searched for him fell apart. There wasn't going to be a passionate kiss as he held me against his chest – his hands were secured behind his back to protect those around him. I wouldn't be throwing myself into his arms and feeling that sense of security and want I had felt with him in Arizona. I wasn't sure if I would even be able to get his attention.

What happened to him?

Evan's eyes moved to mine, and for a moment he closed them for a little longer than it takes to blink. Once he opened them again, the vision of an already broken man seemed to collapse into an even darker hole. Instinctively, I stepped forward. I needed to reach him, touch him, and be sure all of this was real and not some sick nightmare my desperate mind had contrived. I wasn't afforded the opportunity; the police officer who had been arguing with me a moment ago blocked my path. He spoke bluntly, but I wasn't listening to his words.

"Evan?"

Evan's reddened eyes looked away in defeat, and he allowed his escorts to maneuver him towards the open elevator door. Just as he crossed over the line on the floor, his eyes widened, and he looked back to me and called my name.

"Take Odin – please. Please take him with you – make sure he's okay. Please? Will you? Please?"

Odin, of course. He was the shaved-nearly-bald, huge, white dog with a rolling tongue. He kept licking my hand when I tried to fall asleep in the Arizona cabin where I met Evan. I had been amazed at how well-behaved the canine was and how quickly he reacted to anything Evan commanded.

I agreed, naturally. What else was I supposed to do? My head felt like it was full of mush – I couldn't even make any kind of sense of the scene – but of course I would take the dog. As Evan's panicked words to the police captain flowed in and out of my head, I tried to get past the officer near me but wasn't able to push him away.

"Let me talk to him!" I snarled under my breath.

"I can't do that, ma'am," the police officer replied. "You have to understand why I can't do that."

I did, too.

"I'll take care of Odin," I called out to him, and I could see his face relax. "I'll…I'll figure it out. You just need…you need…"

I didn't know what he needed, and the half smile I got in return told me he didn't know, either. His eyes stayed on me as they pulled him backwards into the elevator, and I felt the same connection to him I had felt in Arizona when he handed me a bottle of water and our fingers touched as it passed from one hand to the other.

"Sorry," he said softly, and the elevator closed.

Watching him disappear behind the doors, I knew I would have done anything just to be able to take him back to that moment. I had recognized then how different he was inside despite the hardened outward appearance. William had always looked soft and cuddly on the outside, but inside he was dark, cruel, and vindictive. Evan had the look about him that screamed "stay away from me," but as soon as our bodies intertwined, I had been his.

I didn't know how he had arrived at this point, and I knew if I would have asked Mom, she would have told me to run away as fast as I could in the other direction. I couldn't do that, though. I couldn't just leave him to his fate. If he had done the same to me, I wouldn't have survived alone in the desert.

I wouldn't allow it. He was the only good thing that had ever happened to me in my whole life, and I wasn't going to let him be dragged away from me like this. I would figure out what needed to be done to help him and get him out of this mess he was in. Evan needed someone to help him – to save him.

There was just no way I would turn my back on him now.

ACKNOWLEDGMENTS

Special thanks to everyone who helped pull this together: Chaya and Tamara for their marvelous editing, Adam, Holly and Jada for the fabulous artwork for the cover and video.

I couldn't have gotten it done without all your help!

UNCOCKBLOCKABLE - EVAN ARDEN #2.5

&

OTHERWISE UNHARMED - EVAN ARDEN #3

ARE AVAILABLE NOW

OTHER TITLES BY SHAY SAVAGE

THE EVAN ARDEN TRILOGY

OTHERWISE ALONE - EVAN ARDEN #1
UNCOCKBLOCKABLE - EVAN ARDEN #2.5
OTHERWISE UNHARMED - EVAN ARDEN #3

SURVIVING RAINE SERIES

SURVIVING RAINE - #1

ABOUT THE AUTHOR

Always looking for a storyline and characters who fall outside the norm, Shay Savage's tales have a habit of evoking some extreme emotions from fans. She prides herself on plots that are unpredictable and loves to hear it when a story doesn't take the path assumed by her readers. With a strong interest in psychology, Shay loves to delve into the dark recesses of her character's brains–and there is definitely some darkness to be found! Though the journey is often bumpy, if you can hang on long enough you won't regret the ride.You may not always like the characters or the things they do, but you'll certainly understand them.

Shay Savage lives in Ohio with her husband and two children. She's an avid soccer fan, loves vacationing near the ocean, enjoys science fiction in all forms, and absolutely adores all of the encouragement she has received from those who have enjoyed her work.

Made in the USA
Lexington, KY
27 August 2014